HER WEREWOLF PROTECTOR

WEREWOLF GUARDIAN ROMANCE SERIES

JODI VAUGHN

CHAPTER 1

"*F*an-fucking-tastic." Braxton Devereaux stopped his motorcycle and swiped the blood off his mouth with the back of his tattooed hand. Leaning over, he spit through clenched teeth. The bloody mucus puddled in the frozen winter's ground.

Despite being a werewolf, he preferred the coppery taste of his enemy's blood to his own.

Today had been one of the shittiest days he'd ever had. Considering his lot in life, that was saying something.

His alarm hadn't gone off and he'd shown up late for his bartending job. Once he arrived at work things had quickly gone from bad to worse when one of the customers at the Beaver Tail Strip Club slapped one of the dancers. Braxton had left his position from behind the bar and beat the fucker senseless. The one thing that made him flip his switch like nothing else was some asshole thinking he had the right to hit a woman.

After four bouncers finally pulled him off the guy, his boss had handed him his last paycheck and told him not to come back.

He didn't mind losing his job; he knew he could find something else. He didn't really like bartending that much anyway. He'd only stayed around for the dancers, to keep an eye out for them and make sure no one hurt them. Even tonight, when he was gathering his things, Wendy, the stripper who'd been hit, had wrapped her arms around him and apologized for getting him fired for coming to her defense. She'd said no one had ever done that for her before.

Then she offered him a blow job.

He frowned, now regretting he'd turned down her generous offer. God knows he needed some kind of outlet for his anger before facing his prick of a father.

The frosty January wind ruffled his blue-tipped hair as he set the kickstand on his 1998 Harley Davidson Fat Boy. He dismounted his bike, mentally bracing for walking into his parents' war zone of a house. At thirty-one, his stomach still clenched every time he drove up. His childhood hadn't exactly been picture perfect and as soon as he was of legal age, he'd left. He lived a couple of blocks away in a shitty studio apartment, but it was still too close for his taste.

He'd ridden over after getting a call from one of the neighbors concerned about the loud ruckus coming from the house. The neighbors knew his old man, Remy Devereaux, and were too afraid to go over themselves. They all knew the truth. Braxton had no illusions. He knew exactly what his father was capable of when it came to his mother, Lynette. The neighbors were right to not get involved. It would just make things worse on her.

The hair on his neck stiffened as a desperate chill ran down his spine with each step along the crumbling walkway. The wind howled through the barren winter trees as if in warning of what he'd find on the other side of the door. What kind of shape would his mother be in this time? Busted face? Broken ribs? Bruised kidney?

Braxton wished for the millionth time he could convince her to leave, to get out of Shreveport, Louisiana, while she was still alive. He promised to take her anywhere she wanted, so they could start over, but she never even entertained the idea. Every time he found a new bruise on his mother's gaunt body, she made excuses for his father. The light in her eyes had long gone, leaving behind a shell of a woman who was too afraid to live without a man, even a man that continued to hit her. She'd allowed him to suck out her soul and then crammed in his own convoluted, worthless version of her identity back into her body.

After his last visit, Braxton had discovered fresh bruises on her arms. He'd flipped, wanting nothing more than to wrap his hand around his father's neck and squeeze. She'd begged him not to kill his father, when it was the only thing Braxton had wanted to do. In the end, he'd caved and promised his mom he wouldn't murder the bastard. It was a promise he struggled to keep.

He told himself that he wouldn't keep coming over, wouldn't keep torturing himself over how he hadn't managed to keep his father from beating the shit out of his mother. He should have left Shreveport years ago and never looked back.

Yet he'd stayed, hoping his mother would wake up and realize she was ready to leave Remy.

Until then, he couldn't leave his mother. Deep down, Braxton knew it was his presence that kept Remy from killing her.

He winced as he thought back to the incident two weeks ago. He'd walked in on the scene of his mother crouching in terror on the floor, apologizing and sputtering blood, while his father continued to punch her in the face.

Braxton's gaze had gone tunnel vision, his only thought to the rip the prick apart, limb by fucking limb. He pulled him off his mother and proceeded to bury his fist in the bastard's face, again and again and again, as bone broke under his assault. Remy, being the coward he was, shifted into wolf and overpowered Braxton. Braxton had refused to shift. He hated the wolf part of himself, simply because that was the only thing, besides broken bones and bruised organs, the bastard had ever given him.

Clenching his jaw, he stood on the cramped porch and knocked on the front door. The house with its peeling yellow paint was empty of any rocking chairs or decoration, unlike the neighbors' homes. Even the naked door, void of any wreath, reeked of desperation and hopelessness.

He clenched his fists, ready for the smirking bastard to open the door and ask what the fuck Braxton wanted.

Edgy silence seized his attention.

He turned the cold doorknob, but the door didn't open.

He wasn't surprised. His dad always made sure to deadbolt the door when he was beating his mother. Remy Devereaux didn't like being interrupted when he was in a drunken rage.

He peered into the dark windows and frowned.

That was weird. Even the lamp in the living room was off. For as long as he could remember, his mother always kept that lamp on.

Always.

"Fuck." Braxton tensed his muscles and rammed his shoulder into the front door. Wood split and splintered as the door swung free from the deadbolt.

"Mom," he called out. His breathing, now coming faster, seemed to echo into the voluminous space. An ominous hush stole through the house like an invisible entity, sending his heart racing.

His eyes quickly adjusted to the darkness, and he flipped the wall light switch.

Light flooded the living room but did nothing to alleviate the bleak heaviness that clung to the air. Yet, nothing appeared out of place.

His gaze drifted over the green and yellow plaid couch, raggedy-ass brown recliner, and 1970s coffee table. The drab end tables on either side of the couch held the familiar ugly green glass lamps that his mom had inherited from her mother.

His gaze swept the room. The fireplace was dark and, judging by the chill in the room, there hadn't been a fire for a few hours. The wood floors gleamed from his mother's constant waxing in her attempt to make things perfect in her husband's critical eye.

The pristine appearance of the room did nothing to soothe the unease sliding around in his gut.

"Mom?" he called out louder, panic filling his chest.

He crossed the living room and into the darkened kitchen. His boot slipped sideways as his heel struck a puddle. He reached for the counter to regain his balance.

"The bastard spilled his beer again." Braxton gritted his teeth and flipped the kitchen light switch.

His breath left his lungs in a whoosh.

A crimson spray of blood dripped down the white kitchen cabinets like a toddler's attempt at finger painting. Thick drops trailed down the cupboards and puddled onto the yellowed Formica countertops. The nauseating scent of blood stung his nose and made it hard to breathe. It looked like a fucking horror flick.

Every muscle in his body tensed as tremors racked his frame.

A giant smear of blood trailed from the kitchen floor, around the island, and out toward the dining room.

He took a step, his gut contorting, knowing what he was about to find. His heart beat furiously in his ears. Self-hatred filled him for not getting here earlier. He could have saved her if he'd just gotten here earlier.

His heart stopped in his chest. A lifeless body lay sprawled across the white linoleum floor of the dining room in a pool of reflective blood. The orange afghan from the living room sofa had been thrown across the body, leaving only the badly beaten head sticking out. She didn't even look human.

A cold hard sweat broke out across his body as the room began to spin. Backing up, he grabbed the kitchen island and sucked in a deep breath. Rage melded with guilt until his body trembled.

His father had made good on his promise. Remy had killed his mother.

On shaky legs, Braxton forced himself to step closer. He knelt, his jeans soaking in the pool of thick blood that had leaked out around the afghan. The blanket that was once orange had now been turned into an unrecognizable shade of brown.

He pulled off the afghan. Surprise and then relief flooded his chest as he picked up the heavy gold chain from around the neck.

It was the chain that his father always wore. The corpse belonged to his father, not his mother.

"What have you done?" His mother's heart-wrenching scream tore through the house.

Scrambling to his feet, he faced her. The familiar shadows that hung under her eyes seemed to darken as her frantic gaze darted from him to the bloodied body on the floor. Her hands trembled as she covered her head, trying to make sense of the horrific scene. Despite how abusive he was, Lynette had loved his father with a toxic adoration. Braxton had known one day it was going to end in death. He just always assumed it would be his mother's.

Shaking his head, he held out his hands. "I didn't do this. I found him like this." He stepped closer to take his fragile mother in his arms. She snarled and pushed him away. His heart twisted in his chest at the betrayal.

She stepped closer and then fell to her knees in front of the body, her tan slacks soaking up Remy's blood. She buried her face in her bony hands as she let out a wail. The sound ripped at Braxton's heart.

He bent down to tug her to her feet. She flinched at his touch and screamed, her wild eyes piercing him to the core. "Don't touch me. You killed him."

"What's going on, Lynette? You okay?" Mr. Cooper, the preacher and next door neighbor, rounded the corner and stopped in his tracks. "Holy shit."

"Mr. Cooper ..." Before Braxton could explain how he'd found his father, the preacher was out the door, hurling prayers over his shoulder as he raced back to his own home.

Uneasiness pricked the short hairs on Braxton's neck, warning of something headed his way. His wolf instinct told him something bad was about to happen.

Sirens screeched in the distance and Braxton's heart rate kicked into high gear. He didn't exactly have a sterling reputation with Shreveport's police department. He'd been thrown in jail quite a few times for disturbing the peace. It didn't matter that he'd been protecting some of the dancers from guys who had thought their money could buy more than a lap dance at the Beaver Tail. To the Shreveport PD, Braxton was a criminal. To them, once a criminal, always a criminal.

Dancing crimson and blue lights flickered in from the living room window, momentarily blinding him. His heart fumbled in his chest.

"Hands up. We're coming in," two of Shreveport's finest

called out as they eased their way through the door with guns drawn.

Braxton stood still, unable to look away from his mother as she cradled the mutilated body of the worthless man, a man who hadn't cared less if his wife lived or died.

Deep down, on some level, Braxton was relieved the fucker was gone. Maybe that made him as bad as his father.

"Freeze!" one of the cops yelled out, keeping his gun leveled at Braxton's chest.

Braxton blew out a breath to calm his racing heart, wondering if uttering the word freeze was part of the police protocol. Did they not realize no one had moved since they entered the room?

"Get your hands up!" The bald-headed cop narrowed his eyes.

Braxton slowly lifted his hands over his head. "He's my father." The words tasted acrid on his tongue as he admitted his relationship to the man. "I'm the one that found him."

His mother's frantic wails drew his attention. "Tell them who I am, Mom."

The cops kept their guns leveled at him while addressing Lynette. "Is this your son, ma'am?"

His mother lifted her watery gaze to Braxton and held out her bloody palm. "Why, Braxton? Why did you…"

His chest tightened. "Mom, you know I didn't do this." He took a step toward her. He needed to make her understand he hadn't killed his father.

The cops rushed forward, shoving him face-first into the wall. His cheek collided with the paneling. He fought back a growl as anger surged within him.

"Hands behind your back, buddy."

"Get your hands off me." Braxton gritted his teeth and sucked in a deep breath as he attempted to cage his temper. "I didn't kill the bastard."

"Well, mommy seems to say different." The older cop with the five o'clock shadow clicked the handcuffs around his wrists, tightening them until the metal bit into his flesh, and guided him through the front door.

Braxton squinted against the flashing red and blue lights spilling out across the yard. Neighbors crept out of their houses dressed in robes and slippers, arching their necks trying to get a better look at him, as if he were some kind of attraction from Barnum and Bailey's murderers on parade.

He grunted as the cops shoved him against the side of the cop car and started to pat him down.

"Well, well. Looks like we got us a murder weapon." The older cop pulled a five-inch knife from the inside of Braxton's boot and held it in front of his face.

Fuck. He'd forgotten about the knife he always kept on him. He wanted to tell them if he wanted to kill someone he'd just rip their throats out, that he didn't need a weapon.

The bald cop handed the knife over to the younger cop, who promptly stuck it in a ziplock bag he pulled out of the police car.

"Go ahead and test that knife. You won't find any traces of blood on it." Braxton ground out between clenched teeth as they turned around.

"I guess we'll just have to see, smartass." The cop opened the back door of the police car and thrust him in, slamming Braxton's head into the frame of the door. "Watch your head," the cop sneered before shutting the door.

Braxton ignored the brief blinding pain shooting through his skull and blinked away the blood trailing down his head. As a werewolf, he'd heal soon enough. He wasn't worried about the injury. Holding back the anger that threatened his shift into wolf form was the real challenge. Shifting in front of humans was an absolute no-no in Were Law.

A female's scream shredded the darkness and Braxton's

concentration. He jerked his head toward the house as his mother raced toward them. The young cop grabbed her around the waist, preventing her from reaching the car.

"Let go of my mother, asshole," Braxton growled through the car.

"The ambulance is on its way to check you out, ma'am. You really don't need to talk to the culprit," the younger cop assured her.

"Braxton," she cried out.

"Mom, it's okay. Everything will be okay." Braxton's heart ached at the sight of his wild-eyed mother, clothes smeared with his father's blood.

"You've broken the law, Braxton." Her voice sent a shiver down his spine.

His heart dipped to his stomach. There was no way he could make his mother understand that he hadn't killed his father. Not while she was hysterical.

"That's why we're taking him to jail, ma'am." The cop nodded and shot Braxton a glare before releasing his hold on his mother.

She sprinted for the car and pressed her bloody palms to the window. "They are coming for you, Braxton. And they are bringing judgment with them."

Braxton clenched his muscles as the reality of the situation set in.

He barely registered the ambulance pulling up or the activity of someone taking his mother to sit in the back while a paramedic took her vital signs.

News in the Were community traveled like lightning. The werewolf council in Shreveport probably already knew what had happened. If they believed Braxton had murdered his own father, then he had, indeed, broken the law.

The Werewolf Law.

Breaking the Werewolf Law meant one thing.

The Assassins were on their way to kill him.

* * *

KATE WOLPH TUGGED the starburst-patterned quilt around her shoulders and opened her front door. Stepping out onto the porch, she shivered against the assault of the icy breeze. Easing into one of the wicker rockers on the front porch, she buried her nose into the quilt to keep the January wind from freezing it off. Despite the late hour of three a.m., the woods around her isolated bed and breakfast had a calming effect on her.

The solitude is what had drawn her mother here years ago to buy this particular B&B rather than buying one in the charming town of Eureka Springs. It was the isolation that kept the customers coming back even after her mother died.

Kate swallowed, her eyes stinging with a fresh batch of tears, wondering what her mother would think of the floundering business if she were still alive.

"I'm sorry, Mom," Kate whispered into the cold night air, her escaped tears almost freezing against her cheek. "You were so right about Tom. I should have listened to you. "

Her stomach churned as the bleak memory of the argument that she and her mother had gotten into before the accident rose up in her mind. Kate had told her mom that Tom Hudson had proposed. Her mother had gotten upset and forbidden her to marry him, insisting Tom was nothing but a con artist, and that he was only interested in living off Kate.

Her mother had taken her eyes off the winding road in Eureka Springs for a brief second. That's all it took for their car to plummet off the cliff.

It had taken Kate a month to recover from her physical injuries, but she had yet to get over the gaping wound her mother's death had left behind.

It had taken less than three months after the accident for Tom to leave and take all of Kate's savings with him.

Now, a year later, she was facing the fact that her B&B, the only home she'd known, was facing foreclosure.

She poked her hand out from under the warmth of the quilt and held the bank letter up to the glow of the porch light.

Her heart froze in her chest as she read, and then reread, the looming threat of foreclosure if she didn't make up her missed mortgage payments.

"How can I make my mortgage if I don't have any customers? We're in a recession. Who is going to pay to stay at the Bella Luna Inn when the competition in town is only half the price—plus has a pool?" She clenched her jaw against the sting of tears. She was tired of crying every time she thought about her situation. She needed a solution, not more tears.

Willy Montgomery, the bank president, had given her mother the loan for the Bella Luna years ago. She remembered the first time she'd met him as a little girl. They were walking out of the bank when he'd stopped them. Her shoe-strings had come loose, and he'd bent down and tied them for her.

Strange how such a small act of kindness had stayed with her all this time.

"Maybe Mr. Montgomery will be willing to give me an extension." Kate stood, a flicker of warm hope beginning to spread within her chest despite the winter chill. If she got an extension, then she could start making a plan to draw more customers and turn her business around.

She padded over to the porch railing and slowly exhaled. "I can't lose this place. I refuse to let my mother down. Not again."

The biting winter air stilled and the woods went silent. She looked toward the thick woods. The security light on the side of the house didn't reach that far, leaving that side of the house shrouded in darkness. She had never minded before.

But tonight was different.

Tonight she felt like she wasn't alone.

Wrapping her quilt around her, she hurried to the door. Once inside, she quickly locked the door and peered out the window.

She laughed. "I must be spending too much time alone. I'm starting to imagine things. Now, I'm talking to myself."

She definitely needed some adult conversation. She made a mental note to call her best friend, Beau, the local veterinarian, and set up a lunch date.

The isolation she loved so much was making her imagination run wild.

* * *

"YOU NEED to let me out of here." Braxton tried to stay calm, but he couldn't keep the urgency out of his voice. The urge to shift into wolf pulled at him like never before. If he didn't get out of the back of the police car soon, he was going to rip the inside of the car apart.

"I think you need to remember, hotshot, you have the right to remain silent. So why don't you do that till we get to the precinct." The older cop shot him a glare in the rearview mirror.

"I don't think you understand…" Braxton's breathing increased as the wolf inside him roared to life.

"I understand just fine. What you don't understand, dipshit, is that you are two seconds away from me kicking your sorry ass."

"Look, asshole, I'm telling you if you don't let me out of this car, I'm going to rip your fucking throat out." Braxton's heart raced, the adrenaline of the wolf coursing through his veins. He gritted his teeth, attempting to shutter a growl, but it rolled out anyway.

The Assassins were coming for him, and if they found him trapped in the back of a police car, it would be like shooting fish in a barrel.

He wasn't a fucking goldfish.

"That's it." The older cop pulled the cruiser into a deserted alley, slammed on the brakes, and killed the engine. Turning around, he sneered. "Now we're going to have some fun."

"Ahhh... Jerry, I don't think..." The younger cop's worried gaze flickered between him and his partner. "We should just keep driving to the station."

Jerry glared. "Mike, when I want your fucking opinion I'll ask for it. You got that?"

"Jerry. Your name's Jerry. Like Ben and Jerry's?" Braxton curled his fingers into fists, trying to force himself from shifting in front of the human cops.

"You son of a bitch. That's it." Jerry slid out of the front seat and opened the back door.

Braxton blew out an anxious breath and tried to slow his heart rate. Maybe if he could distract them long enough, he could shift and get the fuck out of there.

His relief was short-lived.

Jerry snatched him out of the car by his hair. Losing his balance, Braxton stumbled against the side of the car.

Jerry slammed his police baton across Braxton's back.

Pain exploded across his shoulders, buckling his knees and sending him into the dirty pavement.

Braxton growled, the pain fueling his body to shift into wolf, to protect himself.

"Jerry, what the hell are you doing?" The second cop held his hands up and stepped between them.

"I'm teaching this white trash some fucking manners." Jerry stepped around his partner, but the younger cop blocked him.

"I can't let you do this, man. This ain't right." Mike rested his hands on his partner's shoulders.

Braxton laughed from his position on the ground.

Both cops turned to him.

"What's so funny, asshole?" Jerry shook off his partner's hold and narrowed his eyes.

Braxton met his gaze and gave him a sinister grin. "I've got something I want to show you."

Braxton relaxed and let go of the chain restraining his inner beast as the shift began to pound through his veins.

He'd lost his job, his mother's faith, and now, his future.

He had nothing left to lose.

Braxton's eyes rolled back in his head as he embraced the wolf. His bones shifted, cartilage stretched, muscles contracted and stretched as power flowed through his veins. His clothes shredded and fell from his body as the beast replaced his human form. His heart raced in his chest, and a deep growl dripped from his lips.

Opening his eyes, he jumped to his paws.

He met the horrified gaze of the two human cops.

"What the fuck?" Jerry held his hands up and backed away, his face white.

Braxton took a step toward him.

Jerry screamed and a dark spot began to spread in the region of his crotch.

He wanted to laugh at the asshole cop wetting his pants, but it didn't seem so funny with the younger cop pointing a 10 mm between his eyes.

CHAPTER 2

$\mathcal{T}$he cop squeezed the trigger.

Braxton leaped. The bullet whizzed past his ear.

Pushing off his back legs, he sprang toward the darkened alley, running hard and pushing his muscles to their limit.

"Stop!"

Ignoring the cop's command, Braxton ran as fast as his four legs could carry him. A second gunshot echoed into the night. He gritted his teeth, expecting the impact of the bullet to penetrate his hide any second.

The pain never came.

He skidded to a stop when he reached a chain-link fence at the far end of the alley. Glancing over his shoulder, he saw the cop running toward him, gun drawn.

He was trapped like a fucking rat. He backed up a few feet, sprinted and jumped, easily clearing the fence beneath him.

The second his feet made contact with the ground, he ran, dodging trash cans and a homeless drunk.

He had to put as much distance behind him as he could

before the Assassins arrived. They were probably already at the police station, waiting to bail him out. Once he was in their custody, they would kill him.

Assassins were the most vicious werewolves, sent to deliver justice, quickly and effectively. No wolf survived and no wolf ever got away.

Braxton raced through the cold night, keeping to the shadows and staying out of sight as he doubled back to his parents' house.

By the time he arrived at the house, everything was quiet. The ambulance was gone and the nosy neighbors had gone back to the shelter of their own homes, their overeager curiosities appeased. Except for the yellow police tape draped across the front door, it looked like any other ordinary street in America.

Braxton's gaze landed on his Harley and he smiled. Thank God no one had tried to take his bike into evidence. It might be old, but it was his baby. Now it was the only thing he had left. Crawling under the neighbor's evergreen shrub, he shifted back into human form.

Something sharp poked him. He winced and rubbed his ass. Fucking holly bush.

He glanced up and down the street, making sure he was alone before venturing out of his safe spot. The last thing he needed was some early-rising housewife to see him running across the yard nude and call the cops on him.

Hurrying over to his bike, he reached inside the saddlebag and grabbed a pair of jeans, a long-sleeved T-shirt, and a pair of tennis shoes. He dressed quickly. His leather jacket and boots were still in the alley where he'd shifted. A Were's natural body temperature ran a few degrees higher than a human's, so he didn't really need a coat to keep him warm. He was a walking furnace.

Still, that leather jacket was his favorite.

Grabbing the Harley, he walked it down a block before starting the engine. No need to alert the neighbors that he was back.

He cast one last look back on his parents' house. Now it was his mother's house. Was she okay? An overwhelming urge to go to the hospital and check on her pulled at his gut.

He shook his head. There was no reason to check on her. She was completely safe. The only danger in her life was now dead.

Braxton had bigger concerns. He had to make it out of Louisiana before the Assassins caught up to him. He had to try to make it to Missouri. It was one of the few states that offered refuge for Weres who were in trouble with the law. Every werewolf in trouble hunkered down in that state.

He straddled his bike, comforted by the feel of steel and chrome between his legs. He started the engine and tore down the street, refusing to look back on a life he no longer knew.

* * *

Dressed in tan pants, a black sweater, and armed with a smile, Kate walked through the doors of First Springs Bank. The lines for the bank tellers were five people deep, and the secretary had her phone pressed against her ear, furiously scribbling something in a folder. It was quite busy for the small town of Eureka Springs.

She hesitated and then took a couple of steps toward the secretary's desk. The woman gave her a warm smile and nodded her toward the empty chairs lined against the paneled wall near her desk.

Kate sat and almost placed her purse on the floor before remembering her mother's superstitious words: *Never put your purse on the floor or you'll never have any money.*

She snatched the bag up to her lap before it had a chance to hit the floor. Not that she was superstitious or anything, but at this point in the game, it didn't hurt to be cautious.

She sat her purse in the chair beside her.

"Why, Miss Wolph. What a pleasant surprise." Oliver Bigsby's grating voice seemed to echo throughout the small bank.

Kate froze, her stomach coiling with irritation. It wasn't enough that Bella Luna was under the threat of foreclosure, now she had the bad luck to run into Bigsby, the land developer who'd been trying to buy her bed and breakfast for the last six months.

Kate glued a polite smile on her face and faced the man. "Hello, Mr. Bigsby."

"If I had known you were going to be in town, I would have made lunch reservations for us."

"What for?" Her smile slipped. Was he deluded or just full of shit to think she'd ever consider having lunch with him?

"So we could talk about your little piece of land." He smiled, his too-perfect teeth looking a little too horsey for her tastes. He ran his manicured hand through his blonde hair and moved her purse out of the chair and onto the floor before sitting.

Clenching her jaw, she jerked her purse up, placed it in her lap and crossed her arms. "I've told you, Mr. Bigsby, I have no intention of selling Bella Luna. To you, or to anyone else for that matter." She turned her attention back toward the secretary, who had ended her call.

"No need to act brave, Kate. A little birdie told me you are in a bit of financial trouble." Bigsby smirked.

"And who would this little birdie be? My ex-boyfriend?" She didn't put it past her ex to try to kiss Bigsby's ass for a little money.

Mr. Bigsby gave her a little nod while attempting a

sympathetic smile.

He looked like Mr. Ed the horse trying to count. She glanced at his feet to see if he was going to paw the ground as well.

"I'm afraid your little vulture has no idea what he's talking about. I've not talked to him in six months, so he wouldn't know a thing about the Bella Luna." She turned her attention back to the secretary and caught the older woman's eye. The secretary stood and beckoned Kate forward with a wave of her hand.

"If you'll excuse me, I have business to attend to." She stood, slung her purse on her shoulder, and strode across the bank.

"Kate, my offer still stands. Keep that in mind."

She cringed, her face heating with embarrassment as the stares from other patrons stung her skin. The other bed and breakfast owners hated Bigsby for driving away their customers. The last thing she needed was for her name to be linked with his.

Keeping her gaze on the secretary, she didn't break her stride until she sat in the leather chair.

She kept her smile on her face and inhaled deeply.

"That's the biggest jackass I've ever come across." The older secretary nodded in Bigsby's direction.

Kate snorted, surprised by the matronly secretary's blunt response. "Actually, I was thinking he looked more like a horse's ass."

The secretary's eyes lit up with amusement. "Yes, that would fit better. Especially with those teeth. The man looks like he's got a mouth full of Chicklets gum."

Kate laughed at the visual.

"Now what can I do for you, dear?" The secretary slid a red lollipop across her desk to Kate and smiled.

"Thank you." Kate twirled the candy between her fingers.

Leaning forward, she whispered. "I'd like to speak to Mr. Montgomery."

The secretary's eyes widened for a fraction of a second. "Mr. Montgomery retired some months ago. His grandson, William Weatherford, is the bank president now."

Kate's heart accelerated, seeming to echo in her hollow chest. "Mr. Montgomery isn't the president anymore?" Mr. Montgomery might have helped her, might have bought her some time until she could get on her feet. How was she going to convince his grandson, whom she didn't know, to help her?

"No, honey." The secretary's brow creased. "But I'm sure our new president can help you. What is it you want to see him about?"

"It's about my bed and breakfast." Her voice, like her heart, cracked a little in desperation.

The secretary nodded and pressed a button on her phone and spoke quietly.

"He's got time before lunch. His office is right down that hall." The secretary pointed and gave her an encouraging smile.

* * *

AFTER POURING her heart out and pleading with the new bank president to no avail, Kate stood outside in the cold winter wind, her last hope dashed. Mr. William Weatherford had been quite different than his grandfather. The new bank president cared more about the bottom line than taking care of his customers.

Unless she paid her mortgage up to date by the end of the month, the bank would begin its foreclosure proceedings.

In order to make that kind of money, she would need to rent out all five of her bedrooms every night for a month.

It was something she'd never done. Ever.

She couldn't even fill up the Bella Luna for one night, let alone thirty consecutive nights.

The more she dwelled on it, the more she saw her hope slipping away.

Tears burned behind her eyes as she hurried down the sidewalk to the alley where she'd parked. She blinked furiously, trying to hold back the tears, and prayed she wouldn't run into anyone she knew.

Even though it was only noon, the tall, historic buildings loomed over the alley, blocking the winter sun's warmth and chilling her to the bone.

Kate swiped at the tears trickling down her cheeks. The urge to get home and curl up in her warm bed made it almost painful to breathe.

She'd never missed her mother more.

Blinded by her tears, she stumbled across the uneven brick pavement and tumbled to the ground. Loose gravel and rock bit into her palms and knees. She didn't bother holding her tears back now. She was alone with no one to hear her.

Under the bruising weight of hopelessness, she hung her head and sobbed, letting the tears flow free.

* * *

THE SOFT SOUNDS of a woman crying drifted down the alley where Braxton had parked his Harley.

He'd driven from Shreveport, only stopping to get gas, and had arrived in Eureka Springs around noon. He knew the biker bar on the Historical Loop was known for their wings and for their reputation of not remembering who came and went. Charles Manson could escape from prison, grab a snack and a game of pool, and when questioned the patrons would claim they never heard of the guy.

He had been starving and planned on stopping long enough to grab something to eat before traveling on to Missouri.

His heart hitched as the female sobs grew louder. The one thing that always got to him was a woman crying.

Easing further into the shadows of the alley, Braxton didn't see anything at first. A small movement on the ground near the dumpster drew his attention. A petite blonde woman was sitting back on her knees, her hands covering her face and sobbing like someone had ripped out her heart.

"Are you okay?"

The woman jerked her head up. Pushing herself to her feet, she stood. The uneven brick pavers caught the heel of her shoe and she stumbled. Braxton wrapped his arm around her waist to steady her.

"I'm fine." She kept her head down, swiping her hand across her face to dry her tears. Her dark blonde hair curtained her face, hiding her features from his gaze.

She pushed his hands away and took a step back. Her heel stuck in another crevice and pitched her forward into his chest. Automatically, he wrapped his arms around her and pulled her into his chest.

"I've got you." Braxton tried to swallow as her sweet scent muddled his brain. His blood heated from the feel of her small but firm breasts pressing into his chest. She might have been petite, but, damn, did she have a body. His dick hardened and strained forward.

Unaware of the physical effect she was having on him, the woman looked down at her foot, wriggling her heel free from the crack. She was so very close. Closing his eyes, he inhaled deep, drawing her delicious scent inside his body, memorizing it. She wasn't a werewolf, but her unique scent was the most fascinating thing he'd ever encountered.

"You smell like fresh snow on cedar trees."

She looked up at him and blinked. Her beautiful brown eyes so serious. "Must be floor cleaner. I mopped before I came into town."

He would have laughed if he hadn't been so startled by her beauty. She could be no more than twenty-five and her teary golden-brown eyes hypnotized him and had his heart racing like the latest Harley Davidson.

He shook his head, but couldn't bring himself to let her go. "No, you smell nothing like floor cleaner."

She cleared her throat and stepped back. Reluctantly, he let her slip out of his arms.

"Are you sure you're…" His gaze stopped at the pendant dangling around her neck. Reaching out, he brushed his fingertips across the moonstone shaped into a crescent moon. It was the same symbol female Weres wore when they were mated.

He narrowed his gaze on her. It didn't add up. Her scent was clearly not wolf, yet she wore the pendant of being mated. He gritted his teeth as jealousy flooded his veins. "Where did you get that?"

She clenched the pendant in her palm. "My mother gave me this when I was a little girl."

He glanced at her bare right hand and relaxed. "I thought maybe your boyfriend gave it to you." Her mother had probably bought the pendant from a pawnshop. Werewolves had money troubles, just like humans, and sometimes were forced to sell their prized possessions to make ends meet.

"I'm single." She blushed and shifted her weight. "Thank you for your help." She dug her keys out of her purse and shouldered her bag. "I need to be going."

Braxton wanted to hold her tight and kiss her senseless until whatever had upset her was nothing but a wisp of a memory. He wanted leaving to be the last thing on her beautiful mind and him to be burned forever in her soul.

25

JODI VAUGHN

He cleared his throat as he struggled to get his lust under control. He didn't have time to get laid. The Assassins were probably closing in on him at this very second. If he didn't get back on the road and make it to Missouri, he wasn't going to live to see another day.

"Maybe I'll see you around." She gave him a shy smile and slid into the driver's seat of her SUV.

His chest tightened as he watched her pull out of the alley and drive away. "No, sweetheart. I'm afraid you won't ever see me again."

* * *

"HE'LL TRY to make a break for the Missouri border." Brutus ground his cigarette butt under his boot heel and glanced at his two Were soldiers. They'd been a team for years now, with numerous executions under their belt. With matching black Harley Davidson V-Rods and dressed all in black, they were an intimidating force when they rolled into town.

"Don't you know those things will kill you?" Lorcan, his second-in-command and ever-growing thorn in his side smirked as he finished gassing up his motorcycle. With his blonde hair and blue eyes, he looked more like a California surfer than a deadly killer. "Or kill us, if you get too close to the gas tank."

As the leader of the Louisiana Assassins, Brutus knew his two partners thought it was funny as hell to ride his ass about his nasty smoking habit, since werewolves never got cancer.

Brutus shot a glare at Lorcan and Killian. "You two assholes better get focused. You know we have a job to do. I've never let a rogue werewolf out of my target, and I sure as shit don't expect to start now."

"We got it, boss." Killian straddled his Harley and started

the engine. The massive beast roared to life. "We're burning daylight. Eureka Springs is only a few miles down the road. Missouri shouldn't be much further from there."

Brutus pulled out of the gas station and back on the road with his soldiers flanking him. His target was clear.

Assassinate rogue werewolf Braxton Devereaux.

* * *

"IF I HAD THE MONEY, I'd give it to you. You know that, right?" Beau Smith, local vet and Kate's best friend, squeezed her hand across the diner table.

After embarrassing herself in the alley and crying all over the gorgeous stranger with the blue-tinged hair and tattooed arms, Kate had driven over to Beau's work. He suggested taking her out to lunch in hopes of getting her mind off the day's terrible events.

"Even if you had the money, I wouldn't take it." Kate pulled her hand away and picked up a soggy French fry covered in ketchup.

"I had a feeling you'd say that. It's that independent streak running through you." Beau sighed and shrugged. "So tell me more about this alley guy."

She flushed. Just the mention of the hot guy made her stomach turn to gelatin and her lady parts tingle. It was an odd reaction, since the stranger was totally not her type.

"I don't know. He came out of nowhere and helped me up. Not really much to tell." She left out the part of when he had held her in his massive arms, she had this overwhelming urge to kiss every part of his incredibly hard body. Beau didn't need to know about that part.

"I'd never seen him before. I just thought maybe he was new in town and you might know who he is." She shrugged.

Beau frowned before taking a drink of his soda. "Doesn't sound like anyone I know."

"It doesn't matter anyway. I've got bigger issues than to be thinking about some hot guy." Kate pushed her plate away and glanced at the time on her cell phone. "I've got to get going. I have to figure out how to get my bed and breakfast booked solid for a month."

"Go by the historical registry. I'm sure those ladies will have some good advice. Maybe they can push the Bella Luna on their website to encourage more visitors."

"I hope so." She stood and took out a ten to cover her tab.

"Put it away. This is on me." Beau waved her money away.

She hesitated and then relented. She shoved her money back in her wallet and dropped it in her purse. "Thanks. Next time I'm getting the check."

* * *

BRAXTON SMILED as he passed the highway sign stating five more miles until Missouri. He'd make it to Branson with plenty of daylight left to drive around the city without worrying if someone was about to put a bullet in the back of his head.

He couldn't help but think about the pretty blonde he'd left in Eureka Springs. He never remembered having such a strong attraction to a woman, human or werewolf, before. A part of him wanted to turn around, seek her out, and make sure she was okay.

Braxton shook his head. That was not even a remote possibility. He was the one in trouble, not her. At least whatever she was facing wasn't as bad as being hunted down and killed. He needed to start looking out for himself and stop worrying about someone who didn't care what happened to him. Old habits died hard.

A loud boom ricocheted down the highway and between the mountains.

His first thought was that his tire had blown out until pain exploded between his shoulder blades and spread like fire to his chest. Confused, he glanced in his rearview mirror to see three Harleys speeding toward him. His heart nearly stopped as he realized he'd been shot.

Assassins.

He gripped the handlebars of the bike as blinding pain spread through his body at a dizzying rate. He tried to tighten his grip on the handlebars in an attempt to keep the bike upright, but the paralyzing effect of the silver bullet was too strong.

The bike tilted to the right. Braxton tried to lean the other way, but his body wouldn't obey. The bike went down hard on the road. His leg was caught underneath as the bike skidded a few feet on the asphalt and toward the cliff. He held his breath, unable to do anything as he, along with his bike, plunged down the mountain.

Disengaged from his Harley, he continued to fall, crashing between limbs and bramble and trees. Pain splintered through his body as bones snapped. Being a werewolf, he could normally survive the fall and his bones would knit themselves back together unnaturally fast. But the silver bullet lodged in his shoulder would prevent any healing.

The silver would slowly poison him as he died a painful death.

His body met the ground in a bone-crushing thud, knocking what breath he had left out of his lungs. Nausea and fiery pain swept through his body in indescribable agony right before his vision grew dim and he passed out.

* * *

BRAXTON BLINKED, his body jerking alive with excruciating pain. Night had fallen and the temperature had dropped several degrees. Pitch-black surrounded him and the bristle of pine needles stuck his face. He wasn't dead.

Yet.

He tried to lift his left arm. White hot pain shot up his arm and into his chest. He knew immediately his arm was definitely broken. He raised his right arm, feeling his body for bone and excessive bleeding. Though no bone stuck out of the flesh, he could feel the awkward bend of the arm.

He shoved down his nausea and continued assessing his injuries. His side burned with each breath, and he knew he had suffered some broken ribs as well. He bent his knees. Despite bruises, his legs were not broken.

He closed his eyes, wondering why the Assassins didn't finish the job. Maybe they saw him fall off the mountain and didn't think he'd survive the drop coupled with the silver bullet.

He shook his head, not daring to give that thought an ounce of hope. It was more likely they were waiting until dark to come back and make sure he was dead.

Urgency flooded his veins. He had to get the hell out of there. His heart thudded against his ribs as he bolted upright. "Fuck!" Pain radiated throughout his core as his stomach twisted in nausea. He leaned over and emptied the contents of his stomach.

He didn't plan to stick around and wait for those assholes to finish him off. He wiped his mouth with his uninjured arm. Grabbing the nearest pine tree, he attempted to stand, but his shaky legs wouldn't bear his weight.

He panted as cold sweat beaded across his forehead.

He had no choice. Not if he wanted to live. He needed to keep going. If he stayed, he was as sure as dead.

Focusing his energy on his inner wolf, he shifted. He

gritted his teeth, trying to not yell as his broken bones twisted into his wolf form. Bones shifted and cartilage stretched. When the transformation was done, he lay on his side, panting. His injuries were still there, but in his wolf form he might have a chance to keep moving. He eased to his feet, growling as the pain reminded him he was running out of time.

He forced one paw in front of the other and began his trek.

He just prayed he was walking toward the Missouri border.

* * *

BRAXTON WALKED for an eternity under the cover of the inky night sky. Although his keen sense of sight helped him avoid running into a tree or stepping in a hole, he had no idea which direction he was going since he had no stars to guide him. His head spun as he pressed on, each step pure agony. Surely he had crossed the Missouri border by now.

Glancing up, he hoped the sky had cleared. He needed those stars to guide his course. Once again, fate, being the bitch she was, had left him without a fucking star in the sky.

His broken ribs cried out with every breath he took, and his body begged him to stop and rest. He knew better. If he stopped, he would die.

A tiny light broke through the thick trees. It must be someone's home. He sucked in another painful breath and pressed on, his eyes never wavering from his illuminated hope of harbor.

* * *

HE'D NEVER RAISED a hand to either of his men, but for the

first time, Brutus really wanted to plow his fist right into Killian's face. They'd had to leave the spot where Braxton had been shot and head to the nearest rest area and wait until dark to continue their search for the rogue wolf.

"Why in the fuck would you think it was a good idea to shoot a werewolf in the middle of the fucking day?" Brutus glared at Killian as they stood on the side of the road. The temperature had dropped several degrees and the scent of impending snow hung heavy in the air.

Killian frowned and shook his head, his expression grim. "He was three miles from the border. He was about to jump the state line. I was thinking..."

"No. That's exactly what you were *not* doing. You were *not* thinking." Brutus aimed his flashlight down the side of the mountain. "You're lucky there was no oncoming traffic. Otherwise, your ass would be sitting in a jail cell for murder. Not to mention the fact that we couldn't even stop and investigate without every nosy state trooper asking if we were having bike trouble."

"It's not murder if there's no body," Lorcan said as he climbed up the steep drop-off. He'd volunteered to go down and investigate while Killian and Brutus stood watch from the road. "From what I can see, there's no body—not a trace of him down there."

Lorcan frowned. "He must be heading to the Missouri border."

Brutus grinned. "Then we need to get there first. And welcome him with a silver bullet to his head."

* * *

"BARRETT, what's so important that you wake me up in the middle of the night to haul my ass all the way over here?" Damon Trahan glared at his Pack Master and all-around badass leader of the Arkansas werewolves, Barrett Middleton. Barrett's office was sparse but neat, with a large desk and office chair that creaked every time Barrett leaned forward. Damon was big, but Barrett was even larger. Damon often wondered how much life the chair had left before it snapped under Barrett's large body of muscle.

He began to wonder if Barrett even had a home to go to, or whether the Pack Master had a bed somewhere in the back. The only time he'd seen his Pack Master was in his office or in the adjoining meeting room when all the Guardians needed to be updated on the status of the Pack.

Barrett leaned back and smirked. "Don't pull that shit with me, Damon. I doubt you and Ava were getting much sleep. I've seen how you two act in the day; I can hardly imagine what you're like at night when no one is looking."

Damon let a slow grin cross his lips. "We're way worse than what you are imagining."

"Okay, TMI." Barrett's expression grew grim as he met his gaze. "We have an issue. The Louisiana Pack has overstepped its boundaries. It seems early this morning a Were crossed into Arkansas."

"So?"

"That Were was being following by three Louisanna Assassins."

"Shit." Damon narrowed his eyes. Assassins were the death squad for werewolves who'd broken the most serious of offenses. Each state had its own Assassins, and they answered only to the Pack Master of their state."Yeah, shit's right." Barrett ran a large hand across his face. "The Assassins broke protocol when they didn't inform me of their mission or even let me know they were crossing into my fucking state. I had to find out from an informant," Barrett growled. "I was going to let it slide. Who am I to interfere with an execution?"

"And now?" Damon cocked his head. Barrett was all about order and following protocol. There was something more to the story.

"I found out the rogue wolf they're after is Braxton Devereaux. The charge is murder." Barrett sighed heavily.

"Braxton Devereaux? From Shreveport?" Chills ran down Damon's back. Braxton had helped him the night he went in to rescue his best friend, Jayden, from a pack of rogue wolves. Those same rogue wolves had kidnapped Ava. The leader of the rogue wolves was captured and Damon, as the role of Ava's mate, had the honors of carrying out the execution. If Braxton hadn't been there that night, things might have gone south.

"So who exactly did Braxton kill to get an execution order?" Damon's gut turned to stone.

Barrett narrowed his eyes. "Braxton killed his father."

Damon gritted his teeth until his jaw hurt. "Well, from what I've heard the fucker was asking for it. It seems Braxton's old man had a habit of using his mom as a punching bag." Damon frowned. "Look, Barrett, even if Braxton did do this, don't ask me to help the Assassins look for him."

"You feel indebted to him. I get that." Barrett sat back in his chair.

"He helped us out in Shreveport. You know I'm right. At least get his side of the story before handing him over to the Assassins."

"The Were Law states I am to hand over any werewolf accused of murdering another werewolf."

"The Were Law also states any Assassins crossing into your territory have to be granted permission before doing so," Damon countered.

"So when this shit blows back, my defense should be, 'They started it.'" Barrett shot him a glare.

Damon gave him a toothy grin. "Always works for me."

CHAPTER 3

*K*ate clutched the baseball bat in her sweaty palm and eased the front door open. She had tried to ignore the soft whimpering coming from outside, but her heart tugged with pity for whatever creature might be freezing to death in the snowstorm that had come out of nowhere.

She had glanced outside the window, but the only thing she saw moving was the steady stream of falling flakes blanketing the ground.

The door creaked. She winced and wondered why she'd never noticed the door making such a loud sound before. She mentally made a note to get some oil next time she was in town.

She flipped on the porch light and hoisted her wooden weapon in the air, ready to swing at anything that attacked.

Nothing leaped from the bushes, nothing barreled out from the woods, nothing snatched her from the porch.

She heaved out a relieved breath. "That was anti-climactic. Pretty much like my ex." She lowered the bat, an idiotic giggle slipping past her lips.

Another soft whine sliced through the winter night, sending chills sprinting up her back. She gripped the bat in both hands, glancing from one end of the porch to the other. Still, she saw nothing.

Another whimper drifted out into the night. She stood still, trying to figure out where the noise was coming from. She took a step and froze.

"Who am I kidding? I know how this shit turns out in the movies. The blonde girl, who is all alone in the house, always gets killed first." She turned, ran into the house, and locked the door. Bat in hand, she went from room to room, making sure her windows and doors were all locked. After making sure the house was secured and no one could get in, she eased toward the living room window and peered out.

She heard the pitiful whimper again. It sounded very much like a dog.

It wasn't unusual for dogs to get hit by cars in this area. Irresponsible people tended to let their animals have free run, and sometimes the unthinkable happened.

She shook her head and headed to the door. She grabbed the bat, just in case Fido decided to snap at her.

She walked out on the porch and edged closer to the steps. She stopped in her tracks and gasped. Her muscles iced over, refusing to move.

Sprawled on the steps was the largest gray wolf she had ever seen.

"Holy sh…"

The wolf let out a pitiful whimper and opened its eyes.

Its eyes were the color of gathering storm clouds, gray and dangerous, and the fur along its upper legs had varied colors of blue and gray, unlike the rest of its body that was a solid grey.

The wolf blinked and closed its eyes, panting out each labored breath.

Sadness stung her heart. There was something familiar, something almost human-like in the animal's expression before he shut his eyes. She set the bat on the nearest wicker rocker and eased closer.

"Come on, buddy. Don't die." Kate reached a tentative hand out and waited for the wolf to open his eyes, sniff her, and growl.

He didn't move.

"I'm going to touch you, okay?" She shook her head and groaned. She wasn't sure why she was talking to the wolf. It wasn't like he could understand her.

Her fingertips dipped into the thickness of his fur. She expected it to be coarse like horse hair, but instead it was silky and soft.

She kept her eyes on his face while her fingers explored his strong body, feeling for broken bones and wounds. She had seen wolves in the mountains, but she'd never seen any this large.

Her fingertips dipped into something warm and sticky. Her gut tightened when she pulled back blood-tinged fingers.

"I'll be right back." She hurried into the house and retrieved some towels and her cell phone. Kneeling down by the wolf, she pressed a white towel against the wound.

The wolf whimpered and opened his eyes.

"I'm sorry, but I've got to stop the bleeding." She firmly pressed the towel against the wound. This time he didn't budge, but his gaze never left her face.

She held out her hand for him to sniff. He strained forward and nuzzled her fingertips.

"You're very loving, aren't you? I bet you've got all the female wolves after you."

The wolf opened its mouth. Its tongue lolled out to the side, its lips curling over its teeth as if it were smiling.

She snorted. That was impossible. Wolves didn't smile.

* * *

BRAXTON DIDN'T REMEMBER the walk to the house. With his blood loss and the silver slowly poisoning his body, he was surprised he'd made it to the house at all. He heard the door open and expected to see some farmer hovering above him with a shotgun aimed at his head. At least then he would be put out of his misery.

Instead, he felt the touch of gentle fingers stroking his fur. Confused, he opened his eyes. To his shock, it was the woman he'd met in the alley.

His female.

Through the blinding pain racking his body, he nuzzled her hand and inhaled her haunting scent.

He even managed a smile, as best a wolf could, when she suggested how loving he was. If only he wasn't hurt, he'd show her just how loving he could be. With her underneath him.

Braxton watched his beautiful woman lift the cell phone to her ear.

He stiffened, lifting his head. Every instinct told him to bolt. She was probably calling the game warden right now, who would probably want to put him out of his misery. A regular bullet wouldn't kill him; it would just hurt like hell. His main concern was the Assassins.

"Easy, boy." She reached out and stroked his head. He leaned into her hand, not wanting her to stop. Her touch was the only thing keeping him conscious and keeping the pain bearable. "I'm calling someone who will help us. He's a vet."

Braxton snarled at the mention of another male.

She snatched her hand away.

He could smell her fear for the first time since she'd found him on her steps.

Lowering his head, he whimpered, hoping she'd understand that he meant her no harm. He waited an eternity until finally she reached out and touched his wound. He knew she was keeping a safe distance from his mouth. Damn, he didn't want her to be afraid. Not of him. Never of him.

He looked up, struck by her beauty and humbled by her kindness. He didn't know many humans who would risk their safety to try to help a wild animal. Yet, here she was, his female, sitting out here in the freezing cold, trying to comfort him.

Pain exploded through his chest, reminding him of the bullet and the reality that he was slowly being poisoned by the silver. He didn't have much longer. The only thing that had kept him alive this long was the fact he was in wolf form.

The second he shifted back to human, he would be dead within minutes.

* * *

KATE GRITTED HER TEETH, irritated that she had to leave Beau a message when he didn't answer her call. She shivered against another blast of wind, the winter air cutting through her thin cotton pajamas. She should have dressed warmer, but hadn't planned on being outside so long.

She glanced at the wolf and frowned. She couldn't leave him outside like this for the night; he wouldn't make it through the night. But then again, she couldn't exactly bring a wild animal in the house either.

"I'll be right back." She raced through the house, gathering blankets and old linens. Stepping out on the front porch, she spread out the old blankets and sheets into a cozy bed in a corner. "At least this will keep the wind off you." She glanced at the wolf still lying on the steps. Her smile faded.

How was she going to get him up the steps? He didn't look like he had the energy to walk. Even though the blood flow had slowed, he panted with every painful breath.

Taking one of the sheets, she folded it in half and spread it beside him on the stairs.

"I'm going to roll you over on to this so I can move you. Okay? It's going to hurt, but I'll try to be as gentle as I can."

The wolf opened his eyes and blinked but didn't move.

Biting her lip, she lifted his head and shoulders onto the sheet. Kate sat back and secured the towel around his wound before sliding her arms underneath his chest and lifting.

The wolf didn't budge.

She straddled him and wrapped her arms around his torso, her cheek pressing into his fur. She pulled, using every muscle in her body. It took three lifts, but she finally managed to move his massive body onto the sheet. She tied the ends together to keep him from rolling out the bottom.

"Good grief, you weigh a ton. I imagine you crush your female partners." She stood and arched her back.

The wolf lifted his lips over his massive teeth once again in a semblance of a smile.

Her face heated. "I didn't mean that. I mean it's inappropriate...you know, for me to say...well, I don't really know you that well and..."

She pressed her lips together and shook her head. "So it's come to this. I'm talking to a wolf about sex."

She grabbed the top of the sheet and wrapped the ends around her hands. "This may hurt a little."

Digging in her heels, she pulled.

He didn't budge.

"Let's try this again." She bent her legs and pulled, yet he still didn't budge.

Kate sat down and looked at the animal. There was no way she was going to be able to move him on her own.

"This is like moving an elephant." It was impossible.

She frowned, remembering her mother's words when she was a little girl and she thought something wasn't possible. A slow smile spread across her face.

The only way to eat an elephant was one inch at a time.

She sat down and positioned her legs on either side of his head. Wrapping the sheet around her hands, she dug in her heels and pulled.

She managed to move the wolf a few inches.

She backed up a step, sat, and pulled again.

Once again, she managed to move the animal a few inches.

Her back screamed in protest by the time she got the wolf onto the porch.

Under the soft glow of the porch light, snow was falling in sheets across the yard. She glanced at her wolf. Her heart tugged for the wounded creature.

"You'll be okay out here, won't you, boy?" Even as she said it, she didn't believe her own words.

The only movement the wolf made was the struggle to breathe, its short, shallow pants coming harder and harder.

"I'll get you some water." Kate hurried back into the house and rummaged through the kitchen cabinets, looking for a suitable water bowl. The closest thing she could find to a dog bowl was a mixing bowl. It would just have to do.

She walked outside and set the bowl of water near the makeshift bed. "Hopefully Beau will get my message and be over here soon." She ran her fingers through his fur and finally stood, some part of her not wanting to leave him. She walked over the porch railing and watched the fast falling snow. Before morning there would be more than a few inches on the ground.

"I guess you'll be okay out here..." Her mouth dropped as the wolf stood and limped through the front door into her house.

"Wait! You can't go inside." He turned at her words, his eyes weak with fatigue and pain. Somehow she knew at that moment if she asked him to come outside, he'd do it.

Stepping through the door, she eyed the giant beast that was now standing in her house. He was even bigger on four legs.

"I guess you can spend the night right here by the door." She went out and gathered up his makeshift bed. Walking inside, she closed the door. She glanced around, but he was nowhere in sight.

"Shit." She dropped the linens and hurried through the house.

When she reached her bedroom, she froze. Lying on his side, with his head resting on her pillow, was the wolf.

"Look buddy, I don't share my bed with just anybody." She wagged her finger at him.

He lifted his head weakly and let it fall against the pillow.

Her heart melted. How could she stay mad at such a helpless creature?

"Okay, but no slobbering on my pillow." She saw his lips curl slightly, and she couldn't help but smile at how expressive he was.

What the hell had she gotten herself into? There was a freaking wolf. In her bed.

She squeezed her eyes shut and shook her head. She glanced at the wolf one last time before closing the bedroom door and heading into the living room. Grabbing a quilt from the closet, she headed for the sofa.

Just her luck. Not only was the wolf at the door, he was now in her bed.

* * *

AMIDST THE BLIZZARD of pain raging through his body, Braxton burrowed deeper into the soft pillow that carried the heavenly scent of the female. It was her scent that had him fighting death with every molecule in his damaged body. It was for her he wanted to live, just to have another minute of her voice, her touch, her presence.

Another bolt of raw pain shot through his chest, reminding him of how short on time he really was. He had lived his life trying to protect the woman who'd given him birth, only to be accused by her of being a murderer.

How could his mother think he'd kill his father? Not that he hadn't entertained the thought, but hell, if he wanted to do it, he would have done it years ago. Then he would have had a chance to live his life, to maybe fall in love and find a mate. Instead, he'd wasted his life in the shit hole strip club in Shreveport, protecting his mother, who didn't even want to be protected.

How fucked up was that?

Braxton sucked in another shallow breath. The image of the blonde female filled his mind, taking the edge off his pain.

An ache of a different kind slapped him across his heart. He wouldn't live long enough to see his female in his human form. He wouldn't have the chance to touch her, to talk, to make love to her.

Braxton rubbed his nose in her pillow, wanting her scent all over him. If he were going to die tonight, he wanted to take her scent with him into the afterlife.

* * *

KATE JERKED awake at the sharp pounding at her front door.

Throwing off the quilt, she padded to the window and peeked out. She quickly unlocked and opened the door.

"I got over here as soon as I heard your message. What's wrong? Did your pipes break?" Beau cast a furtive glance around the room and then back at her.

"There's a hurt animal. I'm not sure what's wrong with him. I think he got hit by a car." Kate glanced over her shoulder and motioned with her hand for Beau to follow.

"So you put it in your room?" Beau lifted his eyebrow.

"Not exactly. He walked into my room when I turned my back."

Beau snorted. "So what is it, a dog or cat?"

"Neither." Kate paused in front of her bedroom, her hand on the doorknob, and looked up at her oldest friend. "It's a wolf."

She opened the door to find her patient laying unnaturally still. Her heart slammed into her chest, and she took a step to see if he was even breathing. Beau grabbed her elbow and jerked her back.

"Are you crazy? That's a wild animal, Kate."

She wiggled free of his grasp and shot him a glare. "I know that."

"Have you forgotten what happened when you were little?" Beau's gaze bore into her making her feel like a ten-year-old.

"No, I haven't." She gritted her teeth. "He hasn't hurt me or even growled at me once." She glanced at the wolf lying in her bed like a very large pet. She sighed when she saw his chest rise and fall. "If he was going to hurt me, he would have done so by now."

"It's a wolf." Beau ran his hand through his hair.

"It's still an animal." She cut her eyes at him. "I don't know how to help him; that's why I called you. You're the vet, can't you do something?"

Beau narrowed his gaze and shook his head. For a second she thought he was going to turn around and leave. Instead, he walked over to her bathroom and pulled out some towels.

"Do you have a leash?"

"For what? I don't have a dog."

"And yet you bring a wolf inside your house," he muttered. "Look, I'm going to have to muzzle him before I start working."

Kate walked up to the wolf and held out her hand under his nose. She let out a breath when his hot breath tickled her skin.

Beau grabbed her by the arm and pulled her away from the bed. "Are you crazy?"

"He won't hurt you."

"Either find something I can use as a muzzle or I'm not touching him." Beau glared long enough at her that she knew there was no way she was winning this conversation.

"Fine." She came back a few minutes later with some rope she'd found under the kitchen sink.

Beau took a step toward the wolf with the rope in hand.

The wolf opened his eyes, lifted his head, and let out a growl between his teeth. Beau froze.

"You need to let him muzzle you so he can look at your wound. He's only trying to help." She propped her hands on her hips and gave the animal a stern look to know she wasn't kidding.

The wolf fell back against the pillow and closed his eyes.

"What are you, the wolf whisperer?" Beau murmured as he slipped on the muzzle. Even with the muzzle secure, the wolf gave a low belly growl. "Easy, boy." Beau stepped back.

"Stop. He's the doctor," she jerked her thumb at Beau, "and you're just going to have to let him look at you if you want to get better."

"I don't think he understands you." Beau slid her a look.

"Stop growling and let him help." Ignoring Beau, she narrowed her gaze at the wolf.

The wolf whimpered and laid his head back down.

Beau's mouth dropped open.

"He'll be good," she said.

Beau's Adam's apple bobbed as he cautiously eased onto the bed.

She held her breath and said a silent prayer as Beau ran his hands across the wolf's chest, assessing the wound.

"He doesn't look like he's been run over. He looks like he's been shot."

The blood in Kate's face pooled in her stomach. "What makes you think he's been shot?"

"There's a bullet-size hole in his fur." Beau frowned. "Maybe someone caught him in their garbage or around their livestock?" He leaned closer. "I think I can see the bullet." He glanced at her. "Do you have any forceps?"

"You're the vet; I thought you were supposed to bring your supplies with you."

"You didn't exactly specify when you called why you needed me. Your message just said for me to get my ass over here ASAP. I tried calling on my way over, but you didn't pick up."

"My cell phone's probably dead." She tapped her finger against her bottom lip. "I have some tweezers in the bathroom, would that work?"

"Go get them."

She returned with the tweezers, a first aid kit, and more towels. Easing down beside the wolf, she rested her hand on his head. "He's got to take the bullet out, okay? It might hurt a little."

"A lot. It's going to hurt a lot. No need to sugarcoat it." Beau looked up at her as he positioned the tweezers over the bloodied wound.

She shot him a glare.

Beau worked the tweezers in the wound as the wolf let out a whimper. Blood spilled out and pooled on the towels that had been positioned beneath the wound. She leaned over and buried her nose in his fur as she rubbed the soft area under his mouth. She kept her hand on the wolf's head to keep the animal calm while Beau worked. There was so much blood. She held her breath, trying to make sure she could feel the wolf's chest rise and fall against her hand.

"Got it." Beau held up the tweezers. Under the lighting, the metal glittered, looking different from any bullet she'd ever seen.

"That's weird. I thought bullets were more grey. That almost looks like a silver bullet." She couldn't suppress a shiver that ran through her body.

Beau's expression shuttered. He blinked and quickly shook his head. "It's probably one of those new Russian bullets. They're always coming up with something new."

She shrugged off the unease that ran up her spine. She was exhausted and she needed sleep. All the stress about her house was making her paranoid. "You're the hunter, you should know."

"His left leg is broken. I'll splint it after I wrap his wound." Beau wrapped some gauze he'd gotten from the first aid kit around the wound. After placing clean towels under the wolf, he stood and rubbed his eyes.

"Want me to help you move him outside?"

"No."

"I don't think it's a good idea to keep a wild animal in your house, let alone your bedroom." He stared at her like she'd lost her mind.

"I'll keep the door locked." She glanced out the window. "The snow's really coming down now. I don't think he would survive being out in that cold. Besides he's lost a lot of blood. I doubt he could do much damage in his condition."

Beau pinched the bridge of his nose and closed his red-rimmed eyes. "Fine. I'll stay."

She held her hands up. "No. You've done enough. Besides, you've got work tomorrow. Go on home and get some rest."

"I don't think you need to be alone with a wild animal. It could attack you."

"Go. I'll be fine. I won't even go into the room tonight. Besides, I don't think it will be able to open the door with its paw."

Beau stifled a yawn and rubbed the back of his neck. "Alright, but you keep that door locked. I'll be back at dawn to check on both of you. If he wakes up and gives you trouble, call me, okay?"

"I will."

She stood at the door and watched Beau's four-wheel-drive head down the road before locking up for the night. She grabbed her bedroom key from the hook in the kitchen and headed down the hall. She stopped in the doorway of the bedroom.

"Okay, boy, I'm gonna lock…" The words faded on her tongue and her breath hitched in her throat. The key slipped out of her hand and landed with a tinkle on the floor.

The wolf was gone. Lying in the middle of the bed, wrapped in gauze, was the hot stranger from the alley.

CHAPTER 4

*B*raxton tried to swallow, grimacing at the fiery pain in his throat. He felt like he'd swallowed fucking lava rocks. What he wouldn't give for one drop of water.

Blinking open his leaden eyelids, his gaze landed on the frilly white curtains draped over the window of the strange room. Snow coursed to the ground, a heavy layer blanketing the earth and hopefully covering his tracks.

He relaxed a little.

Movement from the door caught his eye, and he bristled as he jerked his head around.

It was her. His female.

She stood in the doorway wearing red and black plaid flannel pajamas and looking like the sexiest thing alive. He met her astonished golden-brown gaze. She tugged on her full bottom lip with her teeth as she slowly bent to the floor to retrieve her keys. Her top gaped open, and he got a fantastic view of her perfect firm naked breasts. But it was her scent, God help him, that made him hard as a rock.

He bent his knee and groaned, trying to mask his erection

under the quilt. The last thing he needed was for her to think he was going to molest her and scare her away. He was sure he looked pretty intimidating as it was, covered in tattoos and sporting blue-tipped hair. He probably looked like a thug to someone so beautifully innocent.

He licked his dry lips. "Don't be scared. I won't hurt you."

She narrowed her eyes. "What are you?" She held her hand up. "Wait. Don't answer that." She shook her head, her long, blonde hair brushing against the tops of her pajama-clad breasts.

Damn, he'd never been jealous of hair before.

"I'm dreaming, right? This is one really long dream, and I'm about to wake up because now I know I'm dreaming." Her words came out on one long breath. "I mean, how else would I explain a hot guy lying in my bed instead of my wolf?"

His cock twitched, and he managed a grin even through the pain in his chest. His dick hardened with desire. "You think I'm hot?"

"Duh." She cocked her head as her gaze traveled up and down his body. "You're that guy in the alley. The guy that held me when I was crying."

His breath caught in his throat. She remembered him.

"It's all making perfect sense now."

Had the cops slapped his picture across every TV in America? He sat forward, ready to bolt. Pain ricocheted through his chest, and a groan slipped out between his clenched teeth.

She hurried forward, concern creasing her beautiful face. "Lay back." She pressed her cool hand against his head. He obeyed, sinking into the pillow.

"I don't understand why you're hurt in my dream. I mean, can't I magically make you better?" She met his gaze.

Seeking her cool touch, he pressed his face into her palm

and closed his eyes. So she really did think she was dreaming. He relaxed. "It's not that kind of dream."

"Is it one of those hot sex dreams?"

Braxton's eyes popped open. She stared back at him, completely serious. His cock hardened to the point of pain.

He cleared his throat and winced. "Can I have some water?"

"Sure." She paused halfway to the door and glanced over her shoulder. "Maybe I should call Beau first."

He growled. "Is Beau your mate?"

"Mate?" She arched her eyebrow.

"Boyfriend." Of course she wouldn't understand the term mate. She was human. "I meant is he your boyfriend?"

She wrinkled her pretty nose. "No. He's my friend."

Braxton relaxed. He remembered the man standing over him before he passed out as white-hot pain spread through his chest. He glanced down at his arm, splinted and wrapped. He could feel the bone already knitting itself back together. In a few hours, his arm should be good as new. His chest, on the other hand, was a different story.

"What's with the growling anyway?"

He gave her a droll look. "I'm a wolf in your dream, remember?"

"Oh, right." She shrugged, as if quickly accepting the explanation. "I'll be right back with your water."

Braxton let his eyes drift down her back to the sway of her tight ass as she left the room. He might have a hole in his chest, but he was still breathing.

* * *

KATE WALKED BACK into the bedroom carrying a bowl and glass, both filled with water. She blushed. "I wasn't sure which form you would be in when I got back, so I brought both."

He laughed and hissed in pain from the motion. He couldn't shift right now, even if he wanted to. He didn't have the strength. He downed the water, letting the cold liquid soothe his raw throat. Wiping his mouth with the back of his hand, he handed the glass back to her.

"I take it you've never had a dream like this before." His fingers brushed against hers, sending a jolt of excitement through his body. Had she felt it, too?

A nervous laugh escaped the back of her throat. "No. The only dreams I have about wolves are nightmares."

He stilled, his chest muscles straining. "Why is that? You've got something against wolves?"

"No. They have something against me."

* * *

HER GAZE ROAMED down his naked chest to the sheet that rested low on his narrow hips. She'd never seen a man built as fine as Braxton, in real life, or in movies.

"What do you mean?" His gravel voice made her stomach tingle. An invisible force pulled her to him and made her step closer.

"I was bitten once, when I was a child." She licked her lips, dropping her gaze to his broad shoulders. His arms were completely covered in tattoos, sleeves they were called, while his chest was free of any ink. She wanted to run her fingers across every swirl and curve of his designs until she had memorized every detail. And she didn't want to stop at his arms. She wanted to touch him everywhere.

So what was stopping her? It wasn't like it was real. It was just a dream—and with all the stress she was under, she deserved this.

She reached out her hand, tracing his muscled pec with her finger. His breath hitched, and she could feel him tremble beneath her fingertips, like some unknown power was trying to be released. She grinned at his response to her.

"You have the hardest body I've ever seen." She slid her hand down to his stomach, caressing the rock-hard abs. Her stomach warmed and a sigh slipped past her lips. "I can't stop touching you."

"Then touch me everywhere." He covered her hand with his and slid it down past his stomach, underneath the sheet.

Her fingers brushed against his cock and she gasped. She knew she would never touch him so intimately in reality. But in her dream she could do whatever she wanted. Tentatively, she traced a finger across the wide crest. His cock twitched under her touch. Desire streaked between her legs, and her breasts ached with longing so intense she thought she would explode.

She looked up into his face.

He met her gaze, his gray eyes heavy with lust, a slight smirk playing at the corners of his full lips.

"You never told me your name." His deep voice played across her skin like the ocean breeze, warming and relaxing her. "At least give me your name since you have your hand on my cock."

She swallowed. She should be embarrassed enough to stop and pull her hand away. But she wasn't. This was her dream and she could do whatever she wanted. "Kate."

"Kate. My beautiful Kate." He guided her hand down the length of his cock to the base. He groaned. "My name is Braxton."

"Braxton," she breathed out his name. His hand tightened around hers, showing her how hard to squeeze him as he worked her hand up and down his shaft. Her chest caught as her heart beat in rapid staccato in her ears. "Braxton, I don't usually do this."

"Do what," he breathed out. "Dream about a wolf shifting into a man? Or jack a guy off?" He moaned when she gave him a squeeze.

"I've never done either one." Heated desire poured through her, exciting her to the point that she might come by getting him off. Lust overrode any residuals of embarrassment. It felt too good to stop. Her dream, her rules.

"Have you ever given a guy a hand job?" Keeping one hand on top of hers, he reached up with his free hand and cupped her face.

"No." She swallowed. Her lips parted under the gentle brush of his thumb. "I've never wanted to touch a man as badly as I want to touch you."

"Come here." He pulled her down, his mouth taking hers in a kiss so powerful her knees buckled.

His tongue dove inside her mouth, hot and fevered, and she moaned with pleasure at the invasion. Pressing one knee into the bed, she climbed on top of him and straddled his waist. She released his cock and sat against his bulging erection. They both moaned as she rocked her hips against his.

She leaned down, placing both hands on either side of his face, careful to keep her weight centered on his lap and away from his bandaged chest.

"Damn, Kate. I smell your sweet arousal, how wet you are." He pulled her down into a kiss.

"Braxton?" She closed her eyes as his mouth licked down the side of her neck and sucked. Delicious chills swept across her heated body, and she wanted nothing more than to pull down her pants and sink down on his length.

"Yes, Kate?" he murmured against her parted lips, nipping at the corners.

"Are you really a wolf?" She ran her hand across his chest, her fingertips swirling the bristly dark hairs.

"Does it matter?" He tugged her earlobe into his mouth and sucked.

"No. But, if you are a wolf, don't bite me." She pressed her groin against his.

He chuckled, his laugh deep and sexy. "Don't worry, my sweet Kate. You'll love the way I bite."

"I bet I will." She pulled his face back and kissed him deep, sucking his tongue into her mouth.

His fingers dipped into the back of her pajamas, his hands reaching down to cup her butt. It was like he was branding himself on her. She'd never had a man touch her so possessively. The times she and Tom had sex, their interludes had always left her unfulfilled and never satisfied. Braxton stirred up more passion in her than her ex ever did.

His skilled fingers slid under the back of her panties and made their way further down, caressing up and down between her soft folds.

She moaned.

"Feel good, sweetheart?" Braxton's hot breath against her neck made her tremble.

"Yes." She arched her back, giving him more access. "Don't stop touching me."

"Look at me, Kate."

Her eyes fluttered open, and she held his gaze as he moved his hand around to her stomach and down the front of her pajamas. Her breath came out in hard fast pants and she couldn't look away.

His nostrils flared as his fingers dipped into the wetness pooling between her legs. She shivered as his finger flicked across her sensitive clit. Slowly his fingers slid between her folds, teasing and taunting.

She wrapped her fingers around his wrist and ground against his hand. She needed more.

"Tell me what you want, beautiful Kate."

She swallowed, her mouth suddenly dry. Her face heated as his gray eyes bore into hers, captivating and controlling her in some indescribable way. She'd never been so attracted and drawn to someone like this in her whole life. It was like some kind of black magic.

He unleashed something so primitive and wild within her, it had her wanting more.

His talented fingers continued the exquisite assault between her legs as his intense gaze focused on her, like she was the only thing in the universe that mattered.

"I want you to touch me." The words tumbled out of her lips in a heady rush.

"I am touching you, sweetheart."

She groaned, wishing his fingers were deep within her. "You know what I mean."

"I need to hear it Kate. I need you to say the words."

She let the erotic words fall from her lips. "I want your fingers inside me."

He growled and suddenly his finger was pushing at her wet entrance. His long finger slid partially in. She dug her fingernails into his biceps in ecstasy.

"Fuck, sweetheart. You're so tight." He moved, slow steady pumps, teasing her. But it wasn't enough. She ground her pelvis against his hand, wanting him deeper, but that was impossible with her pajama bottoms on.

"Take your pajamas off." His deep voice sent delicious chills bouncing across her body. Despite his injury, he lifted her off him so she could remove her bottoms.

She tugged at her top and threw it on the floor. The bottoms were tossed in the air. Straddling him once again, she placed her hands on either side of his head. "Why can't I have you in real life? Why does this have to be a dream?"

His lips curved up at the corners. "Maybe this isn't a dream."

She sighed and pressed his hand to her naked breasts. "Nope. Pretty sure it's a dream. Things this good don't happen to me in real life. Just the bad stuff."

Something flashed through his stormy eyes, something sad and hard, like maybe he understood the harshness of life.

She smoothed her hand against his cheek. She wanted to memorize every contour of his face before she woke. He turned his face toward her palm and inhaled.

He reached for her, cupping her face and bringing her down to meet his mouth. She moaned as his tongue teased hers. She melted against him, pressing every inch of her body into his.

"What the fuck are you doing?" Beau's voice rained down on her like a bucket of ice.

She bolted upright and covered her breasts with her hand.

Beau stood in the doorway, his coat shedding snowflakes like a long-haired lab, his face twisted in a mixture of disbelief and horror.

If this was a dream, then why did she suddenly feel like a teenager being caught kissing a boy behind the bleachers?

She opened her mouth to defend herself, to ask what the hell Beau was doing in her dream.

"Where's the wolf?" Beau addressed her but kept his glare on Braxton. "And who the hell is this?"

A growl erupted from underneath her. She looked down at Braxton.

His lips curled over his teeth, glinting dangerously as he pulled her close and glared at Beau. Braxton snagged the sheet and pulled it over her naked back.

Her stomach plummeted as she squeezed her eyes tight. "Beau, tell me this is a dream. Tell me this isn't really happening."

"Which part? That I walked in on you? Or that you were about to molest my patient?"

Her eyes popped open and the blood drained from her face. "Your patient? You know him?"

Beau gave her a hard look, his lips pressed into an angry line. "Yeah. I dug that bullet out of his hide less than an hour ago."

Her head swam as she tried to make sense of Beau's words. She looked down at Braxton. "But, that would..."

Braxton held her gaze. "That would make me a werewolf."

* * *

BRUTUS SHOOK the snow off his massive shoulders and cast a frustrated look around the log cabin that he'd managed to secure on short notice. The house was private and rested in the middle of nowhere, on the border of Missouri and Arkansas. They needed a place to set up base while they located their fugitive.

"Where's Killian?" Brutus turned his attention to Lorcan, who was scouring the fridge once again. The werewolf could eat half a side of beef and be hungry thirty minutes later.

Lorcan tossed him a beer from the fridge in the kitchen. Brutus caught the bottle one-handed. "He's in the shower. We scoured the whole city of Branson and there's been no sign of the fugitive."

Brutus took a long pull from the icy bottle, letting the liquid soothe his parched throat. "I've run the whole length of the area where we saw him go off the cliff. There's no body. Any prints he might have left are covered by this fucking blizzard. Snow's covered any scent I might have picked up as well." They lived in the South where it never snowed. Just his luck mother nature started mind-fucking him with the weather.

"So, what's the plan?" Lorcan leaned against the doorway, stuck a hand in his jeans pocket, and took a drink from his beer. "If we can't find him, do we go home?"

"Have we ever gone home with an unfinished job?" Brutus held Lorcan's gaze and curled his fingers into fists. No fucking rogue wolf had ever gotten the better of him. Not ever.

Lorcan slowly grinned, his white teeth glinting under the low lighting. "No."

"Quitting is for pussies." Brutus stomped to the large picture window and glared out into the dark winter night. He didn't have the patience to wait. It wasn't in his DNA. He was made for tracking and killing. That's what made him an excellent Assassin. This time he was going to have to change up his method of attack.

"So what's the plan, Boss?" Lorcan's voice echoed through the room.

"We wait and watch for him to fuck up. With someone as volatile as Braxton, it won't be long until he makes trouble. When he does, we'll be there. I've got a silver bullet with his name on it." He turned and faced Lorcan. "And I never waste a bullet."

* * *

DAMON TRAHAN SLID out of bed, trying his best not to wake his slumbering mate, Ava. He'd spent the night explaining to her the assignment Barrett had put him on and why he was leaving at dawn. Assignment or not, he didn't like leaving his woman. As fucked up as it sounded, Ava was the air he breathed. Since they'd mated a few months back, he'd yet to spend a night without her.

But he was a Guardian, sworn to protect Arkansas territory. No matter how shitty he felt about leaving Ava, he knew he had to do his job.

He didn't really know Braxton that well, but he felt like he owed the werewolf.

He let his gaze rake over Ava as she slept. Despite the thin sheet covering her nude body, he could still make out every lush curve and contour that he'd memorized with his hands and mouth. He groaned as he pulled his jeans up over his hips, encasing his stiff cock. Ever since he'd met her, he'd walked around with an erection. Good thing she was just as eager to jump him as he was her.

He turned and grabbed his leather jacket off the back of the chair. Warm arms slid around his chest as Ava pressed her naked body against his back. He chuckled, forgetting how good she was at sneaking up behind him.

"Where do you think you're going?" Her silky voice heated his blood to a level he didn't think was possible. "I'm not done with you yet."

He turned and pulled her into his chest. Her silky black hair fell across her shoulders like the finest silk as her green gaze met his own. His hands roamed down her naked back to rest on her tight little ass. Damn, he loved how she felt in his arms. "I thought you'd be worn out by now, baby. We did it, what, eight times last night?"

"Nine. But I'm not counting." Ava licked his neck. His cock twitched.

"You know I have to go to work." He gave her ass a firm squeeze. She moaned and rubbed against him like a cat, teasing him with her body.

"I know." She moved her hand underneath his shirt and scraped her fingernail across his nipple.

"You're not helping." Despite his words, he pulled her closer and kissed her hard, sucking her tongue into his mouth. When he finally broke the kiss, they were both breathless.

"So do you think you'll be back by nightfall?"

He rubbed his thumb across her cheek, stunned by her beauty. His heart tugged in his chest at how much he loved this amazing woman in front of him. She was fucking perfect. He was lucky as hell to have her.

"Hopefully, if I can find Braxton. Hell, he might have already crossed into Missouri territory by now." He shrugged, feeling the weight of the situation on his shoulders. "At least, I hope that's where he's at. The other option is dead."

She cupped his face. "You don't know that for sure."

"I know that Assassins don't miss. Ever. There's been no word that he's been seen. So the only conclusion is that they killed him already."

"He could be hiding. From what you told me about Braxton, he seems to be a survivor. Just like you." She pulled him down for a heated kiss. "I love you."

"I love you, my female." He pulled her close for one last kiss before forcing himself to take a step away. "I'll be back before dinner."

She sat back on her heels, watching him make his way toward the bedroom door. "Any requests for dinner?"

He stopped in his tracks, letting his smirk run across his face. Ava couldn't cook worth a shit. He really couldn't care less what her talents in the kitchen were. She more than made up for them in the bedroom.

"I'll give you one guess what I want to eat tonight."

* * *

KATE SAT at the kitchen island, wrapped in her fuzzy robe and doing her best not to make eye contact with Beau, while he poured her a cup of coffee. She didn't know if she were more embarrassed that she'd been caught naked on top of Braxton or that Beau thought she'd tried to molest a wolf.

Wasn't there a law against that kind of thing? She rubbed her temples at the sudden headache building behind her eyes.

She was losing it. There wasn't any such thing as a werewolf.

She shook her head and looked up to find Beau scorching her with his stare. Geesh, he could melt ice with that look.

"Please tell me he didn't bite you." Beau's gaze hardened.

She flinched. "Of course he didn't bite me. What do you think he is? A dog?"

"No, a wolf," Beau spat out.

Not only was this whole thing not a dream, but the man she was groping had turned out to be a wolf.

Beau slid the creamer across the island to her. "I know this whole thing sounds crazy, believe me…"

"You're asking me to believe the man that's in my bed is a wolf, an honest-to-God, shape-shifting thing you only see in the movies, werewolf?" She crossed her arms and studied her friend. "I mean, if there were such a thing, don't you think I would have heard about it by now? Besides, if this is true, how is it that you know about this and I don't?"

Beau rubbed his eye with the palm of his hand and set his coffee on the counter. "I'm a vet. I've seen some weird shit."

She leaned forward in her chair. "Are you telling me you've seen this before?"

Beau gave a quick nod and looked away.

"You're my best friend. I've told you things I never told my mother." She gaped. "I told you the first time I had sex."

"I know." He gave her a pained look. "That was a conversation I could have done without."

She stood up and crossed her arms. "The point is, I've told you personal things, yet you never even bothered to tell me that werewolves were real."

"Look, I'm sorry, okay?" His shoulder slumped forward as he eyed the floor with interest. "I didn't tell you because I thought it would put you in danger. I thought the less you knew, the better."

"And now?" She slung her hands on her hips.

Beau shot her a hard look. "Now you need to get rid of that guy in your bed. He was shot with a silver bullet."

"So?"

"So, it means someone meant to kill him."

A pain shot through her heart. Why would someone try to kill Braxton? Better yet, what had he done to make someone shoot him?

"Whoever shot him will be looking for a body. When they don't find one, they'll track him down. They will track him right to your front door."

CHAPTER 5

fter a heated debate with Beau over whether or not Braxton should stay, Kate had finally had enough and made Beau leave. She stood at the window, watching her best friend drive away and feeling a little guilty because she'd chosen a stranger over him. She'd never done that before. Tonight held a lot of firsts for her, including making out with a hot guy who happened to be a wolf.

A wolf. She was having a hard time wrapping her head around that one.

She groaned. "Well, I guess I should be hoping for the best. Maybe he doesn't remember me mauling him." She flung herself onto the living room chair and buried her face in her hands. "Of course he'll remember me doing that. Sex is the only thing guys can remember."

Her gut twisted as she realized she couldn't avoid Braxton forever. She needed to go check on him. She stood and gnawed on a fingernail as she cast a furtive glance down the hallway. Sucking up her courage, she made her way to her bedroom. She peeked her head in. She let out a huge breath when she saw Braxton sound asleep.

The sheet was twisted around his naked and chiseled waist while his right leg stuck off the side of the bed. His forehead glistened with signs of fever, and even in his sleep, he grimaced against the pain.

She eased further into the room. Something about him pulled at her, urging her closer .

She brushed his black hair with the blue tips away from his eyes. His muscular tattooed arms screamed bad boy. Trouble was the last thing Kate needed. She had enough trouble of her own.

She touched her hand to his brow.

"Ouch!" She sucked in a breath as she snatched her hand away from the sizzling heat of his skin. Glancing down, she expected to see a blister. It wasn't humanly possible for a man to be that hot and still be alive. Wouldn't his brain be fried from the heat?

"Who are you?" she whispered.

He grabbed her hand, his eyes still closed. She yelped, caught off guard by his quick reflexes. Maybe Beau was right. Maybe she should have kicked Braxton out.

"I won't hurt you." He looked up with red-rimmed eyes.

"How can you be alive and be so hot?"

"Still think I'm hot, do you?" He managed a weak grin.

She snorted. "I didn't mean like that."

His grin faded and so did his grip. "It's the silver."

She leaned closer and laced her fingers through his. "You mean the bullet? But Beau got it out."

"The silver's been in my body, making it hard for me to heal."

"What do you mean? Can you heal yourself, like Wolverine?"

He let out a weak laugh. "Not quite that fast."

"So you should be getting better, right?"

"I'm not sure. I've never gotten shot with a silver bullet

before. I'm not exactly sure how quickly I can heal. Or if I can." He looked down at their entwined hands and frowned. "I'm probably scorching your beautiful skin, aren't I?" He pulled away.

Kate looked down at her hand, missing the heat of his touch. "No burns. See? I'm good." She held up her hand and smiled. "I didn't even notice the heat," she lied.

He held his hand out. She didn't need any more encouragement. She pulled the antique chair closer to the bed and sat, keeping their hands connected.

He sighed and closed his eyes. "You feel so good."

She shivered at his gravelly voice. Her mind conjured up images of what it would be like to be naked and rolling around with this gorgeous man.

He moved and the sheet shifted. She craned her neck, casting her gaze below his waist.

He moaned, drawing her attention up to his face. His eyes were slammed shut, pain etched across his face. Here he was in pain and she was trying to get a peek at his package. She was a bigger jerk than her ex-boyfriend.

"What can I do, Braxton? I've got some Tylenol for the pain."

He shook his head. "No. Tylenol is toxic to my kind."

"Really?" She frowned. "What about chocolate?"

"I'm not a dog, Kate."

"Sorry, I didn't mean it like that." She bit her lip. "I don't have a lot of experience with werewolves. I don't know how to help you."

"I'm teasing." He was staring at her, a softness in his eyes. It made her stomach quiver.

She cleared her throat as her body heated. "I'll go get you some more water." She hurried into the kitchen.

Gripping the edge of the deep kitchen sink, she sucked in a deep breath. What the hell was wrong with her? How could someone she barely knew physically affect her so much?

She filled the glass with water and headed down the hallway.

"Get over yourself, Kate. It's not like he's going to jump you the second you walk into the bedroom." She sighed.

So much for wishful thinking.

* * *

KATE STAYED close to the house for most of the day, wanting to be near in case Braxton's condition worsened. He'd drifted off to sleep and rested for the better part of the day.

With nothing else to do with her nervous energy, Kate took the opportunity to clean. With no paying guests, that particular job was over quickly. The sheets on the beds were already clean. So she went through each room and polished the furniture and swept the floors. After cleaning out the refrigerator, she cleaned out her cabinets and even organized her junk drawer.

Despite her cleaning frenzy, she was too nervous to sit still. She found herself gazing down the hall toward the bedroom with Beau's words of warning about Braxton echoing in her mind.

Was Braxton dangerous? Apparently, someone had thought so or they wouldn't have shot him. It was complicated enough that he'd been shot, but finding out he was a werewolf just added to the mix.

Unable to resist, she gave in to her longing and tiptoed down the hall to the bedroom. She opened the door and peeked in on him. His massive chest rose and fell as he slept soundly. He was all muscle and brawn, and his large frame looked very out of place in the feminine wrought iron bed. Her gaze drifted over the many colorful tattoos that encased both arms, from shoulders to wrists, wondering what each design meant.

Kate licked her lips, feeling a pull in the pit of her stomach. His tattoos were hot. Normally she didn't like tattoos. She preferred clean-cut golfer types.

But on Braxton, she liked them a little too much.

Shaking her head, she headed back to the kitchen and turned on her laptop. Putting her cursor in the search box, she typed in werewolf.

The massive numbers of results for werewolves surprised her. She scrolled and clicked, reading everything she could and quickly losing track of time.

A hard knock on the front door startled her back to reality.

Who could be out in this weather?

She pulled back the lacy curtain at the window overlooking the porch and groaned when she saw who it was.

"What does he want?" She let the curtain drop and clenched her hands. The last thing she needed was Mr. Bigsby poking around and finding Braxton.

Straightening her shoulders, she opened the door.

"Mr. Bigsby, I wasn't expecting you."

"Looks like you weren't expecting anybody." His thin lips slid over his too-perfect teeth as his gaze raked across her jeans and long-sleeved T-shirt.

"Excuse me?" Kate tightened her grip on the doorknob, prepared to shut the door if he couldn't be polite. If he thought he could intimidate her in her own house, he was very mistaken. Until the bank took possession of the property, this was still her home.

"I meant I didn't think you'd have anyone here with the weather like this. I didn't even think I'd be able to make it up your driveway." He glanced over his shoulder at the snowy yard.

Kate narrowed her eyes. "How *did* you manage to make it up my driveway?"

Bigsby's smile widened and he shoved his thumb over his shoulder. "Four-wheel-drive, of course. It's the latest model."

Kate glanced at the blood-red pickup truck with enormous knobby tires. "Of course it is."

"Aren't you going to invite me in?" Bigsby took another step closer and Kate instinctively stepped back, putting as much distance between them as possible.

"Actually, I have a guest and…"

"Sure you do." Ignoring her, he stepped across the threshold and into her living room. He brushed the snow off his jacket and onto her clean hardwood floors. He gave her a smug smile. "See, this is much better than standing out on the porch and talking."

She gritted her teeth and slowly closed the door. Bigsby wasted no time and headed for the kitchen, making himself at home on one of the barstools near the island.

"Doing a little research?" He nodded toward her laptop.

Her stomach lurched. She quickly closed her computer.

"I'm afraid, Kate, that's not going to help you." Bigsby leveled a serious glare at her.

"What do you mean?" Her heart lurched in her chest. Had he seen what she'd been searching for on her computer?

He shrugged his shoulders, causing more snow to fall on her floor. "Come on, Kate, stop trying to hide what's going on. I already know."

"You do?" She grabbed the counter as her head grew dizzy.

His lips curved into a pitying smile. "You're trying to find another bank to refinance your mortgage to save your bed and breakfast."

She blew out a breath. So, he didn't know about Braxton.

"Kate, I know about your money situation." He stood up

and stepped closer, giving her arm a squeeze. She cringed and stepped back.

"I'm willing to make you a very generous offer for this old place."

She gritted her teeth, trying very hard to keep her anger under control. "This old place is my home."

"And it's falling down around you." Bigsby's gaze ran across the kitchen, and his lip curled up over his teeth in disgust. "It doesn't even have granite countertops."

"This house is over a hundred years old. They didn't have granite countertops back then."

Bigsby shuddered. "I know."

Had this idiot ever been in a bed and breakfast before? "I've kept the house as close to the original as possible. That's what people expect from a bed and breakfast."

"What people expect is cheap rates and a continental breakfast."

"From a hotel." She narrowed her eyes. "From a bed and breakfast, they expect character and friendliness and a real breakfast."

Bigsby shook his head. "You don't even have a pool."

Kate threw up her arms. "That's because it's not a hotel." She wanted to strangle him.

Bigsby grabbed her hand. "You don't even have any customers. Face it. You need me, Kate."

She snatched her hand away.

"Kate doesn't need you. She has me." A deep voice growled.

BRAXTON STOOD IN THE HALLWAY, dressed in one of the white robes reserved for guests. The garment was way too small on his large body and the sleeves stopped at his elbows, showing off his colorful tattoos. He held his left arm, though no longer splinted, against his side. Even dressed in the robe, he looked dangerous and lethal. Her heart fluttered in her chest.

Bigsby's eyes widened in surprise as he took in Braxton's size. "Who are you?"

Braxton stepped forward. "I think I need to be asking you the same question."

Bigsby swallowed and tried to force a confident smile. "I'm Oliver Bigsby. I was just checking in on Kate."

Braxton took another step forward until he was chest to chest with Bigsby. "Yeah, well, you won't need to be checking in on Kate anymore. I'm here now. "

A look of disbelief and then outrage crossed Bigsby's face. Kate bet no one had ever talked to him like that before. He opened his mouth and started to speak, but then apparently thought better of it and slammed it shut.

"I see. Goodbye, Kate." Bigsby nodded stiffly and hurried out the door.

Braxton turned his assessing gray gaze on her. "Are you okay?"

She nodded, unable to speak. Did he always roll out of bed looking this damned hot?

Clearing her throat, she nodded. "Yeah, I am. Thank you for that."

"Who was that guy?" Braxton narrowed his eyes and for a second her heart melted a bit. It was almost like he was a little jealous.

"Oliver Bigsby. He's been trying to convince me to sell my home to him for the last few months." She shrugged and walked back into the kitchen, hoping to catch her breath. Braxton followed.

"He doesn't look like the B and B type." He eased himself onto the barstool.

"He's not." She placed a cup of hot coffee in front of him and then hesitated. "You do drink coffee, don't you?"

He raised his eyebrow. "Yes. I do." He lifted the cup to his lips and took a sip. "So what does Bigsby want with your bed and breakfast?"

"He wants to tear it down and build another hotel or motel, something cheap and affordable—with a pool," she spat out the last word. It made her sick every time she thought about it.

"You've told him no."

"Yes, but he knows about my trouble." Whoa. She didn't mean to let that slip. She shrugged and changed the topic. "How's your shoulder?"

His gaze didn't leave her. "I think we were talking about you, Kate. What kind of trouble are you having?"

Why did he make her stomach tremble by just looking at her with those gray eyes? Even how he said her name made her lose her breath.

"It's nothing I want to talk about." She crossed her arms.

Reaching across the kitchen island, he tugged her hand free, his fingertips teasing hers. "What do you want to talk about then?"

Her breath caught and she licked her dry lips. What she really wanted to talk about was him.

He eased back, grimacing as he favored his shoulder. "Let me guess. You want to know about werewolves, right?"

"Will you answer any questions I have?"

He nodded and took another sip of coffee.

She waited a few seconds. "Do you need a full moon to change into a wolf?

"You tell me. Did we have a full moon last night?"

"No." She frowned.

"Then you answered your own question." He looked at her with heavy-lidded eyes, while a delicious smirk played at the corners of his mouth. "It would be better if you still thought I was a dream."

She snorted. "I'd rather have the truth than a lie any day of the week. Believe me."

"Wanna talk about it?" His grin slipped as his expression grew serious.

"Nope." Pushing her coffee cup to the side, she studied him. "Why don't you tell me why someone tried to kill you with a silver bullet?"

"Guess I pissed off the wrong person." His gaze hardened as he looked away, his lips set in grim determination. He was still sexy, but there was a dangerous edge to him now, making her wonder if she should have let him in her home.

She cleared her throat. "If you don't want to talk about it, that's your business. But don't assume I'm an idiot."

His raised his eyebrows. "That's the last thing in the world I would ever call you." He sat forward and reached for her hand again. His face contorted into a mask of pain as he cradled his injured shoulder.

"Let me see." She brushed his hand away from his shoulder to assess his wound. Bright red blood marred the pristine bandage. "Your wound is bleeding again. Let's get you back to bed so I can rewrap it."

A half hour later, after changing his bandage, she stayed by his bedside, watching as Braxton drifted off to sleep.

She couldn't help but wonder just how much danger he was in. What concerned her the most was how much of the fallout was going to end up on her doorstep.

* * *

DAMON WALKED into the smoke-filled bar in Branson, Missouri, a little before ten p.m. Cigarette smoke curled around him in a suffocating blanket, the stench making his stomach turn. He snarled, shaking off the layer of snow from his favorite leather jacket. He fucking hated snow. It was one reason he lived in the South. They were not supposed to get snow.

Glancing down, he grimaced at the wet spots on the leather. He should've listened to Ava and worn the jacket she had bought him, even though it wasn't his style. He didn't have the heart to tell her that it made him look like a pussy. He made it a point never to look like a pussy.

Glancing around, he expected to see a bunch of old timers in the hole-in-the-wall bar, but instead he was greeted with curious stares from pock-marked faces of young meth heads and shifty-eyed criminals. Certainly a mixed crowd tonight at the Old Irish Tavern.

"Beer." Damon straddled the bar stool and pushed his Oakleys over his head. The bartender nodded and slid him an icy long-neck. "Thanks." Damon took a pull and casually looked over his shoulder. Everyone was suddenly very interested in finishing their drinks and paying their tab.

"You aren't from around here." It was the bartender's tone that had Damon's instincts on high alert. Damon crossed his arms and discreetly patted his chest for his Sig Sauer.

"Nope." He took another drink and eyed the big-bellied barkeep. "Are you the owner?"

The bartender reached his hand under the bar and leaned on the counter. "Yeah, I'm the owner. Is there a problem?"

Damon smirked. "No. Just wondering why the owner of an Irish Tavern has a Jersey accent rather than Irish."

The bartender placed his empty hand on the counter and smirked. "Would you believe my mother was Irish and she left this place to me?"

"No. I would believe you got the deed to this place from some underhanded shit you were involved in." Damon met his gaze. "Let me guess, you're some kind of loan shark and when some asshole named Bubba didn't pay up, you took his bar."

The bartender narrowed his black eyes. "Did Bubba send you here to take care of me?" The bartender's hand went under the counter. "Is that why you're here?"

"What? No, I didn't mean, literally, Bubba..." It was the South. One out of every fourth male was named Bubba.

"You go tell that little shit from Arkansas he's never gonna get his daddy's bar back." Chairs scraped across the wood floor as patrons pushed away from their table and made for the front door.

"I don't care how much money he offers, I'm keeping this place. Clear?" The bartender swung a sawed-off shotgun out from under the counter and leveled it at Damon's face.

Damon slowly eased to his feet as anger pulsed through his veins. The desire to shift into wolf was overwhelming. "I didn't come here because of Bubba."

The burly bartender's nostrils flared and he sniffed the air. "Really? Then why do you smell like those damn Arkansas werewolves?"

Damon curled his fingers into fists "Because I'm an Arkansas Guardian, you dumb fuck."

The bartender gave him an arrogant smile. "So Bubba did send you."

"Just because I'm from Arkansas doesn't mean I know Bubba."

"Right." The bartender kept his gun aimed at Damon's head.

"Do you have any idea of how many people named Bubba live in Arkansas?"

"No." The bartender blinked.

"Half the fucking state." Damon pulled out a twenty and slid it toward the man to cover his tab.

"Then what the hell are you doing here in Missouri?" The bartender relaxed a little and rested the barrel of the shotgun against his shoulder.

"I'm looking for some Louisiana Weres."

"I hate Louisiana more than I hate Arkansas." The bartender spit on the floor and then looked back at Damon. "Are these civilian Weres?"

"No. They're Assassins." The bartender's grip slipped and the gun hit the ground with a thud. "Assassins? Who the hell are they looking for?"

Damon shrugged. Werewolves hated Assassins more than they hated rogue wolves, especially in Missouri where there was no Pack Law. "Not sure. What I am sure of is that my Pack Master wasn't very happy when they crossed over into Arkansas and didn't let him know."

The bartender crossed his arms and put his "I don't give a shit" face back on. "So?"

"The Assassins shot a werewolf in broad daylight," Damon growled. The bartender's face went pale. "We don't take too kindly to that in Arkansas."

"Who were they looking for?" Well, now, wasn't he all Chatty Cathy?

Damon laughed. "Funny you should ask. They were looking for a bartender."

The bartender's eyes widened as his face paled.

"So if you see these guys, give me a call." Damon plucked a napkin off the bar and scribbled his cell number. "If I were you, I wouldn't be pulling that gun on the Assassins if they show up here."

"Yeah? Why the fuck not?"

"Because they're not as social as I am and they're using silver bullets, dipshit." Damon made his way to the door, his hand resting on his .45 as he made his way out.

Once outside, he straddled his Harley. He would hit a few more bars tonight, but his instincts told him the Assassins hadn't yet made it into town. If they had, the werewolf population would not be showing their faces like they were.

Where the fuck was Braxton? If he hadn't crossed the Missouri line, that meant he was still in Arkansas.

And probably dead at the bottom of a mountain with a silver bullet in his hide.

* * *

BRAXTON BARRELED DOWN A DARK ALLEY, his lungs struggling for breath as he ran.

They were chasing him. He couldn't stop. He had to keep going. If he slowed down for a second, he was going to be dead.

"Braxton, how could you?" His mother's voice called out to him from the shadows, like vapor. "You are no son of mine."

Pain recoiled through his chest, ripping at his insides. He swiped his hand down his torso, feeling for a gunshot but didn't find an injury. There was no blood, no wound, no gaping hole. His heart dropped when he realized it wasn't a bullet that had ripped his chest in two—it was his mother's devastating words.

Angry and hurt, Braxton stopped running. He lifted his head to the bleak night sky and screamed, hoping to make her believe him. "I. Didn't. Kill. Him."

"Braxton, wake up."

Braxton bolted upright and looked around. The vaguely familiar cozy room of quilts and antique furniture calmed his rapid heartbeats. He sucked in a breath, struggling to get his breathing under control, when he saw Kate sitting on the edge of his bed.

"You were having a bad dream." Kate ran her delicate hand across his forehead. She smiled. "Your fever's broken."

He nodded and glanced out the darkened window. "What time is it?"

"Almost ten at night. You've slept the day away." She eased off the bed and stood.

Braxton reached for her hand. "Don't go." He closed his eyes. He didn't know why he said it. He preferred his solitude and only sought women out when he needed to relieve the sexual tension. But Kate was different. She soothed his soul.

"I'm coming back. I was just going to get you some dinner. I made meatloaf and twice-baked potatoes."

Braxton's stomach grumbled. "Sounds good." He shoved the sheet off, eased his aching body off the bed. He looked around for his jeans and grimaced. He didn't have his jeans— or clothes for that matter. He'd lost them after he shifted. "Fuck."

"You're...you're..." She sucked in a breath.

Her stare was glued to his rigid erection. "Oh, shit. I'm sorry, Kate." He ripped the sheet off the bed and covered his lower half. Where the fuck were his manners? He'd probably scared her half to death, thinking he was some kind of pervert or something.

She dragged her dilated gaze up to meet his and suddenly food wasn't the only thing he was hungry for. "I'll just let you get dressed. The robe is over there on the chair." Face flushed, Kate tried to back out of the room. She bumped into the dresser.

"Kate."

She ran out the room like a shot. Great, he'd probably scared her half to death. There was an innocence about Kate that he'd never encountered before. Innocent women were not his type. They could be hurt too easily. He preferred his women brazen with no strings attached.

Fully robed and with his libido under control, Braxton walked into the kitchen and settled onto the barstool. Though his fever was gone, his shoulder still ached like a bitch.

Kate averted her gaze and placed a plate of food in front of him.

"This looks great." He took a bite and his taste buds exploded with the flavor. "Damn. It tastes even better." The only woman who'd ever actually made him a meal was his mother.

She gave him a shy smile. "My mom started this bed and breakfast when I was just a little girl. I was very young when I learned how to cook and take care of this place. You can't own a bed and breakfast if you don't know how to cook."

"I'm shocked this place isn't packed." He motioned with his fork as he looked around. The house itself was quaint and inviting, and the perfect place for a couple in love to take a romantic weekend.

Her smile dulled. "It used to be full all the time."

"And now?" He got the sense he was probing into sensitive territory, but he wanted to know. If there was a way he could help her, he'd do it.

She sucked in a deep breath. "Now, I'm struggling just to pay my bills. And not doing a very good job of that either."

"What about savings?"

She shook her head. "It's gone. Let's just say I trusted someone I shouldn't have." She pushed away from the island and dumped out the rest of her coffee in the sink.

He nodded. "I can relate to that."

She gave him a look of disbelief. "Really? I can't imagine you'd be fooled by anyone."

He dropped his fork with a clank. Suddenly his appetite was gone. Images of his mother's accusing words and her disappointed face swam around in his head like alphabet soup. "I've learned not to expect much out of people. That way I'm never disappointed."

"Isn't that kind of a lonely life?"

Braxton met her concerned gaze with his own. She had no idea.

He cleared his throat from the emotion threatening to suffocate him. "Do you have a plan to save your business?"

"I've talked to the bank manager to see if I can get an extension. But even with that, I've got to be booked solid for the next month to get back in the black." She sighed. "With the economy in the dump, people aren't as eager to shell out two hundred a night for a bed and breakfast when they can go to a hotel for half that."

"A hotel like the one that douche bag owns." Braxton crossed his arms. He didn't like Bigsby on principle, but when he saw the way that asshole was looking at Kate, his dislike had gone straight to hatred.

"Correct." She plopped down on one of the island stools and rested her elbows on the counter top. "He's been trying to buy me out for months. So far I've managed to keep him away. I realized he was aware of my financial situation when I ran into him at the bank the other day."

"Is that what had you upset when I bumped into you in the alley?" The memory of holding her in his arms as she cried would be forever etched into his soul.

"Yes." Her cheeks turned a pretty pink and she nodded. "I'm sure all of this is boring you to death."

Braxton stood and walked toward her. Inches from her, he pulled her into his arms. She looked up at him; eyes wide. He relaxed his hold, expecting her to pull away. She didn't.

His hands drifted down her back and rested at her slim hips. God, what he wouldn't give to have just one moment with her. "Would you let me help you?"

She frowned. "I don't want your money."

Braxton chuckled. "Good, 'cause I don't have any. I'm just a bartender, so my cash isn't exactly flowing. I'll just have to figure out something else."

* * *

HEAT ROSE in her stomach and then settled in a rush between her legs. All rational thought fled, leaving only images of Braxton in her brain. Visions of Braxton naked—and being under all that muscle—made her clench her thighs together as her body heated a thousand degrees.

"How do you think you can help me?" Her voice sounded like gravel and her body felt like gelatin.

His eyes darkened, and she knew immediately his thoughts were completely in agreement with her own. He leaned down, his hot masculine scent wrapping around her. Then, without warning, his mouth came crashing down on hers.

She relaxed into his embrace, bowing toward him as his tongue sought out her own. Her heart beat loud in her ears as she fought to catch her breath under his scorching kiss. She felt awkward, like a high school girl getting her first kiss and hoping she was doing everything right.

"Your arm. It's not broken anymore." She wound her arms around his neck, pulling him close and not ever wanting to let him go. How did he make her feel like she'd never experienced that kind of passion before? Her ex wasn't a slouch in the kissing department, but damn, he'd never set her panties on fire the way Braxton did.

"Fast healer, remember?"

"Oh, yeah." Her words were but a rush as she rubbed against him.

"Kate." He whispered her name against the side of her neck as he licked and sucked her skin. She gripped him closer, and ground her pelvis into his rock-hard erection.

"If you keep doing this, I'm going to take you right here on the kitchen table."

"Don't do that," she managed to say.

Braxton pulled back. "Why not?"

"Because it's antique." She swallowed. "It might break." She pulled his mouth back down to hers and felt his lips quirk up in amusement.

"Then I'm going to take you to bed." Braxton swept her into his arms before she could say a word. He hissed in pain and stumbled. She slipped out of his arms and stood.

Pushing the robe off his shoulder, she sucked in a breath. A fresh spot of blood spread and saturated the white bandage.

"Come on, I'm getting you back to bed." She tugged on his hand.

"That's what I'm talking about." He smirked.

Kate suppressed a laugh and did her best to give him a stern look. "I don't mean for that. You need to lie down and rest. Your wound is bleeding again."

"It's just a little trickle."

"It's more than just a trickle. " After a little nagging, she got him settled into bed and redressed his wound. They kept up the small talk while she doctored his injury. By the time she was done, his eyes had drifted shut and he was lost once again to sleep.

Kate continued to stay by his side, studying the stranger in her bed and wondering why she felt such a strong connection to someone she hardly knew.

* * *

"IT'S STOPPED SNOWING." Brutus stood at the window of the snowbound cabin, his hands behind his back as he stared out into the night. The security light cast the snow-covered yard in an eerie yellow glow. The muscles in his legs jumped, impatient to get this mission over with. He fucking hated waiting.

"I hate snow." Lorcan plopped down on the couch with a bag of chips and slung his feet up on the coffee table.

Brutus turned and glared. Lorcan needed to be on his guard. This was not some fucking holiday in the mountains. "He has to be found."

"Bastard's still going to be hard to track. There's a good four inches covering his tracks." Killian spoke from his perch on the kitchen barstool of the cabin, where he was busy slamming down another shot of Southern Comfort.

"Hell, I think the son of a bitch is dead, buried under a blanket of white." Lorcan snorted.

Brutus glared at the two men. "Maybe he is. Maybe he isn't. The point is, I need to be sure. If he's not dead, then we need to make him that way. Understood?"

CHAPTER 6

*B*raxton had seen a lot of women do a lot of things on their knees, but he'd never seen one on their knees trying to disassemble a dishwasher. Kate had half of her amazing body buried in the dishwasher with her tight little ass sticking out. He was getting hard just watching her wiggle.

"Shit."

His eyebrows shot up at her profanity. She didn't strike him as the type of woman to curse. She was too gentle, too shy, too ladylike.

She scrambled out of the cave of the dishwasher and stood with a plastic piece pinched between her fingertips. "Do you know how much it costs to replace this thing?" She cocked her head and narrowed her gaze on him.

He shook his head. "No." He had no idea what that part was.

"Me either, but I bet it costs a lot." Kate blew a strand of her blonde hair out of her eye and propped her hand on her hip. "Do you know if it's supposed to even look like this?" She waved the dangly plastic in the air.

"No idea." She was looking for his advice and he had none to offer. He wished he'd been more handy growing up, but back then all he had thought about was staying out of the house and away from his father's fists.

"I thought men knew all about this manly stuff."

Braxton held his hands up. "I'm a bartender and ride a Harley. I know how to fix every kind of engine ever built. But when it comes to appliances, I'm lost. The lightbulb in my microwave went out and I went and bought a new microwave, because I couldn't figure out how to get the damn light out."

Her lips quirked up in a smile and it had his heart racing. Everything about Kate had his body reacting like a teen in puberty. It had taken all his restraint not to jack off last night when he woke up thinking about her.

"Why don't you just call a handyman?"

"If I could afford to pay someone to fix my dishwasher, I wouldn't have bothered taking it apart." Her shoulders slumped in a look of defeat.

He hated that lost look on her face. "Let me have a look."

After a few minutes inside the appliance, Braxton grimaced and stood.

"Yeah, I'm not even going to lie and say I know what's wrong. I have no clue."

She laughed. "Don't worry about it. I have to go to town anyway for groceries. I'll just take this part to the hardware store and see if they can talk me through how to fix it." She laid the plastic piece on the island by her purse. "Do you want to ride along?"

He shifted his weight. "I would, but—" What the hell was he supposed to say? I'm a fugitive and I'm trying to lay low?

"Ah. I got it." Her eyes shifted to his wounded shoulder. He didn't see fear in her expression, only concern. "Do you think whoever shot you is still looking for you?"

"I don't know." Probably. They were Assassins trained to kill. They didn't give up or give in until the job was done.

He turned to the window and glanced out at the snowy landscape. It would have been quite the romantic setting if there weren't three lethal killers searching the woods for him right now. "I'm hoping the snow buried my tracks. I saw the weather report on TV this morning and they said Missouri was getting another four inches of snow tonight."

Kate's face went pale. "Is that where they shot you? In Missouri?"

"Just outside state line. When I was shot, I fell off my bike and rolled down the hill." His heart sunk as he thought about his beloved Harley. It was the one thing he treasured more than anything and now it was nothing but twisted metal.

"Hill? There are no hills going into Missouri. You mean to tell me you rolled off the side of the mountain?" Kate's hand flew to her neck and the blood drained from her face.

"Well, it wasn't like it was Mount Everest." He shrugged. Sure fucking felt like it, though.

"Jesus, Braxton, then you walked all the way here?"

He shoved his hands in his jeans pockets and looked away. "I saw your light through the woods. I knew I was dying. I didn't want to end up dying alone in the woods for the raccoons to eat. So I crawled to your front porch." He felt like a complete pussy. She must think he was a really weak male.

"Was my house the first one you saw?" Her soft voice made him take a step closer, his body humming with desire.

"I passed some others, but they had a negative energy. Yours didn't. When I got close enough to read the name, Bella Luna, I knew I had picked the right spot to die."

She stepped into his arms and wrapped her arms around his waist, burying her face in his chest. God, she felt so small and fragile and perfect. He tightened his arms around her, breathing in her unique scent that stirred his cock.

"I'm glad you didn't die, Braxton."

"Say that again." He closed his eyes as he memorized the soft feel of her body against him.

"I'm glad you didn't die."

"No, say my name."

She looked up, her beautiful lips parted. "Braxton."

With one word from her, he was under her spell. She didn't even know the hold she had on him.

His mouth found hers, licking inside her hot mouth. She tasted better than his wildest fantasy, sweeter than the finest chocolate.

He snaked his hand under her sweater and cupped her firm breast. She moaned and arched into his palm as his fingers played with her nipple.

He murmured against the crook of her neck. "I want you, Kate. I want you naked, in my bed, under me."

She slid her hands around his neck and pulled him closer. "I want that, too."

Braxton groaned, pulling away long enough to tug her sweater over her head, his fingers brushing against her flat stomach.

A door slammed, startling them both. Braxton quickly pulled Kate behind him and growled.

"What the hell is going on, Kate?"

* * *

KATE, wearing her jeans and bra, stared back in horror at Beau from behind the safety of Braxton's back.

"Don't you knock? You have horrible timing, do you know that?" Kate's face heated as her embarrassment shifted into anger. She scrambled to get her sweater over her head. She wasn't a child, dammit. She was a grown woman.

"I've been trying to call, but you're not answering. I came by to check on you." He walked over to the phone, picked it up, and frowned. "Your phone's not working. Have you called the phone company?"

"How can I call the phone company if my phone doesn't work?" Kate gave him a disbelieving stare.

"Smart-ass." Beau glared.

"Watch how you speak to her," Braxton growled and advanced toward Beau.

Kate placed her hand on his arm. "It's okay, Braxton. Beau and I grew up together. I'm sure he's called me worse."

"Dude, you should hear some of the names she's called me." Beau snorted. He tossed a brown paper bag on the kitchen counter. "I brought you some clothes from the thrift store. It might be safer around here if you had some clothes on." He arched his brow at her. "Get your phone fixed, Kate."

Kate chewed her lip and glanced at the dead phone. "I'll go by the phone company when I run into town today for groceries."

"Don't forget the hardware store," Braxton murmured.

"What do you need at the hardware store?" Beau asked.

"I need a part for the dishwasher." Kate cocked her head. "You wouldn't happen to know anything about a dishwasher, would you?"

Beau held his hands up. "Don't look at me. I only work on animals, not appliances."

"What are the odds that the two men currently standing in my house are appliance-challenged?" Kate sighed.

"Actually, I drove out here to make sure you were okay since I haven't heard from you." Beau cut his eyes at Braxton. "Needed to make sure he didn't eat you."

Kate's face heated a million degrees. Braxton turned and

looked at her. He grinned slowly, looking very much like a predatory animal.

"Oh, God. Enough with the mental image already." Beau palmed his eyes. "I take it your shoulder and arm are healing." He nodded at Braxton.

"They are." Braxton picked up the bag. "Thanks for the clothes."

"So why don't you tell me what I'm dying to know?" Beau glared.

"And what would that be?" Braxton snarled.

"Exactly how did you wind up with an Assassin's bullet in your body?"

* * *

BRAXTON HELD his breath for a brief second before meeting Kate's astonished gaze. When he exhaled, he took a slow, deep breath. The scent of male wolf hit him. He jerked his gaze back to Beau, who was standing there smirking.

"Yes. I'm a wolf, too."

"What?" Kate rounded on her friend. "You're a werewolf? What the hell, why didn't you tell me?"

"I kind of figured you'd freak out. Like now."

Braxton narrowed his eyes at the vet. How come he hadn't picked up on his scent before?

"I use a camouflage spray to hide my scent," Beau answered the unspoken question. "Besides, the silver in your system dimmed your sense of smell. That's why you didn't scent me."

Beau narrowed his eyes on Braxton. "Now that we've cleared that up, let's get to the real question. Just how the hell did you get an Assassin's bullet in your shoulder? Who did you kill, Braxton?"

Kate paled, her pretty caramel eyes widening. At that

89

moment, the sliver of trust he'd earned faded from her eyes. It hit him in the middle of his chest like a baseball bat.

"I didn't kill anyone." Braxton kept his eyes on Kate, trying to make her believe him by sheer will.

"Assassins don't go around killing innocent werewolves. We both know that."

Braxton rounded on the vet. "I'm not a fucking liar."

Beau held his gaze, daring him to look away. To look away was a true test of lying. All wolves knew that.

Kate swiped the keys off the counter.

"Kate, wait." Braxton grabbed her elbow. She flinched out of his grasp.

"I'll be back. Sounds like you two have a lot to discuss."

* * *

KATE DIDN'T REMEMBER the drive into town. She'd been too caught up in replaying the conversation between Beau and Braxton and trying to make sense of it all.

Was it possible that Braxton was a killer? She'd made bad decisions before, but to bare herself to a killer was unthinkable.

She shivered and turned up the heat in the SUV.

Her gut told her he wasn't a killer. But her gut had also led her to believe her ex was a good guy. Look how that turned out.

She didn't doubt for one instant that Braxton wouldn't hesitate to get into a fight and do some serious bodily damage, but to actually kill someone? That was quite another thing.

Her shoulders sank along with her stomach.

She didn't have an excellent track record when it came to men. She'd thought her ex had hung the moon. It wasn't until he ran off with her life savings and put her in a dire financial situation that she realized how wrong she'd been.

Was she wrong about Braxton, too?

She parked in front of the hardware store and cut the engine. She snuggled down further in her winter coat as she climbed out. The winter breeze stung her cheeks as she hurried to the door.

Mr. Thurmond, the owner of the hardware store, smiled warmly when he saw her. "Hello, Kate. What brings you in today?"

Kate gave him a sheepish grin and held up the dangly plastic part. She hoped she was standing in front of the man who could give her much-needed advice. "You wouldn't happen to be able to tell me how to get my dishwasher running again, would you?"

* * *

BRAXTON GRIPPED the windowsill as he watched Kate's SUV disappear down the snow-covered hill and out of sight. He should go after her and explain, but it was light out and he didn't know whether the Assassins were still out there looking for him. The last thing he wanted to do was to get Kate hurt.

"She's always been too trusting." Beau busied himself with pouring a cup of coffee. "I knew the moment she brought Tom home it wasn't going to work. I never trusted that shifty-eyed son of a bitch."

Braxton swallowed, his gut burned with anger. "I would never hurt Kate."

"Braxton, face it. No matter how this thing plays out, Kate's going to get hurt."

"What do you mean?"

Beau set his coffee cup down. "If the Assassins find you,

they are going to kill you. If they don't find you and think you are dead, then you'll be on your way out of town out of Kate's life, forever on the run and looking over your shoulder."

Braxton hardened his gaze.

Beau scrubbed his hand across his face and sighed. "Look, I don't know what's going on between you two, and frankly, I don't want the play-by-play." Beau shivered. "Jesus, Kate's like my sister, so I don't need the visual. But what I do know is how she looks at you when you walk in the room."

"How does she look at me?" Braxton glanced away, waiting to hear the next few words come out of the vet's mouth.

"Like you're her hero."

"I'm nobody's hero." He'd tried to be that for his mother, to save her from the monster his father was, and look where it got him. As much as he loved his mother, she would never have left his abusive father. The pattern was set and the routine learned. He couldn't save someone that didn't want to be saved.

"While I'm here, let me have a look at your shoulder." Beau waved him over to the barstool.

"Nice way to change the topic."

Beau snorted. "I have to admit, I've never actually seen an Assassin's bullet before. And I've never heard of anyone living after they were shot with one. You must be one lucky son of a bitch."

Braxton shook his head. He didn't have a lucky bone in his body. He never did. "It's not luck. I'm just cursed to keep on living."

* * *

KATE LIFTED the trunk to her maroon SUV and began

loading up her groceries. She didn't normally buy this much when she didn't have guests at the B&B. But judging how much Braxton had put away at the last few meals, she'd gone ahead and stocked up. He ate as much as a family of four, yet there wasn't an ounce of fat anywhere on his body.

"Can I give you a hand with those?" A deep male voice came from behind her.

"No thanks, I've got it." She turned to give the stranger a polite smile but froze. The man had to be as tall as Braxton and just as broad. Dressed in jeans and leather jacket, he wore sunglasses that obscured his eyes. She shivered as her gaze landed on a vicious scar that ran down one side of his cheek. The hair on the back of her arms stood at attention. Danger seemed to pulse off him in waves.

"Are you sure you don't need any help?"

"I'm sure." She turned back and quickly began tossing the white grocery bags into the SUV. She needed to get out of there.

She slammed the door shut and spread her keys between her sweaty knuckles. She saw that defense move on TV one time. If he took a step closer, she was prepared to stab him in the balls.

"I'm looking for someone who passed through here a few days ago. He's a friend, and he didn't meet up with me at our designated destination." The stranger cocked his head. "Can you take a look at a photo for me?"

Cold fear ran up her back as the stranger held out a picture of Braxton. She swallowed hard and shook her head.

"I'm sorry. I've not seen him. Have you tried asking down at the restaurants on Main Street? They get a lot of traffic and maybe someone saw him there." She gave him a tight smile.

The stranger held her gaze and then finally nodded. "Thanks, I'll do that."

She forced herself not to run and jump into her car. The last thing she needed was this stranger getting suspicious. With her heart pounding in her chest, she took her time putting the shopping cart back in the cart corral and walked back to her car. She started the engine and glanced in her rearview mirror. The stranger didn't move but watched as she pulled away.

With shaking hands, she forced herself to take several deep breaths. As much as she needed to get home, she drove slow and took the long route home just in case the stranger got the urge to follow her.

* * *

BRAXTON FROWNED as he watched Kate pull around the back of the Bella Luna and park. Why wasn't she parking in the front of the house?

He hurried out the back door, ignoring the pain in his shoulder. "What's wrong?" He opened her car door and studied her expression.

She shook her head, her face strained and pale. "Is Beau still here? Never mind. I need to get these groceries inside."

He gathered up the groceries in both hands, leaving only a couple of bags for Kate to carry inside. "Beau left a couple hours ago." As much as he didn't like the vet, he was grateful for the clothes Beau had dropped off for him.

"We need to talk." Kate went about her work of putting the groceries away, worry straining across her face, her mouth pulled into a thin line.

"About what Beau said…" Braxton forked his fingers into his hair and swallowed. He was going to have to be honest with Kate.

Kate balled up an empty plastic bag in a white-knuckle grip and turned to face him. "I was stopped in town today by some guy. He was big, like you. From the looks of him, I think he was one of you."

"You think he was a werewolf?" His gut clenched and his fingers curled into fists as white-hot anger flooded through him "Did he hurt you?" he growled.

"No." Her mouth fell open and she took a step back.

Crap. He'd scared her.

He kept his voice calm and forced his hands to unclench. "What did he say?"

"He said he was looking for a friend. I knew he was looking for you before he even showed me your picture."

"Shit. He had a picture?" He went to the living room, pulled back the lace curtain with his finger and peered out. Nothing. He went to the back and scanned the back yard. Maybe she hadn't been followed home.

"I need to know exactly what happened," Kate pleaded.

Braxton turned to face her. The knot in his throat matched the one in his stomach. He knew she deserved the truth. After all she'd done, he at least owed her that much.

He reached out and took her hand, awed by the crackle of electricity that washed over him every time they touched. He walked over to the couch and sat, pulling her down beside him.

Leaning forward, he rested his elbows on his knees and took a deep breath. "I guess I need to start from the beginning."

* * *

KATE KNEW that whatever he was about to say may just change her opinion of him, forever.

She saw the anguish in his gray eyes. "My father was an alcoholic. When he got drunk, he liked to hit things."

Her heart stopped. She reached for his hand. "Did he hit you?"

"Yes."

She squeezed his hand as she swallowed back the revulsion of such an act.

"But when I went through puberty at thirteen, things changed. It was the first time I shifted into a wolf. My father came home drunk one night and was angry that I didn't put my bike in the garage. He hit me. It was the last time he made that mistake."

"What did you do?"

"I shifted and beat the shit out of him." He gave a joyless chuckle. "Surprised the hell out of both of us. I would have killed him if my mother hadn't begged me to stop."

Kate squeezed his hand. "I'm glad."

He looked at her. "That I stopped?"

"No, that you beat the shit out of him."

He stared at her for a few beats and then glanced away. "After that, he never laid another hand on me. But the beatings didn't stop for my mother."

"He hit your mom?" Anger stirred in the pit of her stomach. She'd never experienced domestic violence, and she couldn't begin to fathom living in that kind of situation.

Braxton's gaze hardened. "Yeah. After a while she stopped telling me about the beatings because she knew I'd kill him. He made sure to hit her where no one could see the bruises. I just thought he'd stopped. When I found out he was still abusing her, my mom said that she had forgiven him because she loved him. I tried to get her to leave. I told her we could leave Louisiana and go anywhere in the world she wanted. I told her she could be safe and that he'd never hurt her again."

"But she wouldn't leave." Kate already knew the answer.

"No, she wouldn't."

"So you stayed and tried to protect her."

"Yeah, well, that didn't work out so well for me."

"What happened?"

He shifted in his seat. "I told you I work in a bar."

"Yes."

"Well, the bar happens to be located in a strip club."

Kate flinched, uncomfortable with the image of hot, naked strippers walking around in front of Braxton. "I see."

"It was just a job, Kate. I didn't go to college and a lot of places won't hire a guy looking like me." He held out his tattooed arms and gave her a self-effacing smile.

"People should judge others by their heart, not what's on the outside." Although to her, the outside looked pretty damn hot.

He brought her hand to his lips and brushed his lips against her knuckles. Her heart sped up at the touch of his warm mouth.

"Back to what I was saying." He kept her hand in his as he continued on. "One of the customers hit a dancer when she refused to have sex with him. I saw him when it happened and I jumped on the guy."

"You might look tough and untouchable, but I'd bet you always try to save the damsel in distress." Her heart tugged for her tattooed hero.

He looked away, embarrassed. "Trust me, I'm no one's hero."

She begged to differ.

He forked his fingers through his blue-tipped hair and shrugged. "After the fight, I was fired. On my way home, I got a phone call from my mom's neighbor saying there was some yelling coming from my parent's house. The neighbor was an older lady, and she knew how big an asshole my dad was. Anyway, I rode over there."

"I didn't really notice how quiet everything was as I was walking up the driveway. I guess because I was still going over the fight at the bar in my head and wondering where I was going to find work.

"There was blood everywhere. For a minute I thought maybe my mom had killed him in self-defense, but when she walked in a few minutes later, I realized she hadn't done it. She screamed and asked why I killed him."

"Oh, Braxton." Kate went to hug him, but he held up his hands, obviously needing to finish his story.

"I told her I didn't kill him, but she didn't believe me. By that time, someone had heard her screams and called the cops. The police barged in, guns drawn, and my mom told them I was the killer."

"But Braxton, you didn't do anything. You wouldn't have murdered your own father."

He stood and rounded on her. "Kate, don't fool yourself. Don't let yourself believe that I am an honorable man. Don't think if the opportunity had presented itself that I wouldn't have acted on it."

She pressed back further into the couch, both shocked and frightened at Braxton's sudden fury. His lips curled over his gleaming white teeth and his gray eyes glinted with lightning rage. He had never looked more dangerous than he did at that moment.

She tried not to show any fear, but something must have spilled onto her face. He relaxed, backed up, and dropped his gaze to the floor.

Her heart splintered. He needed her now more than ever. Standing up, she made her way to him. She pressed her palm to his cheek and met his gaze. "I think you are far more honorable than most humans. You tried to protect your mom. You protected those girls who found themselves forced to strip because they need the money. You even protected me from Oliver Bigsby when he came to my house." Her smile softened as she brushed her thumb across his lips.. "Braxton, I think the world is a much better place with you in it."

* * *

BRAXTON'S CHEST shifted as a heaviness fell away, like ice falling from a branch after a snowstorm. Kate stared at him as if he were worth something. No one, not even his mother, had ever looked at him like that. Kate was practically a stranger, yet she could see him better than anyone else he knew.

He pulled her into his arms, her lithe body pressing into the hard plane of his own. God, she fit. She fit him like no one else. Right now, he needed her more than his next breath.

She lifted her face and he bent his head, angling his mouth across hers. Her soft warm lips slayed him, left him breathless. Right now, air was the last thing he needed.

What he needed more than anything was Kate.

* * *

KATE GASPED and pressed deeper into Braxton's strong embrace. The outline of his muscled abs against her sent delicious shivers through her body.

He growled. She tightened her arms around his neck, rubbing her hardened nipples against his chest and wanting to crawl up his body. Everything on the man was hard and hot. Everything.

He pulled back, his eyes dark with primal desire. "If you don't want this, tell me now."

He was actually asking permission to ravish her. No problem there. Ravage away.

"I want this." Her words came out hoarse and dry. She

licked her lips as her gaze drifted to his bandage. "How are you feeling?"

"Horny." He hauled her up into his arms as if she were weightless and strode to the bedroom. "Does that answer your question?"

Kate tightened her arms around his neck and mentally said a prayer of thanks for remembering to wash her sheets that morning.

Her heart sped up as he laid her on the bed and pressed his warm body into hers. He kissed her gently, their tongues sliding against each other. The taste of him, male and hot, had her arching upward. The kiss changed, became more urgent, more forbidden, as he laced his fingers through hers, pinning her hands on either side of her head. Her eyes drifted shut as he trailed his hot mouth down to her neck. His tongue darted out and licked the sensitive spot near her ear.

"God, I love your scent. It's so fucking sexy."

She moaned and wrapped her legs around his lean waist, grinding against him. "Less clothes. Now."

He chuckled and released her hands. He skirted his hands under her sweater and pulled it up and over her head. His heated gaze dipped to her pink lace-clad breasts.

"Pretty." He trailed a finger across her bra as she struggled to catch her breath under his touch.

He ran his large hand down the valley between her breasts, setting her skin on fire.

"Braxton," she panted as she rubbed her legs together to ease the ache.

"Easy, baby. I need to take my time, to make this last." He scalded her with his gaze as his fingers dipped to her jeans. He unzipped and tugged her jeans off.

He eased off the bed, pulled his tight T-shirt over his head. She raised up on her elbows, unable to tear her gaze away as he divested himself of the rest of his clothing. If Braxton was hot with clothes, he was magnificent without them.

He grinned slowly as his gaze held hers. "You like what you see?"

"Oh, yeah." Kate swallowed as her gaze dipped down to his straining erection.

His stormy eyes dilated with animal lust. He straddled her, pinning her down with his hard body. He met her gaze. Something far more intimate passed through his eyes before he bent his head and covered her mouth with his. She wrapped her arms around his neck, pulling him closer and loving how good he felt against her.

His dipped his head until his lips brushed against her bra-covered breasts.

"Yes." She arched as he sucked her nipple into his mouth. His fingers fumbled with the clasp in the back for just a second before he eased her arms out and tossed the bra onto the floor with her other clothing.

His mouth was on her once again, a combination of fire and heat, as he teased her nipple, making her writhe underneath him.

"More." She gripped his silky hair between her fingers and pressed his face against her breasts. For the first time in her life, she thought she would orgasm from just his mouth alone.

He tortured one breast with flicks from his tongue before changing direction and kissing his way to the other one.

"I want you inside me." She panted out the words, desperate for him.

He lifted his gaze to hers as his tongue darted out to lick her nipple. "Not yet. I want to watch you come while my mouth is on you."

He grinned wickedly and kissed his way down her body,

pressing his lips against her stomach. Her heart raced. When he reached her panties, he caressed her through the lace.

She bucked against his hand.

His fingers skidded across her panties and then dipped underneath the material and into her wetness. His nostrils flared as he growled. With a swipe of his hand he ripped her panties off in one swift motion.

His eyes devoured every inch of her as if she were cake. She shifted, uncomfortable at being spread like that before him. Instinctively, she closed her legs.

"Don't hide yourself from me, baby. I need to see all of you."

She swallowed and let her legs fall open.

"You're so fucking beautiful."

Kate's heart catapulted in her chest at his reverent words.

She gripped his shoulders, pulling him up for a kiss.

"Braxton, I can't wait any longer. I want you inside me," she panted against his mouth.

He chuckled and kissed his way down her body.

Kate gasped as his mouth covered her clit.

"Oh, my God." She meant to push him away, but her fingers were wired to another part of her brain. She fisted her fingers in his hair and held him against her wet core as he licked her.

His tongue slid across her clit, teasing and stroking.

"Don't stop. Please don't stop."

He sucked her sensitive clit into his mouth, gripping her hips and not letting go.

Hot pleasure flooded every inch of her body. She pulled his hair as she came, crying out his name while tremors racked her body.

* * *

BRAXTON HAD NEVER TASTED anything as sweet as Kate. When she called out his name with her orgasm, his chest filled with pride knowing that he'd done that to her delicious little body.

He was nowhere near done. He wanted to make her come again.

Crawling up her body, he positioned himself between her thighs, her creamy skin brushing against his legs. He almost stopped and buried his face back between her legs again. He could go down on her all day and never get enough.

Braxton looked into Kate's liquid gaze and growled. He positioned himself against her wet entrance and pushed.

"Fuck," Braxton murmured, pushing himself into her snug heat.

Kate moaned and tried to pull him closer.

"Wait, baby." He froze, afraid if he moved another inch, it was going to be over too soon. She was tight, so fucking tight.

"I can't wait." She dug her nails into his hips, pushing him further inside until he was buried balls-deep. His scalp prickled and every muscle in his body tensed as he forced himself not to move.

"Braxton." Her breath caressed his neck as she moaned his name.

"Feel good?" His voice came out like sandpaper and he wasn't even sure what he'd said. All he could feel was her heat around his cock.

"Please, Braxton. Please don't stop."

"I couldn't stop even if I wanted, baby." Her body fit him like a silk glove, threatening to make him come too fast.

He moved slowly at first, grinding against her in a torturous dance. Every moan and hitch in her breath urged him to slow down to make it last and make it good for her.

Her legs locked around his ankles and she bucked. Pleasure raced down the base of his spine, threatening his self-control. He moved faster, thrusting in and out, until their bodies were wet with sweat and sex.

"Oh, God, Braxton." She moaned out his name as she climaxed, tightening around him like a vise.

He moved faster, thrusting harder. His balls tightened, pleasure streaking through his body straight to the end of his cock, exploding in the hardest orgasm he'd ever experienced.

When the last tremor left, he collapsed on top of her. She wrapped her arms around his back, holding him close.

"You okay?" he whispered in the crook of her neck as he inhaled her scent.

"Yeah, though I'm not exactly sure what you did to my body. That's never happened before."

He lifted his head and gazed down at her. "You've never had an orgasm before?" He grinned, knowing that he'd given her something no other man had.

"No."

Braxton stilled, watching her face flush with embarrassment.

"Have you ever given yourself an orgasm?"

She squeezed her eyes shut. "No. I guess I wasn't sure how to work the equipment."

"I may not know anything about appliances, but I know how to work your equipment just fine." Braxton kissed her neck and rolled off. Laying on his back, he pulled her close and tucked her into his arms.

Caressing her cheek, he forced her gaze to meet his. "I'm glad that I was the one to give you your first orgasm." He pressed his lips to hers.

His hand drifted down her back to rest on her hip. He let his eyes drift shut, savoring the sweetness of being wrapped in her arms.

"Braxton?"

"Yeah, baby?"

"Do you think that guy I ran into in town is still looking for you?"

He stopped his caress, every muscle in his body stiffening. He didn't want to lie, but he didn't want to upset her either. Werewolf laws were strict and could be viewed by humans as cruel. In the end, he decided on telling her the truth.

"Assassins don't give up until they have the body of their target. They always need confirmation."

Kate buried deeper into his chest and shivered against him. He tightened his hold.

Braxton frowned. "I'm surprised they tracked me this far. I would have thought the snow would have covered my trail. I'm not sure that it's safe for me to even stay here."

Kate raised up on her elbows. "I don't think they know you're here. From the conversation I had, it made me think they are just back-tracking. That big guy said you might have come through Eureka Springs. I don't think they found your tracks." Her eyes softened. "So you don't have to leave. Not yet."

Braxton's heart caught in his chest. He didn't want to leave her. Not ever. For the first time in his life, he felt like he was home. "Then I'll stay. For a little longer at least. But if it looks like you'll be in danger, for any reason at all, I'll leave."

She pressed her mouth to his lips. The gentle kiss soon turned hungry.

This time when he slid inside her, he took his time, loving every inch of her, like it was their last moment on earth.

* * *

KATE SAT on the kitchen stool as Braxton flipped the pancake in the air and caught it in the skillet. His chest muscles flexed with each movement.

With the next flip, he caught the pancake on a dainty pink plate, stacked two more on top, and set it in front of her. "Hope you're hungry."

She was hungry, just not for food.

"How is it?" Braxton looked over his shoulder as she took a bite.

"It's good, really good." She held back an appreciative moan. "How'd you learn to cook?"

Braxton shrugged, the muscles playing across his shoulders with the movement. "I learned pretty early. When I was younger, my mom would tell me to stay out of my father's way whenever he was around. So I usually waited until they were out of the house to get something to eat."

Kate's fork froze halfway to her mouth. "Your mom made you miss eating meals? Just to appease your father?"

Braxton shook his head. "It wasn't like that."

Trembling with anger, Kate sucked in a breath and carefully laid her fork on the plate. "Then, what was it like?"

"I don't know. She just didn't want me to upset my father and end up getting hit." Braxton slid his plate next to hers and sat. "It doesn't matter. It was so long ago."

It did matter. She wanted to wrap her arms around Braxton and show him how much he mattered. How could a mother neglect her own child? What kind of mother did that?

She looked at him under her lashes as he quietly ate his breakfast. She didn't want to bring up painful memories, so she let the issue go.

She gave him a playful elbow to the side. "I've never had a guy cook me breakfast before."

"Yeah?" Braxton gave her a devastating grin. "Looks like you are having a lot of firsts today."

Her face heated. He was right. He'd given her a lot of firsts today.

"Do you do this all the time? Cook for women after ravishing them?" She waved her fork over her plate.

Braxton's grin slipped, his gaze boring straight to her heart. "I've never cooked for a woman before."

Her heart melted like a snow cone in the middle of July. "Looks like there are a lot of firsts for both of us today."

Bam! Bam! Bam! Three sharp knocks to the front door had Braxton grabbing his shirt and heading for the living room.

She grabbed his arm and dug in her heels, holding him back. "What are you doing? You can't answer the door. What if it's the Assassins?"

He took another step and she tightened her fingers on his bicep. Her heart pounded in her chest.

"If you get caught now, you won't have a chance to find your father's killer."

Braxton thinned his lips, and she knew he was contemplating his options.

"Braxton, please. I don't know what I'd do if you got hurt, or worse." She swallowed the lump in the back of her throat. She was an idiot. She was falling for a guy who wouldn't be around much longer. Even if he did find the killer and things were resolved, Braxton would want to go back to Shreveport to be with his mom. His home was in Louisanna, not here with her.

He cupped her face between his massive hands and stared down at her with such tenderness it made her chest tighten.

The visitor pounded out three more hard knocks.

Kate gripped his wrist. "Please, let me answer the door. If it's those guys, you can have a chance of escaping out the back door."

He brought his mouth down on hers and kissed her hard. As much as she wanted the kiss to never end, she pulled away and shoved at his chest. "Go."

She waited until Braxton was out the kitchen door before

making her way slowly to the front door. Kate glanced at her reflection in the mirror over the table. Damn, she looked like she'd been rolling around in bed with a hot man.

She tightened the belt on her robe and counted to ten before opening the front door.

Her heart dropped to the floor. Standing right in front of her was the same man that had approached her in the parking lot. She thought she had been so careful about not being followed back to the Bella Luna.

The stranger whipped off his Oakleys and glared at her with intense blue eyes.

"Where is he?" he growled.

"Where is who?" She suddenly wished she was a gun owner. Here she was, standing in front of a guy who outweighed her by at least a hundred and fifty pounds, and she had nothing to defend herself with.

The dark stranger blew out an impatient breath. "Braxton. Where is he?"

Holy shit. "I don't know any Braxton." She gave him her best poker face. She sucked at poker. She sucked at lying in general.

The Assassin stuck his hand through his jet-black hair and closed his eyes."I know Braxton is here. I can smell him all over you."

CHAPTER 7

*K*ate lifted a lock of hair and sniffed. Smelled like mango and apricots to her.

The stranger growled. "I don't mean your hair. I mean I can smell his scent on your body."

She opened her mouth and clamped it shut, both embarrassed and outraged.

"Listen, I'm…"

A growl rumbled through the house. She turned just as Braxton rushed past her and tackled the stranger, knocking him to the hardwood floor.

* * *

"You know I can't let you live," Braxton growled. "If I do, you'll have the other Assassins on Kate's doorstep within the hour." Braxton twisted the stranger's hands behind his back as he held him down.

"Braxton, get your large ass off me before you really piss me off."

Braxton stilled, the familiar voice catching him off guard. Slowly he released his hold and rolled off. Damon leaped to his feet in a front flip.

"Damon?" Braxton narrowed his eyes.

"Yeah, it's me you dumb fuck." Damon dusted the imaginary dirt off his leather jacket with a scowl.

"Wait, you know him?" Kate stuck her thumb in Damon's general direction.

"Yeah." Braxton nodded slowly.

"Is he one of the Assassins?" Kate gave him a wide-eyed look.

Damon scowled. "I'm no fucking Assassin."

"He's a friend." Or so he hoped.

"Well, don't start having a Lifetime movie moment with me. I'm already mated, dickwad," Damon snarled.

Braxton gave him a fist bump and laughed. "Don't worry. You're not my type. By the way, how is Ava? Is she still playing Little Red Riding Hood?"

"Only in my bed." Damon cut his suspicious gaze at Kate. "And you are..."

Braxton placed his hand on the small of Kate's back. "Damon, this is Kate. She owns the Bella Luna."

Kate cast a wary glance at Damon before she accepted his outstretched hand. "Nice to meet you. I think."

Braxton snorted. "You won't think so once you've seen him get angry."

Damon glared at Braxton and then turned his attention to Kate. "Pleasure to meet you."

Kate motioned toward the kitchen. "Would you like some coffee?"

"Yes, thank you. I see you have better manners than Braxton." Damon jerked his thumb in Braxton's direction as he followed them into the kitchen.

Braxton rested his arms on the kitchen island and cut his

eyes at Damon. "I suppose you know what happened in Louisiana. I need to know something. Are you here to start trouble?"

Damon snorted. "Actually, I think you already took care of that." Damon muttered his thanks to Kate as she offered him a hot mug of coffee. "I'm here because the powers that be aren't very happy with what you've done."

Braxton straightened. "I didn't kill my father."

Damon shrugged. "From what you told me I wouldn't blame you if you did. He sounded like a prick." He lifted the mug to his lips.

"Then why are you here?" Braxton caught the hesitancy in his friend's expression as Damon's gaze flickered over Kate. "You can speak in front of her. She knows what I am, what we are."

Damon eased onto a kitchen stool and nodded for them to sit. "Barrett sent me here because those Assassins have broken Arkansas Pack Law. The moment they crossed the Arkansas border, they failed to inform Barrett they were in the territory. That's a big no-no. Then they shoot you in our state—in broad daylight—risking exposing us to humans. Needless to say my Pack Master isn't exactly feeling rainbows and puppies toward the Louisiana Pack."

Hope swelled in Braxton's chest. Maybe Barrett could help him. He didn't know the Pack Master that well, but he did know that Barrett was fair. "Did Barrett send you to help find my father's killer?"

Damon shook his head, looking pained. "He's gone to Louisiana to raise hell with their Pack Master about letting those Assassins loose on Arkansas territory. He's working on getting you a formal Tribunal in Louisiana. He sent me here to bring you to Little Rock and make sure they don't kill you before that happens."

"What's a Tribunal?" Kate looked between him and Damon.

"It's kind of like a court for our kind."

"A court for werewolves?" Kate cocked her head.

"Yeah." Damon cringed. "No offense, but it feels weird discussing this with a human."

"Kate's cool." Braxton wrapped his arm around her shoulder and tugged her into his chest. She relaxed against him.

Damon nodded. "A Tribunal is a court for Weres when there is a dispute or a law is broken. There are certain laws that, once they are broken, carry an immediate judgment."

"Sounds like a lively bunch," Kate deadpanned.

"It's a fucking barrel of monkeys." Damon took another sip and nodded. "You make good coffee. Better than Ava." Damon cut his eyes at Braxton. "Don't ever tell her I said that."

"Is Ava your wife?" Kate asked.

"She's my mate."

Braxton turned to her. "Being mated is a stronger bond than being married. Once you are mated, you are bound together for life."

"What happens if there is infidelity?" Kate looked from him to Damon.

"There is no infidelity. We are not like humans, Kate. Once we find our mates, it is impossible for mated couples to have sex with anyone else." Braxton had never considered being mated. But now, looking into Kate's eyes, he couldn't help but wonder what it would be like.

"So the equipment doesn't work." Kate raised her eyebrow.

"Right." Damon grinned.

"Back to the topic at hand. Look, Damon, I appreciate you

coming all this way, but I can't leave with you. If I leave, the Assassins will find me. I don't mind dying. But I'm not ready to die for something I sure as hell didn't do."

Damon set the coffee cup down with a clink. "Doesn't matter what you want. I have my orders. You have to come back with me."

"And I have to find the killer. At least that's what I was trying to do before those assholes put a hole in me." He absently rubbed his shoulder. The pain had eased up a day or two ago, leaving behind a slight ache.

Damon lifted his chin, a frown creasing his brow. "How the hell did you survive a silver bullet, anyway?"

"Kate's friend is a vet. He dug it out of my shoulder and patched me up." Braxton pulled his shirt up to his almost fully healed wound.

"Nice job. I take it he's a Were too?" Damon asked.

"Yes." Braxton squeezed Kate's shoulder.

"I've got to hand it to you guys. You know how to keep your paranormal species a secret. Until I found Braxton on my porch, I had no idea werewolves even existed." Kate snorted.

Braxton nodded at his friend. "Looks like you came all this way for nothing."

Damon glared. "I still have my orders."

"We both know how much you hate following orders, Damon. Besides, you kind of owe me."

Damon straightened. "Owe you? For what?"

"For helping you get Jayden out of that trouble down in Shreveport."

"Help? All you did was handcuff me to the bar in that strip club," Damon growled.

Kate's mouth dropped open. "Braxton handcuffed you to a bar?"

Damon lifted his brow. "With a pair of fuzzy pink handcuffs."

Kate grinned. "Okay. I'm afraid to even ask."

"Hey, they weren't mine. Someone left them at the bar." Braxton held up his hands. Fucking Damon.

"So you keep saying." Damon's expression grew grim. "Since you managed to hide out here without the Assassins finding you, it might be wise for you to stay put."

Braxton relaxed. That would give him more time with Kate. Even if it was just one more day, he'd take it.

"And since you're staying here, that means I'll be staying here, too." Damon stood.

"Wait a minute." Braxton shook his head, not liking where this conversation was going.

"This is a bed and breakfast, isn't it?" Damon glanced at Kate.

"Yes."

"Good. How much is it a night?" Damon reached for his wallet. Guilt and jealousy stung Braxton's gut. He didn't have the funds to pay Kate for her hospitality and everything she'd done for him. Yet, here was Damon, pulling out cash earned from his highly profitable position as one of Arkansas's Guardians. He had to hand it to Barrett for paying his employees so well.

"The usual rate is two hundred dollars a night, but since it's the slow season, I charge a hundred and nineteen."

Damon shook his head. "I'll pay the full price. You have no idea how much I can eat. Ava has to buy groceries twice a week." He pulled out a wad of hundred dollar bills. "Cash okay?"

Kate nodded, her eyes widening. "Cash is great."

"Good. Put me down for a week." He counted off eleven hundred dollars and handed it to her.

She looked up at Damon and shook her head. "This is too much."

"The extra should cover any additional expenses, like food. I wasn't kidding about eating a lot."

Kate stared at the wad of cash in her hands. "Thanks. I'll just put this up." She grinned and then headed to her bedroom.

Making sure she was out of earshot, Braxton gave Damon a pointed look. "You can't stay."

"Why not? It's a bed and breakfast and she apparently needs the money." Damon looked over his shoulder and out the window. "I didn't notice any cars outside. Since I've been here, I haven't exactly heard the phone ringing off the hook with people booking a room."

Braxton gritted his teeth. Damon was right. Kate could use the money. He just wished he had the money to help her out and not Damon.

"Besides, I wouldn't be doing my job if I didn't stick to you like glue." Damon slapped him on the back. "So are you going to tell me what's going on?"

Braxton rubbed the back of his neck. "I already told you. I was accused of a crime I didn't commit."

Damon shook his head. "No, not that. That, I got already. I mean, what's going on with you and the human." He nodded toward Kate's bedroom.

"Her name is Kate and nothing's going on." The lie stuck in his throat like an apple. A lot was going on; he just needed to figure out what it was.

"Does she know that?"

"What are you, Dr. Phil? I never pegged you for a relationship specialist." Braxton gave him a dry look.

"Fuck you."

"No, thanks, I'm into blondes."

"So I've noticed." Damon reached for his coffee. "Don't you find it a little strange that Kate hasn't freaked out about you being a werewolf?"

Braxton eyed him. "Of course she freaked out."

"Really? What did she do? Go running for the hills?" Damon looked out the window. "Never mind, we *are* in the hills."

"Smart-ass."

"Did she call the cops when you shifted?" Damon crossed his arms over his chest and stared at him.

Braxton shook his head. "No."

"Did she call her friend the vet to come shoot you?"

"Of course not."

"So you're telling me a human woman saw you shift into a wolf, helped dig a silver bullet out of your shoulder, and let you stay here in a secluded bed and breakfast? No questions asked?"

"What the fuck are you getting at, Damon?" Braxton curled his fingers into fists.

"I find it hard to believe that Kate is being nice to you out of the goodness of her heart. I mean, who's to say she's not using you for her own benefit?"

"If anyone's using someone, it's me using her," Braxton muttered. Vivid images of Kate naked, under him, flashed through his mind. He remembered the way she held his gaze when he held her close, her body responding to his every touch.

"So it's like that."

Braxton gave him a murderous glare. "Change the topic."

"For now. But, I still find Kate's reaction to the whole wolf thing out of place." Damon shrugged. "I mean, when Ava saw me shift, she did at least scream."

"Did she try to run away?"

Damon scratched his whiskered chin. "She tried, but I didn't let her."

"So maybe it's just you that women run away from." Braxton smirked.

Damon grinned wickedly. "Maybe, but at least I got one to stick."

* * *

THE PHONE RANG, jolting Kate out of a deep sleep. Since Damon's arrival, he and Braxton stayed up late, discussing the situation with the Assassins. Exhausted, Kate had given up playing hostess and gone to bed.

She blinked back the cobwebs in her sleepy brain and answered the phone.

"Hello?"

"It's Beau. Glad to see your phone is fixed."

Kate eyed the alarm clock. Six o'clock. He had never called her before seven in the morning. "What's wrong? Is everything okay?"

"No, it's not. Something's happened."

"What?" She sat up in bed, fully alert.

"Someone discovered a dead body."

A wave of nausea enveloped her. "Where? Who was it?"

"It was a construction worker on Oliver Bigsby's crew. They found him dead at the construction site." Bigsby had broken ground to erect his next eyesore of a hotel on an area just on the outskirts of town. The more hotels he built meant less business for the B&Bs in town.

"That's horrible. How did he die?" Please don't say he was bitten by a wolf. She held her breath, waiting for his answer.

"He was shot through the eye with a nail gun. Death by nail gun doesn't exactly fall under the accident category."

Her blood turned to ice in her veins. With a trembling

hand, she pulled the quilt up to her chin in a feeble attempt to ward off the shivers racking her body.

"Kate, you still there?"

"Yeah, I'm here."

"I know it's none of my business, and I don't need you to remind me that you're a grown-ass woman, but I can't help but think this has something to do with your houseguest."

"Which one?" She cringed. Though Braxton had not been out of her sight since he arrived, Damon, on the other hand, was another story. She didn't know where he was half the time.

He snorted. "The house guest that happens to be a wolf."

"Again, which one?"

"Christ, Kate. Please don't tell me there's another Were staying in your house."

"Okay. I won't." She slunk back into the covers as unease slunk into her stomach.

"I knew I should have kicked his ass out the minute I saw him. I should have known he'd bring more Weres around." She held the phone away from her ear at his acrid words. "I should have listened to my gut."

She shook her head as her shoulders slumped. "Whoever killed that guy wasn't one of my Weres. That I know." She hoped her voice held more conviction than her gut. She wasn't exactly the best judge of character. The last guy she trusted was her ex. Look where that had gotten her. On the brink of foreclosure and one step away from being homeless.

God, she was a mess.

She cleared her throat. "Thanks for the update. Somehow I feel like if a werewolf were going to kill someone, they would have done it without the use of a nail gun."

The line went silent for a beat. "Maybe you're right. They usually rip the victims' throats out. Doesn't change the fact that I don't like the idea of you putting yourself in the middle of whatever shit Braxton has found himself in."

She smiled a tiny smile. If he really thought Braxton was capable of murder, Beau would have thrown him out on his ass the minute Braxton had confided in them.

"Please tell me the new Were in your house is not wanted for a crime."

"He's not. He's actually some kind of Arkansas soldier."

"A Guardian?" She didn't miss the surprise in his voice.

"Yeah. Someone named Barrett ordered him to find Braxton and make sure he stays alive until there is a Tribunal. Do you know Barrett?"

"I've never actually met him. He's the ruling Pack Master over Arkansas, and from his reputation, very lethal. Anyone that crosses him ends up on the losing end."

"I'm not sure if I should feel safe or scared." Kate tugged on her lower lip.

"Probably a little of both. How's the patient doing by the way?"

"Great." More than great. He was totally fine, hot, and gorgeous. She licked her dry lips. "His wound has healed up nicely."

"It will take some time to get the silver completely out of his system. He was damn lucky it didn't hit his heart. Otherwise he'd be dead."

Kate shivered at the image of Braxton's lifeless body on the side of the highway.

"What are your plans for the day?"

"I've got to go back into town. The bank president called and wanted to talk about my loan. I'm hoping it's good news and not an eviction notice."

"Alright, honey. Good luck. And Kate?"

"Yeah?"

"Call me if you need me."

"I always do."

* * *

KATE SAW Bigsby standing in front of the bank, holding the door open and smiling like he'd won the lottery. She snarled. He certainly didn't look like someone who'd just lost one of his workers to such a brutal death.

She stepped closer and swallowed. "I'm sorry to hear about your employee."

His smile left his face in a hurry as he sought to look mournful. "Thank you. It was quite a shock, I must say."

"What a horrible way to die." She didn't bother suppressing the shudder that ran down her back.

Bigsby's cold eyes found hers and he gave her a quick nod. "Yes, well there's nothing to be done about it now. Life does go on." Just like that, his smile was plastered back on his perfect face.

Unease coiled in the pit of her stomach as his façade of self-assurance slipped across his face. What did Bigsby know that she didn't? Surely she wasn't about to lose her home. Surely there was something right in the universe where the little guy who worked hard all his life would prevail.

"I must say you look lovely today, Kate."

"Thanks." She gave a polite smile and then hurried past him and into the warmth of the bank.

"There is something different about you. You have a glow."

Her foot caught the edge of the rug and she stumbled. The only thing that would have that effect on her would be Braxton Devereaux and the multiple orgasms he'd given her.

"Must be my new lotion." She kept walking, hoping he would just leave her alone.

"I was hoping to talk to you before your meeting with Mr. Weatherford."

She froze. Slowly she turned and faced him. "How did you know I have a meeting with the bank president?"

He shrugged, and a sinister smile crept across his face. "I know a lot of things in this town. For instance, I know that guy you've got up at your place is bad news."

She curled her fingers into her palms as her blood boiled. "I don't think my houseguest is any of your business."

"You don't know anything about him, Kate. Where did he come from? What does he do? He certainly doesn't look like he can hold down a job with all those tattoos." He frowned, his perfect brow creasing.

She sucked in a breath and chose her next words carefully. "I still own the Bella Luna and I honor my clients' privacy." Bigsby was either afraid that her business was picking up or he was jealous at how hot Braxton was. She bet it was a little of both.

"As far as his tattoos go, I like them. I think they're hot."

His eyes rounded in disbelief, and she bit the inside of her cheek to keep from smiling. She fought the urge to tell him in detail of the tattoo on Braxton's back, just to rub it in his face.

His lips puckered into a tight circle. "You need to be careful who you let into your bed and breakfast. You're so isolated and if there was trouble, no one could help you."

A shiver ran across Kate's back.

Bigsby gave her a curt nod and walked past her to the first open teller.

She hurried toward the bank president's office. The bank secretary looked up from her computer screen and smiled warmly.

"You can go on in, Kate. He's waiting for you."

She straightened her shoulders and stepped through the door.

The bank president smiled and waved her toward the empty chair while he wrapped up his telephone conversation. She took a deep breath and braced herself for the next few minutes.

* * *

"You really gonna eat all that?" Braxton looked at Damon's plate overflowing with food.

"What are you trying to say?" Damon narrowed his eyes as he curled his arm over the edge of his plate and pulled it closer.

"Five ham sandwiches, two bags of chips, a liter of Dr Pepper, and almost a whole pie."

"So?"

"So? If I ate like that I'd be five hundred pounds and couldn't get my fat ass on my Harley." Braxton's stomach dropped as reality set in. He no longer had a Harley. His Harley was long gone at the bottom of the mountain.

"I just recently started eating this much. It's like I can't get enough food. Yet, I don't gain an ounce."

"Probably from all that sex you're getting."

"Probably right." Damon took a large bite out of his sandwich and smiled.

"I'm getting sex. So why am I not eating like an elephant?" Braxton folded his arms across his chest.

Damon finished off his sandwich and swallowed. "Are you having sex every three hours?'

Braxton's mouth fell open. "Every three hours at night?"

Damon snorted. "Every three hours around the clock, man."

"You're shitting me." Braxton had never lacked getting

laid. There was a time in his life when he didn't go longer than a few days before sleeping with a willing female. But that had been years ago when he'd hit his teens and his sexual drive was so intense. The last few years he'd been less interested in the physical act of sex. He'd started wondering if there was something more for him in the world. But sex every three hours?

"Yes, it's possible." Damon smirked and began tossing back the first bag of sour cream and onion potato chips. "I see the jealousy written all over your face." Damon poured the soda in a glass. "I think it has something to do with being newly mated. It's like I can't get enough sex. And as for Ava…" He whistled.

"What?" Braxton leaned forward

"She's insatiable. Always wanting more. Always demanding more." Damon smiled and wiggled his eyebrows. "I can't get her off my dick."

"This mating thing is starting to grow on me."

Kate walked into the kitchen. "What's starting to grow on you?"

From the innocent look on Kate's face she hadn't heard their conversation. Good. Mating was the last thing he wanted to discuss. Even with Kate.

"We were talking about the mountains, about how different Eureka Springs is from Shreveport." Braxton shot Damon a warning look not to open his big mouth.

Kate laughed as she placed her purse on the kitchen island. "We don't seem to have much going on in Eureka Springs."

"It's like Mayberry. I'm betting the crime rate here is zero." Damon took another bite of his sandwich.

Kate paled. "Actually, now that you bring that up…"

"What?" Braxton straightened.

"Beau called me early this morning." Kate licked her lips.

"He said someone discovered a dead body." Kate's gaze drifted from him to Damon.

Damon shrugged and continued to eat. "Don't look at me. I was here with you guys all night."

"Was it somebody you knew?" Braxton reached for her hand.

"No." Kate swallowed. "It was one of Bigsby's construction workers."

"The guy who's trying to buy your B&B?" Braxton frowned.

"Yeah."

"People get killed on construction jobs all the time. Hell, I heard someone in town talking about someone falling to his death while working on that old hotel on the top of the mountain here." Damon crumbled the now-empty potato chip bag and tossed it in the garbage.

"This guy didn't fall." Her slender throat worked up and down as she swallowed. "He was shot through the eye with a nail gun."

They both turned to her.

"So he was murdered." Braxton glanced at Damon before looking at Kate. "Do they have any suspects?"

"No, but they are looking at anyone new that might have come to town recently." Her voice cracked.

Braxton knew there could be cops showing up on Kate's doorstep any time now, questioning his whereabouts at the time of the murder. Cops he could handle. It was the Assassins he was worried about.

"Maybe you should head back with me." Damon scowled.

"And leave Kate here with some murderer on the loose? Forget it."

"Maybe Damon's right," Kate spoke.

"What?" Braxton's chest tightened.

"It sounds like you'd be better protected under the

Arkansas Pack Master." Kate looked at Damon. "What's his name?"

"Barrett Middleton."

Kate nodded. "Barrett can give you protection while you figure out who killed your father."

Braxton stilled. "Is that what you want? Me gone?"

* * *

KATE'S LIPS trembled as she fought back the urge to scream that she didn't want him to leave. "I think you should do what's best for you."

"She makes a good point. You need to listen to her." Damon stood and put his empty plate in the sink.

"Stay out of this, Damon," Braxton growled.

Damon held his hands up and backed away. "I'll let you two figure this out. Kate, do you have ESPN?"

Kate nodded. "Yes. On the living room TV."

After they were alone, Braxton took a step toward her. "Kate—

She held up her hand and shook her head. If he touched her now, she was going to lose any self-control she had and beg him to stay. She couldn't be that selfish. "Don't say anything. We both knew that you wouldn't be staying forever."

The hurt on Braxton's face hit her like a punch in the gut. As painful as that was, she needed to do what was best for him.

"I see. If that's what you want, then I'll leave." Braxton averted his eyes before making his way toward the bedroom.

Kate took a step to go after him but stopped. Her nails bit into her palms. The last thing she wanted to do was hurt him. Even though it had only been a few days, he'd come to mean a lot to her.

"You're doing the right thing. He'll understand," Damon said quietly behind her.

"If it's right, then why does it hurt so much?" Kate turned and headed outside, needing the cold, snowy air to freeze her tears.

* * *

BRAXTON STORMED into the living room ready for a fight with Damon. "Just so you know, I'm not going with you."

Damon stood, his mouth set in a grim line. "You're not exactly in a position where you have a say, Braxton. I have a job to do and I intend on doing it."

"I intend on finding my father's killer."

"You think you're smart enough to evade those Assassins forever? They are killers, trained from the time they were old enough to walk to seek out and kill. You got lucky, but you won't escape their bullet a second time."

"I can try." Rage burned through him. He wasn't going to give up without a fight.

"You'll lose. I've seen Assassins track down Were Guardians who had gone rogue. Once Assassins have a bead on you, they will be relentless in hunting you down until they are sure you are dead." Damon shook his head. "They don't care if you're guilty or innocent. All they care about is getting the job done. That's it. At this moment, to them, you, Braxton, are the job."

Braxton shoved his hand through his hair. What Damon was saying was right. But his heart told him to do something else.

"Come with me and…" Damon's phone rang. He growled at the interruption and pulled it out of his pocket and answered.

Damon's entire expression softened.

"I don't know, sweetheart. I won't be home for dinner. Things aren't going as planned." Damon gave Braxton a pointed look like it was all his fault.

Braxton headed into the kitchen. Would he ever have someone in his life like Damon did? Would there be a day when someone was waiting for him at home, someone calling and asking him what he wanted for dinner? Would he ever have a mate? Would that mate be Kate?

Braxton swallowed, startled at his romantic thoughts. What the hell was wrong with him? He'd never entertained the idea of having a mate before. Not after how he grew up. He would never want to raise a child in an environment like that. Yet here he was entertaining the idea of a life with a female who wasn't even a wolf.

The hum of someone pulling up the driveway pushed away any fantasy thoughts.

The Assassins. They'd found him.

Braxton hurried to the front window where Damon stood next to him with his hand on his gun.

"Assassins?"

"Not unless the Assassins have traded their Harleys for a minivan, a sedan, and a Volkswagen Beetle."

The vehicles rolled to a stop. Groups of women began piling out of the cars.

"Did Kate mention she had guests coming in?" Damon shot him a glare.

"No. In fact, she's behind on her mortgage and heading toward foreclosure because business has been so bad."

Customers were exactly what Kate needed. From the expression on the ladies' faces, they were sure to book a room.

"Leslie, I don't know. This place looks so isolated," a younger woman who'd gotten out of the VW mumbled as she walked across the yard.

"Yeah, but it's got character," one woman offered. She smiled and lifted her gaze to the snow-covered pines.

Braxton snorted at the women's interaction. He didn't know their names, but he already liked the one who said the place had character. If Kate got all those women booked for the weekend, that would help her business.

"Kate needs to get out there then," Damon said.

"I'll go check out back. If those women knock, go answer the door," Braxton called over his shoulder.

"I'm not answering the damn door. What do I look like? A butler?" Damon hollered after Braxton.

Braxton bounded down the steps and out into the snow-covered yard. The wintery air made his lungs ache as he sucked in a chilly breath. Kate was nowhere to be seen. Maybe she'd headed into the woods. Trampling through the fluffy snow, he stopped at the tree line. He closed his eyes and sniffed. He caught her sweet scent but it wasn't coming from within the woods. He changed direction and headed toward the storage shed off to the side of the house.

Opening the door of the shed, he stepped inside. Kate stood, gripping the counter of the potting bench as her head hung down. She looked like he felt. Broken.

His heart twisted in his chest.

"Kate."

She stiffened and then slowly turned.

"There are some people that just pulled up. Looks like they are needing a place to stay."

A flicker of surprise flashed across her face. "Guests?"

He shrugged. "I think so. They were talking about whether or not they were going to stay."

"Did you talk to them?"

"No, I just heard them talking."

Kate rubbed her hands on her jeans and hurried past him. "Did you invite them inside?"

"Well, no. I thought you were outside. When I didn't see you greeting them, I came looking for you." Braxton rubbed the back of his neck as he followed after her. They entered the front yard. The cars were still there, but the ladies were gone.

Kate stopped suddenly. Braxton plowed into her back. His hands came around her waist, steadying them both.

"They must be inside." Braxton's hands slid up and squeezed her shoulders.

"Inside?" She turned and stared up at him with wide eyes. "With Damon?"

CHAPTER 8

*B*raxton hurried inside the house. Damon wasn't exactly Mr. Personality, and most women found him downright intimidating.

He braced himself as he rounded the corner in the living room, ready to apologize to Kate for Damon scaring off her customers. She needed those customers if she were going to have a chance at saving her home.

All the ladies were in the living room, with Damon standing in the middle, looking uncomfortable. Instead of keeping their distance, they were all eyeing him like a lion looking at a steak.

"What's your name?" The younger girl who'd been bitching about the Bella Luna being too isolated leaned closer to Damon.

"That's Damon." Braxton narrowed his eyes in warning at his friend. "Damon's my favorite name. I'm Felicity." Felicity stepped closer to Damon and smiled.

Another woman tugged on Damon's arm. "Damon, how long are you staying here?"

Damon glared and pulled out of the woman's grip. "I was just leaving."

"You can't leave. We just got here." An older woman with a pageboy haircut pressed her lips together.

"Hi, everyone." They all turned at Kate's voice.

Damon eased himself out of the circle and moved to stand by Braxton.

"I'm Kate. I'm the owner of the Bella Luna." She gave everyone a warm smile. "Are you ladies interested in booking a couple of nights with us?"

"Well, we were, but…" One of the older ladies' gaze zeroed in on Braxton.

"Are you a guest here, too?" Felicity gave Braxton a feline smile as she stroked her own throat.

Kate reached for his hand. "Actually, he's more than a guest."

All the ladies' eyebrows shot up in understanding. Braxton bit his lip to keep from smiling. So Kate was claiming him, was she? Two could play at that game.

Braxton reached for her, pulling her into his arms, and kissed her.

He expected her to hesitate, to pull away at the public display of affection, but she didn't. Instead, she laced her fingers around his neck and kissed him back.

Damon cleared his throat. Braxton finally pulled away. Kate's heavy eyes made him want to throw her over his shoulder and lock themselves in her room for a week. Hell, for eternity.

"*Awwww*. That's so sweet," one woman whimpered.

"Sweet, my ass. That was hot. Like fuck-me-up-against-the-wall hot."

Braxton and Kate turned their shocked gaze upon the women. Damon snorted.

"So, if he's yours, what about him?" Felicity pointed at Damon.

Damon's eyes grew wide and he held up his hands. "Sorry. I'm taken, too."

"Well, shit. Don't that figure. All the hot ones always are." An older lady crossed her arms and cocked her head at Damon. "So, I'm guessing you're faithful to your woman?"

Damon looked offended. "Of course. I'd never cheat on Ava."

That garnered another round of *awwwws* from the ladies.

Kate cleared her throat and glanced at Braxton. "Are you ladies looking to have a girls' weekend?"

"We're here on business."

A blonde-haired lady wearing a blue twinset frowned. "I thought we were here to get drunk and write smut."

"We are, Jackie. But I'm writing this off on my taxes, so we're officially here on business."

Felicity snorted.

"So you're all writers? What kind of books do you write?" Kate asked.

"We write everything, hon. I'm Felicity and I write romantic suspense. This is Jackie; she and Myrtis write paranormal romance. Leslie writes contemporary romance. Danielle and Barbara write historical romance. That's Lynn over there. Don't let the shy act fool you. She writes erotica."

Braxton felt Damon edge closer to him. He didn't blame the guy. The way these women were openly staring at them pushed the boundaries of lewd.

"Wow. All of you ladies write romance? How exciting. Are any of you published?"

"Lynn's the only one published right now. As for the rest of us, we were hoping to spend our time here writing during the day and drinking at night. Who knows? It might result in a best seller. Do you have internet?"

Kate's face fell. "I do, but the snowstorm knocked it out. I'm not sure when it will be back up. I could call and…"

"No!" All the women answered in unison.

Felicity shook her head and grinned. "It's better if there's no internet. That way we'll spend the entire weekend writing and not looking at the internet or checking email. Isn't that right, ladies?"

They all nodded.

"Do you have enough room for all of us? The last B&B we stopped at only had three rooms open."

"She has four rooms open," Braxton spoke up. "You girls don't mind sharing a bed, do you?"

"Of course not. In fact, it would be better on my wallet if we did." Myrtis smiled. "And since Lynn is the published writer in the group, she can have a room to herself."

"So how much is it a night?" Felicity looked at Kate.

"Well, the rate is two hundred dollars plus tax. It includes a full breakfast and cookies and wine at five in the afternoon."

"How come I didn't get cookies and wine?" Damon scowled.

"Because you ate everything in the house," Kate deadpanned.

"That sounds so romantic." Barbara sighed.

Kate frowned. "What? Damon's appetite?"

"No. The cookies and wine."

"How much wine are we talking about? Because we're just letting you know, we can throw back some liquor," Myrtis said.

Felicity waved her hand in the air in a dismissive gesture. "Ignore her. We brought our own alcohol. The last bed and breakfast we stopped at said no alcohol. We were beginning to wonder if Eureka Springs was a dry city."

Kate laughed. "It's not a dry county. That's for sure. And alcohol is definitely allowed at the Bella Luna."

"What a relief." Barbara sighed. "I was beginning to think we were going to have to stay at that hotel just outside of town. You know, the one next to the construction site with all the police tape around it."

Kate went pale.

Braxton squeezed her hand to keep her from saying anything.

"I'm afraid there was a death there last night."

The ladies let out a collective gasp.

Too late. Braxton rubbed his hand down his face. She needed to bring in customers, not scare them away.

"I'm not sure what happened, but..." Kate's voice trailed off.

Lynn's eyes widened. "Was it an accident?"

"Was it suicide?" Barbara's mouth dropped open.

Felicity arched an eyebrow. "Was it murder?"

Kate looked up at him. "I believe the police are ruling it as a homicide."

"Murder! I knew it!" Felicity pumped her fist in the air while the other ladies shot her a glare at having guessed correctly.

"Sorry. We're writers and we sometimes get excited over the weirdest things." Barbara laughed. "It makes for great fodder for our novels."

"Yeah." Felicity's eyes grew wide with excitement. "On our last trip to New York, we were almost kidnapped by this crazed taxi driver and held for ransom."

Myrtis snorted. "We were not. That cab driver wouldn't let you out of the car because you refused to pay him."

"Fifty bucks for two blocks. That's criminal." Felicity crossed her arms.

Braxton shook his head. These were the craziest women

he'd ever seen. And he'd seen a lot of crazy during his stint bartending in a strip club. "Are you ladies interested in seeing the rooms?" They needed to quit yapping and book the damn rooms already.

"Nope."

Sadness filled Kate's eyes.

"We don't need to see the rooms. We'll take it." Barbara clasped her hands together.

"Really?" Kate brightened. "The rooms are ready now if you'd like to get settled in."

"That would be great." Felicity plucked her keys out of the depths of her oversized purse. "Let's unpack first. Then we can head back into town for a late lunch at that place Lynn pointed out."

Barbara looked horrified. "You mean that hole in the wall? I'm not sure it's safe, Felicity."

"We don't want safe. We want excitement for our novels." Felicity gave a sly grin. "Besides, if there's trouble, I got this." She pulled a .45 handgun out of her bag.

"Holy shit, Felicity. Put that damn thing away." Danielle flapped her hands up and down nervously.

Braxton shoved Kate behind him. "Do you have a permit for that?" Crazy women and guns did not mix.

"Sure do. Concealed carry permit right here." As Felicity waved her license, her gun swung around and pointed at Barbara, who had the good sense to drop to the floor.

"Jesus, give me that!" Myrtis grabbed the gun and pointed it at the ceiling. "Who the hell would give you a concealed weapon permit?"

"The guy teaching the concealed weapon class. Plus, he asked me out to dinner."

"Great to know there are assholes out there willing to give a crazy woman a gun for a piece of ass." Myrtis glared.

Damon and Braxton snorted. The women turned and looked at them.

Braxton sobered and nodded. "If you ladies unlock your trunks, we'll be happy to take your luggage to your rooms."

"We will?" Damon arched his brow.

Braxton elbowed him hard in the side.

"Why, aren't you two gentlemen?" Barbara gushed and then locked her gaze on Braxton as she cocked her head. "Do you know who you remind me of?"

Braxton stiffened. Holy fuck. Had his face been splattered over the five o'clock news?

"A pirate."

"Excuse me?" He had fucking blue streaks in his hair. No pirate had blue streaks in their hair.

Damon laughed out loud.

Braxton shot him a glare and jerked a thumb in his direction. "What about Damon? Who does he look like?"

Barbara gave him a thoughtful look. "He looks like a vampire."

Damon looked horrified as Braxton barked out a laugh. "I do not look like a fucking vampire."

"Damon! You can't say the F-word in front of these ladies!" Kate hissed.

"Why not?" Felicity shrugged. "We say it all the time in our writing. Don't we, Lynn?"

Lynn smiled. "Fuck, yeah."

"Plus, we need to be around alpha males like you two. You know, to listen to how you really talk. Don't edit yourselves for us." Barbara smiled warmly.

Braxton looked at Damon. "Well, you see, we were planning on leaving today."

"Oh, you can't do that! I need an inspiration for my hero and you two gentlemen fit the bill," Barbara pleaded.

"Yeah. You can't just leave us helpless women here alone while there's a madman on the loose," Felicity offered.

"I don't think you are exactly helpless." Braxton nodded toward the .45.

"Are you kidding? What if I hear a bump in the night, get up to investigate, and end up shooting Kate who couldn't sleep and is making homemade cookies because that's what she does when she's got something on her mind."

"You wouldn't really shoot me would you?" Kate's voice quavered the tiniest bit.

Felicity smiled broadly. "Not on purpose."

"If you ladies will excuse us, I need to have a word with Kate." Braxton guided her toward the kitchen.

Alone in the kitchen, he glared at her. "I think you need to tell them they can't stay."

"Why would I do that? Are you crazy?" she hissed.

"I'm not the crazy one wielding a .45. Did you see the look in Felicity's eyes? I don't think she's right in the head." He tapped his temple for emphasis.

"I'm not telling them they can't stay. They're not crazy. They're just writers. Besides, I need the income. If the bank sees I'm bringing in customers, then I might have a chance against foreclosure."

Kate's face lit with the hope. He doubted she'd survive a foreclosure. It would crush her.

Braxton blew out a breath. "They can stay, but on one condition."

Kate crossed her arms and narrowed her gaze on him. "What's that?"

"I stay, too."

* * *

KATE STOOD in front of the living room window, watching

Damon and Braxton retrieve the luggage out of the cars. She grinned as Damon dropped a bag, cursed, and straightened. From the posture of the two males, Braxton had to be telling him he wasn't going anywhere.

A few minutes later, they were stomping back through the house and following the group of writers to their rooms. Kate busied herself in the kitchen, checking her supplies and making a list of what she needed to pick up. She had enough for breakfast in the morning, but would have to head into town afterward to replenish her stock. The writers popped in the kitchen to grab their room keys and tell her they were heading out and might be back late.

"What the hell am I supposed to tell Barrett?" Damon followed Braxton in to the kitchen.

"Tell him you couldn't find me." Braxton grabbed a soda out of the refrigerator and popped the top.

"I already told him I found you, dumbass."

"Then tell him you lost me again." Braxton gave his friend a broad smile.

"I..." Damon growled as his phone began to ring. He snatched it out of his jacket and slid his finger across the screen. "Hello?'

Damon's face softened and then a smile broke out across his lips. Speaking in a hushed voice, he walked into the living room.

"Must be Ava." Braxton stepped up behind her and wrapped his arms around her waist. She let herself lean back into the strength of his warm chest.

"How long have they been together?" Her heart melted as he rubbed his bristled chin against her cheek.

"A few months, I think."

"So they are still in the honeymoon stage."

Braxton chuckled. "The honeymoon stage is never over between mated Weres."

She tilted her head back to meet his gaze. "You mean they never get tired of being around each other?"

"Nope. Not to mention the sex gets better every year."

Her mouth dropped open. "Better? How can it get better than when we..." Her words drifted off as his hand found her breast. She moaned and arched into his greedy hand.

"You feel so damn good." His hoarse voice sent delicious electricity straight to her core.

"Son of a bitch," Damon snarled as he strode into the kitchen.

Braxton quickly moved his hand and shot Damon a dirty look.

"What's wrong?" Kate pulled away from Braxton's arms and hurried to the refrigerator, pretending to search for something in order to give her body time to cool down.

"Ava's really pissed. She thought I'd be home by now." Damon propped his hands on his hips and sighed. "Jesus, she flipped when I told her I was at a bed and breakfast. I told her I was here on a mission. It's not like I'm sitting around playing footsie with Braxton and eating bonbons."

Kate giggled at the image of the two males. "I don't have bonbons, but I do have some cookies and some wine."

Damon brightened a little. "Almost forgot about that."

Braxton snarled. "Save your cookies and wine for that writer group. Don't waste them on him."

"Damon's a paying guest too, Braxton," Kate admonished.

"Yeah, Braxton." Damon flipped him the bird.

Braxton arched an eyebrow. "I doubt he even drinks wine."

"For your information, I drink Pinot Noir."

"Are you fucking with me?" Braxton widened his eyes.

"It's Ava's favorite." Braxton laughed.

"You're *so* mated."

Kate grinned and pulled out a bottle of wine. "I'm out of red wine. But I do have Pinot Grigio."

"I'll try it. Just so you know, I'm not as sophisticated as your boy there." Damon shoved a finger in Braxton's direction. "He's the expert on all things alcoholic."

"Fuck off." Braxton scowled.

"Thanks." Damon straightened when she handed him a platter with cookies and a glass of white wine.

* * *

KILLIAN STARED out of the window, his gaze skittering across the yard in search of some kind—any kind of movement. If he had to stay one more day in this cabin, he was going to fucking lose it. He flexed his fingers and leaned his neck side to side in an attempt to release some of the anxiety and anger that was slowly building up. He hadn't expected a bartender to give him so much trouble. He was an Assassin, and he'd never let a contract kill get away. He hated lose ends.

He turned as Brutus came out of his bedroom.

Brutus nodded for Killian and Lorcan to follow him into the next room.

"I've heard from the Pack Master of Louisiana." Brutus's deadly voice bounced off the walls. "We seem to have pissed off a lot of people by not getting that bartender."

"Who would have thought a civilian would be so hard to kill?" Killian eased himself into a chair and steepled his fingers.

"Who have we pissed off?" Lorcan cocked his head.

"Other than our Louisiana council, we now have the Arkansas Pack Master raising hell about shooting a werewolf during the day." Brutus glared at Killian

Killian shifted uncomfortably.

"Now more than ever, it's important that we find that

fucker and take him out. The longer he's out there, the more we risk exposing our race to the humans. Then we'll be the ones with silver in our asses."

"I might have a lead," Lorcan offered.

"What is it?" Brutus asked, his eyes doing that "changing from blue to green" thing they did when he was getting all amped.

"I overheard a group of ladies at a restaurant down in Eureka Springs. They were talking about some bed and breakfast where they were staying. She was describing some guy that was staying there. Could be our guy."

"Which bed and breakfast?" Brutus scowled.

Lorcan frowned. "She never said the name."

Brutus let out a slow breath. "Do you have any fucking idea how many bed and breakfasts there are in Eureka Springs?"

"A fucking lot." Lorcan arched a brow with his signature smart-ass reply.

"We need to leave within the hour. It could take days to find the right one."

* * *

BRAXTON COULDN'T TAKE his eyes off Kate, completely in awe of everything she'd accomplished on her own. She'd managed to get a three-course breakfast cooked by the time the writers came down to eat the next morning.

"Damn, this is good," Damon said around a mouthful of eggs Benedict.

"Thanks. I could give you the recipe for Ava." Kate took a sip of her coffee.

Damon snorted. "Ava only cooks in the bedroom."

"Ahhh. Isn't that sweet, girls!" Barbara cast moon eyes at Damon. Damon scowled and ducked his head.

Braxton snorted. Since the writers had come down for breakfast, they'd constantly flirted with both him and Damon.

Braxton had choked on his coffee when Lynn had asked him to lift his shirt so she could see his abs. Though they seemed harmless enough, Braxton wanted the women to know that he only had eyes for Kate. She was the only one allowed to see his abs.

Since the writers arrived, he hadn't had much time alone with Kate. She'd been a constant blur of activity, going from one task to another as she efficiently ran her business.

After breakfast, they had loaded the dishwasher and turned it on. Whatever part she'd gotten at the hardware store, she'd replaced and gotten the appliance working again. His respect for her grew immensely.

His stomach warmed as she moved upstairs to make the beds. He followed to give her a hand.

"They've only been here one night and already the rooms are a mess." Clothes and books were scattered along the floor, while two laptops were plugged into an outlet by the door. He arched his eyebrow. "I had no idea women were so messy."

Kate smiled, walked around the side of the bed and positioned the comforter. "Pull your side up."

Braxton tugged the comforter to the top of the bed and smoothed out a wrinkle. She tossed him a pillow and he caught it midair.

"The solid color pillows down first. Then the striped." Kate lined up pillows on her side of the bed and Braxton followed her lead until there were ten pillows in place.

"Why do women insist on having so many pillows on a bed? You only need one to put your head on."

Kate laughed, the sound rippling through him like waves. "We want the bed to be cozy and inviting."

His heated gaze fixed on her. "Your bed is always inviting."

Kate's smile faltered and her pupils dilated. She licked her lips as her gaze traveled down the length of his body and stopped at his crotch.

That was all the encouragement he needed.

* * *

KATE'S BREATH caught in her throat as Braxton stalked around the bed until he was face to face with her, closing the distance between them. Her nipples peaked against her shirt, the heat radiating off his hard body too much to ignore.

She needed to stop him before things went too far. They shouldn't be looking at each other like they were. They weren't even in her bedroom.

Somehow her head didn't relay any of that information to the rest of her sex-starved body.

Braxton wrapped his hands around her waist and pulled her against him. His dilated gray eyes stared down at her like she was the prey to his predator. His mouth came down on hers, possessive and hard. She didn't even have time to draw in a breath before his tongue was inside her mouth.

Kate fisted her hands in his silky, blue-tipped hair and clung to him, wishing they didn't have clothes between them. She needed him inside her now.

He lifted her and she wrapped her legs around his narrow waist. He pressed her back against the wall, grinding against her already damp panties.

"Braxton," she panted. Her heart beat loudly in her ears as her stomach quivered. "This is a bad idea."

"Feels like a pretty good idea to me." His teeth nipped at the sensitive spot beneath her ear.

"Looks pretty good, too."

Braxton stilled. Kate held her breath. Looking across his shoulder, she saw Felicity standing there with her fellow writers behind her, all looking very entertained.

"Oh, my God." Kate buried her face in Braxton's shoulder. How could she face her clients now?

"Well, don't stop now," Danielle whined as she held up a pen and notepad. "You were just getting to the good stuff."

She lifted her face and unwrapped her legs from Braxton as he let her slide to the floor. She averted her gaze as she smoothed down her clothes.

"Damn it, Felicity. I told you not to interrupt them. Now how am I going to write my sex scene?" Myrtis scowled.

"You're going to have to do more than just watch someone have sex to write a good sex scene, Myrtis." Felicity snorted.

Myrtis glared at the younger girl. "Just because I'm older doesn't mean I don't know what goes on in a bedroom."

"Knowing what goes on and getting it down on paper to make women hot are two different things. I've told you a hundred times, when you write a sex scene you need a deeper point of view. Stop telling what he's doing and start *showing* what he's doing. You know with his hand, his mouth, his cock."

Braxton paled. "I've got to go help Damon."

Kate scowled at Braxton's retreating back, irritated that he was leaving her alone with these women.

"So how long have you two been a thing?" Felicity smiled.

"Are you two going to get married?" Danielle cocked her head.

"How's the sex?" Lynn pushed her glasses up on her nose.

Kate stared at the group as her face heated. "Please, don't hold anything back."

Barbara chuckled. "You've got to forgive us, Kate. Writers are a different breed. We like to live in our heads, our own fantasy worlds. When we actually see the love and chemistry between a couple like you and Braxton, it gets us all excited."

Her stomach bottomed out. "Like me and Braxton?"

"It's not just the way he touches you. It's the way he looks at you." Felicity sighed. "Wish a guy would look at me like that."

Kate bit her lip trying to stifle the words, but her curiousity got the better of her. "How does Braxton look at me?"

"Like you're his everything." Barbara smiled.

Hot tears burned the backs of her eyes. If that was true then maybe, just maybe, Braxton wanted her just as much as she wanted him. And not just in bed.

"I don't know what to say." Kate busied herself by picking up a wet towel and avoided meeting their eyes.

"How long have you two known each other?" Myrtis asked.

"Not that long."

"Say, he's not in any kind of trouble, is he?" Myrtis narrowed her eyes.

Kate jerked her head up. "Of course not. What makes you ask that?"

Myrtis' gaze relaxed and she shrugged. "Just making sure he's not the killer that's running around town."

Kate felt the blood leave her face.

"Good grief, Myrtis, leave Kate alone. Of course Braxton's not a murderer." Felicity snorted.

"That's good to know. I would hate to write my next book based on a murderer." Lynn unplugged her computer and settled in the middle of the bed.

"You want to write about Braxton?" Kate wasn't sure how she felt about this.

"Yeah. I'm thinking an erotica involving the hero and heroine who get snowed in together at an isolated cabin. He's the hero and you're the heroine, of course."

"Me?"

"Of course, you. You guys look great together." Barbara picked a book off the floor and shuffled through the pages. "So, ladies, what do you say we settle in for some productive writing time?"

Kate left the ladies to their writing and headed downstairs. Between the guests and her two werewolves, she had exhausted her food supply.

She needed the drive to clear her head and put things back in perspective.

* * *

"MOTHER FUCKER." Barrett Middleton walked out of the Louisiana Pack Master's house and into the cold darkness, seething. His breath came in white puffs as he stormed back to his Harley Davidson Streetglide. He'd gone into the meeting with the Louisiana Pack Master expecting Edward Boudier to at least try to make amends for letting his Assassin dogs loose in Arkansas territory without asking permission. What Barrett got was a Pack Master who didn't give two shits about stepping all over another state's boundaries. Edward hadn't even cared that his Assassins had shot a Were in broad daylight. All Boudier wanted to know was if Braxton was dead.

Edward Boudier was lucky that Barrett didn't knock him the fuck out.

Gritting his teeth, he pulled out his phone. It rang before he could punch in a phone number.

Growling, he held the phone up to his ear. "Hello?"

"Barrett, I need to talk to you."

"Ava, how'd you get this number?" He narrowed his eyes and made a mental note to get his number changed ASAP. Only the Guardians were allowed access to his direct line.

"Damon gave it to me in case of an emergency."

Barrett stopped in his tracks. "What's wrong? What's the emergency?"

"Damon's not home. That's the emergency."

Barrett ran his hand down his face. He had enough problems without having to listen to Ava bitch about missing her mate. Every time they were in the same room, they were on each other like dogs in heat. Damon probably couldn't take a piss without Ava holding his dick.

He snarled. "Look, Ava, Damon's on a mission. He'll be home as soon as it's over."

"Nope. Not good enough. I need him home now." He envisioned her standing there pouting, her arms crossed over her chest like a child who didn't get her way. "Either get him home now or tell me where he is so I can go to him."

Barrett growled. "What part of 'on a mission' did you not understand? I can't have you compromising his position just because you want some cuddle time."

Ava snorted. "I need more than just cuddle time, Barrett."

"I could have lived my life without ever having an image of Damon's hairy ass and you going at it like two rats in a wool sock."

"Damon doesn't have a hairy ass. In fact, it's quite…"

"Enough." He straddled his Harley. "You're just going to have to sit still until Damon has completed his mission."

"I can't do that. I'm going crazy waiting around for him."

"Why don't you go over to Granny's? I heard she's having a party tonight. That will take your mind off things." Barrett chuckled.

Barrett disconnected before Ava could say another word. No doubt her comments wouldn't be very ladylike.

* * *

"SON OF A BITCH." Ava glared at her cell phone after Barrett hung up.

"Ava. Such language from a pretty girl. You should be ashamed." Granny gave her a disapproving look before licking a wrinkled finger and turning a page in her new sex toy catalogue.

Ava raised an eyebrow as Granny turned to the edible underwear page. The old lady saw nothing wrong with selling sex toys until the cows came home, but she took exception to cursing. The irony was laughable.

"Barrett won't tell me where Damon is." She flounced down on the sofa, feeling restless and irritated.

"Damon's working, dear."

"Yeah, and he's staying at a bed and breakfast." It was totally not fair.

Granny looked up with a wistful look in her eye. "A bed and breakfast. I always wanted to stay at a bed and breakfast."

"You and me both." Ava shook her head. "What kind of mission is it when you have to stay at a bed and breakfast? That doesn't make sense to me."

Granny tapped a bony finger to her lip. "Maybe if you check Damon's tracking device, you can find out where he's at."

Ava stilled. "Damon has a tracking device?"

"Of course. Barrett puts them on all his Guardian's phones just in case they get hurt—or worse."

Ava frowned. "So how do I check the device if it's on his phone?'

"It's connected to his computer. Look for an icon shaped like a footprint. Click on that and it should pinpoint his location."

Ava's face broke into a wide grin. "Where do you get all

your information, Granny? You should totally be a private investigator."

Granny waggled her eyebrows. "I keep my ear to the ground. Nobody expects an old lady to be listening. They always underestimate us geriatrics."

Ava stood and pulled Granny into a hug. "I don't underestimate you. I think you're wonderful."

"Well, thank you, dear." Granny smirked. "Don't think you're going to that bed and breakfast by yourself."

CHAPTER 9

"*D*on't leave me alone with them," Damon said as soon as Braxton walked in the back door.

Braxton had gone into town to see if he could find anything out about the murder. Although he couldn't prove it, he had a feeling that his father's murder was somehow connected.

"With who? The scary writers?" Braxton smirked. He couldn't help it. Damon was built to intimidate, but once those writers cornered him in the living room to ask him questions it was like someone asked him to skin his granny.

"Keep laughing, pretty boy. They'll be on you next."

"I doubt that. They know I'm with Kate." Braxton slid onto the stool at the kitchen island and reached for a cookie. The oatmeal raisin sugary confection melted in his mouth.

Damon's lip quirked up. "They actually have a topic that is right up your alley."

Braxton sat up. "What?"

"The women were discussing alcohol and roofies."

"Jesus. Why?"

Damon shrugged and pulled the cookie platter closer.

"They said it's for their book." Damon took a bite and lowered his voice. "But I don't think so. I think they're planning to roofie my ass."

Braxton choked back a laugh. "Don't be so paranoid. They're writers. It's their job to make shit up."

"Yeah, well. Just so you know, I had to throw you under the bus."

Braxton leaned closer. "What do you mean, Damon?"

"I told them you were a bartender and could answer all their alcohol questions."

Braxton closed his eyes and slowly let out a breath. "You think maybe I could get them drunk until they pass out?"

Damon gave a thoughtful look. "I don't know, man. That one woman, Myrtis? She's mean as a snake and looks pretty hardy. Think it'll take a lot of alcohol to take that one out."

"What are you two talking about?" Kate scowled at Damon and pulled the plate away. "These are for my paying guests."

"I am a paying guest," Damon argued.

"Yeah, but you've already eaten two plates today." Kate frowned. "You don't happen to have a tapeworm, do you?"

Braxton snorted.

Damon's expression grew somber. "Nope. No tapeworm."

Kate nodded as some unspoken communication passed between her and Damon. Kate gave Damon's arm a squeeze before heading outside.

Envy pinged Braxton in the gut. He glared at Damon, but Damon was too busy staring into his glass of soda. What the hell was that about? Pushing off the island, he went in search of Kate.

His heart warmed when he spotted her dragging heavy limbs from the woods toward the backyard.

"Here, let me. It's too heavy for you." Braxton hefted the limb over his shoulder. "Where do you want this?"

"Over there. It's for the fire pit." Kate picked up the ax off the ground to cut the limb into manageable firewood.

Braxton shook his head. Positioning the limb between his hands, he brought it down on his leg and snapped the wood in half.

Her eyes widened at his strength.

Damn. He kept forgetting she wasn't like him. She wasn't a werewolf. She wasn't used to seeing physical strength like his.

He cast a quick glance at her and froze.

Her gaze dilated as her lips parted. Her tongue swiped across her beautiful lips in a slow, torturous motion.

She wasn't looking at him in fear. She was looking at him like she wanted to rip his clothes off and fuck him to death.

His cock hardened.

Dropping the wood, he yanked her against him. Despite the heavy coat she wore, he could feel her body yielding to him. He growled before bending his head. Her cold lips quivered and opened under his mouth. His tongue tangled with hers, tasting her sweet mouth until he was dizzy with lust.

Her hands slid down his back to cup his ass and squeeze. He groaned.

She was going to fucking kill him.

They couldn't do this right now. The guests were probably standing at the window, gawking and taking notes. He pulled away, brushing his knuckles across the cold satin of her cheeks as he stared into her dewy gaze.

"What was that back there?" He nodded across his shoulder.

"My hand on your ass."

He grinned. "No, I mean back in the kitchen. That interchange with Damon."

Kate blushed. "Oh." She shook her head, her blonde hair

brushing the soft curve of her breasts. "Damon's missing Ava. I feel bad for him." She shrugged. "I know how he feels."

He stiffened under the assault of the words. "Are you missing your ex?"

She grimaced. "God, no." Her eyes met his. "But I know I'm going to miss you when you go."

Warmth spread through his chest, blossoming into a feeling so wonderful he couldn't describe it with words. He needed this woman, more than he could ever express.

It scared the shit out of him.

He gave her a tight hug and turned her toward the fire-wood. "So what's with the fire pit?"

Her face fell in disappointment that he didn't reciprocate but she quickly recovered her composure. "I thought the girls would like their wine around the campfire."

"It's pretty cold. I don't think they'll last very long out here."

"I overheard them talking at breakfast about wanting to experience Eureka Springs in the winter. Wine around the fire pit has long been a tradition at the Bella Luna." Kate shivered and crossed her arms as a gust of winter wind played with her hair. "I remember when I turned sixteen, my mom let me have my first glass of wine." She grinned, staring at the cold fire pit as if seeing a past memory come to life again. "We had a full house, and that night we sat around the fire and had cocktails."

"Your mom sounds like she was pretty special."

A sad smile touched her lips. "She was. She was my best friend."

"Sounds like you had the perfect life." Quite the opposite of what Braxton had grown up with.

"It was until…" Kate bit her lip.

"Until what?"

"Until I met Tom. I brought him home and Mom immediately didn't like him." Kate let out a rueful laugh. "I didn't understand why. Tom was charming the entire time. I thought my mom would adore him. Boy, was I wrong. After he left, she told me that there was something about him she didn't trust."

Braxton listened. As a bartender, he was used to having intoxicated women confide their secrets to him. More often than not, he would half-heartedly listen while trying to make sure they had a designated driver to haul them home.

Not with Kate. He wanted to know every detail about her life. He couldn't stop listening to her if he tried.

"What happened?"

Kate winced. "I got into an argument with my mom. I couldn't believe that she wasn't happy that I'd found someone who adored me." She bit her lip and glanced away. "I was such a bitch to her that night."

Braxton took her hand between his palms. "I can't ever imagine you being a bitch."

Misery fell across her face and she shook her head. "I was definitely a bitch." She blew out a breath. "I continued seeing Tom—against my mother's wishes, of course. Our relationship was never the same." She cleared her throat. "We were arguing about Tom the night of the accident. She lost control of the car and ran off the cliff. I lived and she died."

"Oh, God, Kate." He pulled her into his arms. She could have been killed. Just the thought tipped at his heart. He ached for the pain she still carried. She melted into him as if soaking up his strength. He wanted to take away every painful memory and give her a life of happiness and joy, but he knew that was impossible.

They were impossible.

Weres only mated other Weres. Sure, they could date or have sex with humans, but they never mated humans. Never.

When Damon met Ava, he didn't know she was a Were.

Maybe Kate was a Were, too, and she just didn't know. If Kate were a werewolf, he would be able to smell it now that the silver had left his system.

He inhaled deep. Her sweet scent of snow covered evergreen filled his head. His heart dropped in his stomach, his last thread of hope snapped. She didn't carry the scent of wolf. No, Kate definitely wasn't a Were. There could never be a future for them.

"I'm sorry. I shouldn't have told you all this." She smiled a little as she swiped the silent tears off her cheeks with the pads of her fingers, unaware how his heart had just fractured into irreparable shards.

"Don't be. I'm glad you shared that." His throat tightened. "I wish I'd had that kind of relationship with my mom. Sounds like your mom loved you fiercely."

She nodded. "She did. All mothers do."

Braxton snorted and released her. Bleak childhood memories settled on his shoulders. "Not all." He cleared his throat, embarrassed that he hadn't been raised in the kind of love that Kate had grown up with.

Her hand brushed his arm. "All mothers love their children, Braxton."

Braxton swallowed. This was one topic he wasn't ready to discuss with anyone, let alone Kate.

"I need to go see what Damon's up to. I think those writers are making him nervous." He made his way toward the house.

"Braxton?"

He stopped and looked over his shoulder. "Yeah?"

"We're not finished with this conversation." She cocked her head. "And just so you know, my mom would have loved you."

Warmth exploded in his chest as his eyes widened. The concept of someone's mother loving him hit him like a ton of bricks. He'd learned to live half a life, not expecting love. Kate's words humbled him and made his eyes ache.

He nodded once, shoved his hands in his pockets, and headed for the safety of the house.

* * *

THAT NIGHT, after having wine by the fire pit for the women, Kate managed to usher everyone inside. The ladies didn't want to leave, insisting they needed to experience the full effects of standing in the snow. She told them the only thing they were going to experience was frostbite and hypothermia, which would lead to amputation of important lady parts. That finally got the writers moving.

Braxton stood in the kitchen, looking through her liquor cabinet. She'd promised that Braxton would make cocktails for everyone if they came out of the cold. She cut her eyes over at Braxton's broad back and smiled as she lined up the martini glasses on the kitchen counter.

"I can't find the shaker." Braxton turned to her.

"I've got one." Myrtis tossed the silver canister to Braxton. Braxton caught it one-handed.

He arched an eyebrow. "You always carry this?"

"To all my writing retreats, I do." Myrtis lifted her chin. "With all these bitches, I'm always in need of a drink."

Barbara walked up behind Myrtis, shaking her head. "Goodness, Myrtis. You shouldn't be so blunt."

Myrtis turned. "Why not? You know every one of you get under my skin after a day of plotting and critiquing." Myrtis crossed her arms and scowled. "I feel like you've eaten me alive."

Felicity walked in with a large brown paper bag. "Okay, Braxton. Here's what I brought."

He peered in and his eyes widened. "Damn, you come prepared."

Felicity shrugged. "Danielle drove into town to get the rest of the stuff to make chocolate martinis."

Braxton chuckled and began unloading the bottles of vodka, rum, and tequila. "Well, while the rest of you are waiting, I could make a Long Island Iced Tea."

"Perfect." Felicity rubbed her hands together and headed back into the living room with the rest of the ladies.

Kate cocked her head as Damon entered the kitchen. "Do you think they drink like this all the time?"

"I don't know. But they are starting to scare me." Damon eased onto the kitchen stool and watched Braxton pour the different alcohols into the mixer. "Especially that Myrtis one."

Kate wrinkled her nose and poured herself a glass of chardonnay. "Myrtis? She has to be at least sixty-five."

Braxton poured a shot of tequila and shoved it toward Damon. Damon tossed it back without flinching. "I see the way she keeps looking at me."

"Yeah, how's that?" Braxton smirked, as he mixed the liquors in the silver canister.

"Like she knows what I look like naked."

"Yikes." Braxton shuddered.

"What are y'all talking about?" Myrtis walked into the kitchen.

Kate choked on her wine.

Myrtis slapped her on the back. "You okay?"

Kate nodded and cleared her throat. "Just went down the wrong way."

Myrtis turned her attention to Damon, let her gaze drift down his body, and smiled. "Hate it when something in your mouth goes down the wrong way."

"I've got to go check on something." Damon jumped up from the kitchen stool and hauled ass out the back door.

Myrtis frowned and joined her friends in the living room.

"Are those ready yet, Braxton?" Felicity walked over and rested her arms on the back of an empty kitchen chair. "The natives are getting restless."

Braxton finished pouring the bourbon-colored drink into a highball glass he'd pulled from the cabinet. "Long Island Iced Tea." He held out the glass to Felicity, who cradled it between her palms.

She took a sip and closed her eyes. "Mmm. This is really good. The best I've ever had, actually."

"Thanks." Braxton tossed the kitchen towel across his shoulder and held out a second drink for Kate.

Kate shook her head and waved her hands in protest. "I better not. I lost count of how many liquors you put in there."

Amusement lit his eyes. "Are you afraid?"

Her stomach tilted.

He grinned and held out the glass. "Go on. You've worked really hard today. You deserve a little happy hour."

"What happens if I start making a fool out of myself in front of my guests?" She raised an eyebrow.

"You won't do that. I'll take care of you."

Yep, she definitely wanted Braxton to take care of her. In the most carnal way possible.

Kate swallowed and pulled at the neck of her sweater as her body heated.

She reached for the glass, her fingers brushing against his. Sweet awareness shot across her skin. She looked up into his heated gaze. Apparently he was feeling the same way.

She studied the drink before taking a sip. The liquid slid down her throat and warmed her stomach in a comforting way. She closed her eyes and moaned. "Oh God, that's good."

She opened her eyes and her heart stuttered. Braxton gripped the countertop, his arms flexing under the tight black T-shirt as his breathing increased.

The women were in the next room and Damon was somewhere outside, trying to stay out of sight.

For right now, they were alone in the kitchen.

Braxton crooked his finger at her. "Come here."

She set the glass down and shook her head slowly.

"Kate. Now." His voice was raspy and commanding and it made her panties wet. She knew without a doubt what would happen if she went to him. He'd take her right there, her jeans pushed down and her sweater pulled up, on the kitchen table. He wouldn't care about the numerous set of eyes watching while he ravished her body.

"I don't think so."

"Why not?" He scorched her with those stormy gray eyes. She tried to step back, but her stubborn body wouldn't obey.

"I'm afraid."

"Of me?" A brief flicker of hurt coursed through his eyes.

"No. I'm afraid of losing my shirt." She would have blushed if she wasn't already so damned over heated. What the hell was wrong with her? She never would have said something like that to her ex. But then again, Braxton was nothing like her ex. Even though he was a werewolf, he was a far better man than Tom would ever be.

"You should be more worried about losing your panties, Kate."

* * *

BRAXTON PUSHED off the counter and stalked around the obstacle until he was inches from Kate.

Mine!

Maybe he would have thought twice about what he was

159

about to do if she hadn't been standing there looking all flushed and licking her lips, like she was starving. He could smell her arousal from where he stood.

She wanted this as much as he did.

He pulled her into his arms, devouring her mouth with his. She went limp and sighed. He went hard and groaned.

If he kept her in bed for the next forty years, he still didn't think he'd get enough of her.

He pulled away roughly, holding her face between his palms. "Where."

It was more of a statement than a question.

"My room."

He swung her up into his arms before she could change her mind and hurried to her bedroom. He kicked the door shut and set her on her feet.

"Lock it." Kate's husky voice made him want to rip her clothes off and thrust into her tight little body. He clenched his jaw as she gripped his T-shirt in her hands and pulled it up over his head.

He fumbled for the lock just as her hot mouth closed over his nipple. He sucked in a breath and wrapped his fingers around the back of her neck, urging her on. "Damn, baby, that feels good."

She sucked hard, sending shivers through his veins. He tried not to plunge his fingers down her jeans and into her wet panties.

"Your turn." He kicked off his jeans and growled. She had too many fucking clothes on.

He slipped her sweater over her head and tugged her jeans down, his finger sliding over her silky skin. He groaned in appreciation. She stood before him in nothing but a lacy peach bra and matching panties.

She blushed.

"I like it when you do that." He gathered her into his chest and whispered against her neck. Reaching around, he unhooked her bra.

"When I do what?" she asked breathlessly.

"When you blush. Makes me feel like the big bad wolf."

She nipped his shoulder. "You *are* the big bad wolf."

Braxton quickly stripped off her bra and tossed it to the floor. His mouth closed around her taut nipple. She moaned as he teased and sucked the bud into his mouth. She tasted so fucking sweet. She arched under his mouth, pulling his head closer.

"More," she moaned, her words shooting straight to his dick.

He swept her up into his arms and laid her across the bed. He liked the way her gaze drifted down his body and rested on his hardened erection.

"Big bad wolves are insatiable."

Kate sucked in a breath and dragged her gaze back to his. "Thank God for that."

Braxton knelt between her legs and hooked his thumbs in her panties. She rose up on her elbows to watch as he tugged them off.

He bent his head and licked at her sweet core.

"Braxton." She fisted her fingers into his hair. "Don't stop."

"I won't stop. I won't ever stop." That's how he fucking felt. .

She jerked her hips to his face, her breathing growing faster. When he felt her body tremble, he closed his lips around her clit and sucked.

* * *

KATE CRIED out as she came, her body trembling under Braxton's wicked mouth. Wave after wave of pleasure racked her body until she was unable to move. When the tremors finally subsided, he slid up her body and between her legs.

She moaned as he filled and stretched her body.

"Damn, baby. You feel so good," he whispered between kisses. She clenched around him, earning another groan.

He moved against her, thrusting in and out at a torturous pace until she was writhing against him. She dug her nails into his back, needing more. "Faster, Braxton."

He chuckled. "No, sweetheart. This is going to be slow and delicious."

Her breathing hitched and she clutched him closer. He seemed to sense her impending orgasm and moved faster, thrusting until her orgasm swelled and crested.

This time when she came, Braxton was right there with her, clinging to her hips and moaning her name.

* * *

BRAXTON GATHERED Kate into his arms, caressing her naked back with his fingertips. He'd never been more at peace than when he was holding her.

"Hmmmmm..."

He grinned and looked down into her smiling face. "I take it you found that satisfactory?"

"Are you kidding? I found that more than satisfactory. In fact, I never thought I could have an orgasm that intense."

Braxton grinned, feeling pretty damn pleased with himself. "I aim to please."

She laughed and playfully hit his arm.

A loud crash had Kate bolting up in bed.

"What was that?" Kate pulled the comforter across her body. He'd been so busy trying to get into her panties that they didn't bother to pull the sheets down.

"The sound of drunken writers." Braxton rolled off the

bed and tugged on his jeans. She slid off the bed and gathered her clothes, quickly dressing.

"I hope no one got hurt," Kate threw over her shoulder as she hurried down the hall. "A lawsuit is the last thing I need."

Braxton gave her arm a reassuring squeeze. "Stop worrying... I'm sure no one got hurt."

"You might want to rethink that last statement." Damon hurried past them into the living room.

Braxton came to a halt. Kate crashed into his back.

Standing in the middle of the living room and looking like an angry Goddess was Ava. Ava had a handful of Felicity's shirt and was holding the girl a foot off the ground. Damon wrapped his arms around Ava's waist, trying to pull her away, but she wouldn't let go of Felicity.

Kate rushed forward. "Who the hell are you? Get your hands off her."

Ava let go of Felicity and scorched Kate with a glare.

Braxton pushed Kate behind him. "What's going on, Ava?"

"I want to know what the fuck Damon is doing at a bed and breakfast with a bunch of women." Ava turned and glared at Damon, who ran his hand across his face

"That would be my fault." Braxton glanced at Damon. "Barrett sent him for me. I refused to leave. Damon is only doing his job."

"Yeah? Who the fuck is this?" Ava shot a venomous glare at Felicity.

"She's one of my guests," Kate answered and stepped in front of Ava.

"Really? Then why was she telling Damon to take his shirt off when I walked in the door?" Ava hissed.

Kate rolled her eyes. "Because she's a writer." She swept her arm across the room. "They say obscene things that they don't mean."

"Plus, they're drunk," Damon offered. He tried to wrap his arms around his mate, but Ava only growled.

"I am not drunk, thank you very much." Myrtis propped her hands on her hips. "I can handle my alcohol, unlike the rest of these bitches."

"I hear ya, sister. I can drink anyone under the table." Granny emerged from the kitchen holding a shot of tequila in her wrinkled hand.

"Granny, put that down." Damon let go of Ava and tried to take the glass away from the old lady.

She spun away on her heels, downed the shot, and then smirked while handing over the empty glass. "Here you go, Damon."

"Is this your granny?" Kate's widened gaze landed on Damon.

"I am, honey. I came with Ava when she found out Damon was here." Granny gave Kate a smile. The old lady picked up someone's Long Island Iced Tea. "I've always wanted to stay at a bed and breakfast, but I never had the chance. I've been so busy with my work that I don't have the time. So I decided to make time."

Kate smiled. "What kind of work do you do?"

"I am gainfully employed in the sex industry."

The room went silent as all eyes landed on Granny.

Damon rubbed his eyes. "Damn, Granny. Would you quit saying that?"

"Sex industry?" Felicity grinned. Lynn looked intrigued. The other writers looked horrified.

"Of course." Granny took a sip of her Long Island Iced Tea. "This sucker has quite a kick." Granny's gaze landed on Braxton. "Hon, did you make this?"

"You know it." He chuckled. He'd always liked Granny. She didn't pull any punches and had a kind heart.

Damon stilled and looked at Braxton. "Wait a minute. How do you know Granny?"

Braxton hesitated.

"I know him from the strip club," Granny offered.

"The strip club?" Damon grimaced and waved his hand. "Never mind. I don't want to know."

"Well, I want to know." Felicity had apparently recovered from her brush with Ava. She edged closer and gave Granny a look of utter fascination.

Kate gave him a confused look. It was too much to explain so he just shrugged.

"Granny sells a lot of her...merchandise to the dancers at the club." Braxton frowned at Granny's now-empty drink. "You might want to go easy on those."

"Another round, barkeep." Granny held out her glass to Braxton. "It's been a long drive, and I fully intend to enjoy myself while staying at a B&B."

Damon sighed. "There's no room, Granny."

Felicity shook her head. "Actually, you can stay with Lynn." She cut her eyes at her friend.

Lynn's lips curled up in an uncertain smile.

"Oh, I don't know. I'm not used to sharing a bed." Granny's eyebrows shot up. "At least not with another female."

The women erupted in laughter.

"Come on. It will be fun." Felicity took her hands. "Besides, you can give us a lot of information about the kinds of things you sell."

"My sex toys?"

"Please, Ava, if you love me just a little, beat me over the head until I pass out," Damon pleaded with his mate.

Ava's lips quirked up, obviously enjoying Damon's discomfort.

Braxton mixed up another cocktail and passed it to Granny.

Granny looked around the room at the women. "You guys want to know about my sex toys?"

"Of course." Felicity elbowed Barbara in the side.

Granny sighed. "It would be easier if I just showed you."

Lynn's smile disappeared, replaced by genuine interest. "Do you have them with you?"

Granny took a sip. "Yep. Brought an extra suitcase just so I could make everything fit."

Kate leaned into Braxton. "Is she serious?"

"As a heart attack." Braxton wrapped an arm around her shoulder and tugged her against him. "She's a live wire when she gives her sex toy presentation."

"Okay, I have to see that," Kate murmured.

Granny emptied her glass and plunked it down on the side table. "Okay, you talked me into it. I'll stay. On one condition."

"What's that?" Damon frowned.

"I get to give my full presentation of my sex toys. That way, you ladies can procure the merchandise so you can get the full experience." Granny wagged her gray eyebrows.

"Is that okay with you if Granny shares with Lynn?" Felicity looked at Kate.

Kate shrugged. "It's fine with me."

"Great."

"Damon, be a dear and take my stuff up to my room." Granny patted his arm.

Damon snarled as he headed out the door. Ava followed after him, bitching the whole way.

"Are they married?" Felicity narrowed her eyes.

Braxton grinned. "Yes, and then some."

"I thought she was going to rip my throat out." Felicity rubbed her neck.

"What did you do to get her so upset?" Braxton looked at Felicity.

"She was telling him to take off his shirt...while she copped a feel." Barbara shot Felicity a disapproving look.

"Felicity." Kate crossed her arms and frowned.

"What? I didn't know he was married." Felicity managed a sheepish look. "Usually men that don't have a wedding ring are available."

"I think it's best if you stay away from Ava." Kate pursed her lips.

"You think?"

"Yeah, honey." Granny tapped the bottom of her glass, trying to get the last few drops out. "She may look all dainty, but Ava can kick some serious ass."

Damon came back. "Your luggage is in your room, Granny."

"That's a good boy." Granny patted his cheek and then faced the ladies. "Oh, and just so we're clear. I may be sleeping with a girl, but I am not a lesbian."

CHAPTER 10

"Where have you been?" Damon narrowed his gaze at Braxton.

Braxton shrugged out of his leather jacket and averted his eyes. "Just went into town."

Damon raised an eyebrow. "For what?"

"Seeing if I could find out anything about that murder." Braxton eased onto the barstool.

Damon cocked his head. "That guy was a human. It has nothing to do with us."

Braxton bristled. "It has everything to do with Kate. That's the point."

"You risk too much for that human." Damon took a step and Braxton stood, bristling.

"Back off, Damon." Braxton fisted his hands, anger surging through his body. The wolf side called to him, urging him to shift. "You would risk the same thing for Ava."

"That's different. Ava is my mate," Damon gritted out.

"What the hell's going on here?"

Both males turned at Ava's voice. She stood in the

doorway of the kitchen, her arms propped on her hips, looking like she'd just rolled out of bed.

Braxton swept his gaze at Damon. The Were's jeans were unzipped. Damn, maybe they both had just rolled out of bed.

Damon pulled her into his arms and kissed her.

Braxton cringed. "Jesus, do you two mind?"

Damon pulled back and laughed. "That's the pot calling the kettle black."

"What are you talking about?"

"I'm talking about all that noise I heard last night." Damon rolled his eyes.

Braxton's eyes went wide. He thought he'd covered Kate's cries of ecstasy with his mouth. Maybe he hadn't.

"Never knew you had a nickname." Damon looked a little horrified. Ava snickered.

"Name? What are you talking about?" He didn't remember Kate calling out anything other than his name.

"Give it to me good, Big Daddy," Ava cried out in mock ecstasy.

What the fuck? He didn't remember that.

"That wasn't Kate." Granny walked in and opened the refrigerator and pulled out a bottle of water.

Everyone stared.

"Was it you?" Ava giggled.

"No, sassy mouth. It was Barbara."

Damon turned green and Braxton felt the same way.

"Barbara? The older lady that writes historicals?" Ava gaped.

"Yes. She bought something to keep her company last night. It's the Big Daddy line of dildos and comes in all shapes and sizes."

"Oh, hell. She said dildo." Damon swiped a hand across his face, as if trying to erase the mental image that had been conjured up.

Braxton closed his eyes, trying to go to his happy place.

Ava chuckled.

"Stop laughing. It only encourages her." Damon scowled at his mate.

"What's everyone talking about?" Kate walked in and set the laundry basket on the island. She looked around the room.

"You don't want to know," Braxton murmured.

She frowned. "Yes I do."

"We were talking about the sounds Damon and Ava heard coming from a bedroom last night. They thought it was you, but I told them it was Barbara and one of my dildos." Granny took a dainty drink.

Kate's mouth fell open as her face turned bright red.

Braxton leaned down and whispered in her ear. "I told you, you didn't want to know."

Kate clamped her mouth shut and grabbed her laundry, mumbling something about chores as she escaped from the kitchen. Braxton followed on her heels.

* * *

KATE GRIPPED the sides of the washing machine with both hands, her head bowed. She wanted to melt into the floor. "Please tell me it really wasn't me they heard."

Braxton buried his face in her hair and laughed. "No, it wasn't. I was pretty good about keeping you quiet last night. All night."

She turned in his arms and faced him.

She ran her hands up his arms to his shoulders, the simple touch setting off a fire in her belly.

They'd made love half the night, yet it wasn't enough. She wanted him again.

Braxton pushed away. Disappointment stung her chest

until he reached the door of the laundry room. Shutting the door, he twisted the lock.

Her eyes widened as her heartbeat sped up. "What are you doing?"

"I want you naked and I want you now." He accentuated every word with a heavy step until he was towering over her.

"But, we're in the laundry room." She glanced at the window blinds. "And it's daylight."

"I don't care." Braxton covered her mouth, his tongue seeking out her own.

She moaned and melted against his body. Braxton slipped his hands under her thighs and lifted, setting her on top of the washing machine.

His mouth stayed on hers as his hands skirted under her sweater. She nearly cried out as his fingers found her nipple.

She gasped and arched against his hand.

Panting, she lifted the hem of his shirt, her fingertips dipping into the deep grooves of his defined muscles.

He leaned down so she could pull the shirt over his head.

"Your turn." His fingers gripped her shirt and tugged. It went sailing to the floor. He pulled her close, his hard chest rubbing against her soft bra-clad breasts.

He sealed his mouth over hers, licking the seam of her lips. With a flick of his fingers, her bra gave way and she quickly wiggled out of it.

His fingers danced at the front of her jeans, unsnapping and unzipping.

"Lift."

She planted her hands on the washing machine and arched her hips. She hissed when the cool metal of the washing machine hit her bare ass.

He grinned, took a step back and freed himself from his tight jeans. He met her gaze and took himself in his hand before stepping between her parted thighs.

Her breathing increased as his fingers stroked gently down her thong. His fingers dipped in the side. He growled low before lifting his finger to his mouth and sucking her arousal off.

She laced her fingers behind his neck and pulled him to her lips. "Now, Braxton. I want you now."

He pulled her panties to the side and coated his dick with her wet heat. She moaned as he thrust, burying himself deep inside of her. She shivered around the enormous length of him.

"Fuck." He buried his face in the crook of her neck.

She dug her fingers into his shoulders as he moved slowly. "Please, Braxton, faster." She needed him out of control and wild.

"Baby, if I go faster I'm going to come too soon." His mouth clamped down across hers, and he slid his fingers between the tight space of their bodies and flicked her clit.

She gasped.

"Feel good?" he groaned out.

"Yes," she panted, clinging to him like he was her lifeline to this earth.

His fingers stroked over her clit in a circular motion while his thrusts grew faster. Pleasure spread throughout her body as she began to climax. She tensed, and then she went limp as her orgasm crashed over her in a blinding display.

* * *

BRAXTON THRUST DEEP, his body shaking with the effort to hold back his own pleasure until Kate found her orgasm. It was a rule. The female always came first. And they always did. But with Kate, Braxton almost broke the one rule he'd always kept.

As Kate cried out, he held on for a few more seconds and

then went over the edge with her, burying deep within her tight body as he spilled his release inside her.

Her fingers caressed up and down his back. He found the touch soothing and comforting. It was something he could get used to every night.

And it scared the hell out of him.

He straightened and gazed down into the eyes of the woman he'd just made love with.

She giggled and slapped a hand across her mouth.

He frowned. "What's so funny?

"I'm sorry. I've just never had sex on a washing machine before. It sounds like something out of a romance book."

He relaxed. "Well, don't go telling those writers. I'm sure they'd love to know how you liked it." A slow grin crossed his face. "So, how did you like it?"

"It felt wrong."

He frowned. "Wrong?" That certainly wasn't the answer he was expecting.

She shook her head, her hair falling in blond waves across her shoulders. "I need a better word. It felt wicked." She glanced away, her cheeks flaming.

"Wicked?" He tipped her chin with his finger, gently forcing her to look at him. "I like wicked."

She grinned. "I kind of thought you would."

"What other things have you never done, my sweet innocent Kate?" Braxton rubbed his thumb across her bottom lip.

She blinked rapidly, and for a moment he expected her to change the subject and make an excuse to get away.

"I've never given a blow job."

Braxton felt like the ground shifted under his feet, and he reached for the side of the washing machine.

Kate pushed at his chest as her face turned red with embarrassment. "I need to go."

But he didn't budge. "Wait. Are you saying you've never gone down on a guy?"

She crossed her arms over her chest and glared. "If you're going to make fun of me, then you can leave."

Braxton stared at her. "Make fun of you? Why the fuck would I do that?"

"Because I'm not experienced like all the other girls you've been with."

"No, you're not." She was so much more than what he ever deserved.

She tried to shove him out of the way.

"That's what I love about you."

She stilled and gave him a suspicious look. "You do? I thought guys liked experience."

Braxton snorted. "Baby, guys like to teach a woman what they like."

She arched an eyebrow. "Really?"

"Yes, really." His gaze zeroed in on her lips, fantasizing about how they would feel around his dick.

She leaned in close. "Show me what you like."

He swallowed and closed his eyes as his dick hardened at the thought. "Don't tempt me, baby."

"I want to tempt you." She reached down and gripped his dick, already hard and ready for round two.

Braxton opened his eyes and groaned. Her eyes were hungry.

"Step back."

He obeyed her. How could he refuse her anything?

She released him and hopped off the washing machine. He watched as she slid to her knees.

She looked up at him. "Tell me if you don't like something."

Was she fucking kidding? What would he not like?

Her hot, wet mouth closed over him and he groaned at the pleasure. Her heavy-lidded gaze stayed on him as she flicked her tongue over the tip and then sucked him deep into her mouth.

"Fuck, Kate." He threaded his fingers in her silky hair and rocked into her mouth. She moved back and dipped her head to caress his balls with her tongue before sucking each one into her mouth.

"Jesus Christ, Kate. You need to slow down." Braxton wasn't quite sure how he managed to get the words out. He was all sensation, feeling every flick of her tongue and suck of her beautiful lips.

"Am I doing it right?" She gazed up at him with such tenderness and lust, it almost made his knees buckle.

"Hell, yes. It feels good. Too good."

She sucked him harder and deeper into her white-hot mouth. Each torturous lick of her tongue sent pleasure streaking down his back. He wasn't going to last much longer if she kept sucking him like that.

"I'm going to come." He tried to pull her head back, but she didn't budge. Humming her approval as she looked up into his eyes, he thrust hard, seeing stars as his orgasm overtook him. He came hard, spilling his seed into her willing mouth. She held him tight, sucking and swallowing until he was spent.

She smiled and slid up his body. Braxton forked his fingers through her hair and pulled her into a deep kiss, tasting himself on her tongue.

She pulled back and smiled as she watched him under her lashes. "Did I do okay?"

"That was the best blow job I'd ever had."

"Really?"

"Yes." It was the truth.

"Hey, Kate. I need to use your washing machine," Granny

called out from the other side of the locked door and jiggled the door knob. "Why is this door locked?"

Kate scrambled for her clothes, tugging them on. "Just a minute, Granny." She glared at him as he slid his jeans up over his hips. "Hurry up!" She threw his T-shirt at his face.

Still in the slow afterglow of his orgasm, he couldn't make his limbs move any faster. Had fate fucked him one more time, giving him the woman of his dreams only to snatch her away? Pack Law clearly stated that wolves mated wolves. End of story.

Which meant his life just got a little more complicated.

* * *

BRAXTON AND DAMON pulled into Eureka Springs just after dark. Braxton put Kate's SUV in park and surveyed the near-empty streets in the small town. The snow had probably kept most people at home, but there were still a few locals scurrying along on the side streets, trying to find the closest restaurant to pop in for a drink and seeking shelter against the brutal winter wind.

"We're supposed to be keeping a low profile. Riding into town doesn't fit into that description." Damon scowled.

Braxton white-knuckled the steering wheel in a death grip. "I need to find my father's killer to clear my name before the Assassins find me. I can't do that by sitting around on my ass all fucking day. Besides, I had to get out of the house. I think one of those writers tried to get into the bathroom while I was taking a shower."

"I hear ya." Damon let out a shiver. He nodded out the window. "You really think your father's killer is in Eureka Springs?"

"No. But there is a biker bar in town that caters to Weres, and I want to know if anyone there knows anything."

"What they probably know is that those fucking Assassins are coming for you. They had to pass through here before they caught up and shot you." Damon slipped his Oakleys over his eyes. Braxton wondered if Damon really liked the glasses or if he wanted to look more intimidating. Knowing the wolf, probably both.

"I don't know a single Were that likes Assassins."

"And I don't know a single Were, that when cornered, wouldn't hesitate to give up your location or information about a wanted target." Damon looked over his glasses. "Right now, you're the target."

"Glad to see you have complete trust in the Were species."

"Fuck you." Damon showed him the back of his middle finger.

"Like I said, brother, not my type." Braxton pulled into the parking lot of the bar right off the main drag.

He eased out of the SUV and made his way up the rickety wooden steps leading into the bar with Damon following close behind. Like the rest of the small town, the bar was built around the top of the mountain, curving to fit nature's own landscape.

The scent of whiskey, stale beer, and cigarettes hit Braxton like a wall the second he stepped inside. Having worked in a bar most of his adult life, he'd come to welcome those scents. Now, after being in the fresh air at Kate's house, those same scents made him want to gag. The change of scenery seemed to have changed his tastes as well.

Braxton sidled up to the bar with Damon flanking him. The bartender gave him a nod of acknowledgement from where he was busy pouring a round of shots.

"What can I do for you guys?" The bartender rested his beefy arms on the counter while his slit-like eyes assessed both of them.

"Jack." Damon angled his body where his back wasn't to the door and kept his gaze sweeping the room.

Braxton smiled. For the brief time he'd known the guy, Damon never sat with his back to the door. The wolf trusted no one.

"Beer." Braxton leaned against the bar and took a cursory glance around the darkened room.

The tables and booths were full of Weres, mainly males with a couple of females sitting in their laps.

"You guys new to the area? Or just passing through?" The bartender slid their drinks across the counter.

"Passing through." Braxton looked the Were in the eye.

"Well, if I were you, I'd keep going." The bartender wiped the counter with a bar towel.

"Why is that?" Damon leaned closer.

"'Cause there's been some trouble in town. A murder." The bartender cocked his head. "Cops around here don't think it was someone in town. Which makes everyone passing through a suspect."

"Did you know the guy that was killed?" Braxton took a long drink of his beer.

The bartender shrugged. "I'd seen him around. He tried to come in here a couple of times but quickly realized he didn't exactly fit in."

"Because he wasn't a Were?" Braxton arched his brow.

"Because he was an asshole."

"Do you know where he worked?" Braxton turned his full attention to the bartender.

"Yeah, he worked for that builder that's been putting up those cheap hotels around here. Bigsby is his name."

"Did he start some trouble in here?" Damon pushed his shot glass to the bartender and was quickly given a refill.

"He tried hitting on the females and they didn't exactly

like it. After that he stayed to his own kind, the low-life human bars."

Damon snickered.

Braxton scratched his cheek with his middle finger. He judged people by their own actions. Not on what race they were.

"Easy." Damon chuckled. "I'm sure Kate's different."

"Kate? You talking about Kate Wolph?" The bartender gave him an astonished look.

Braxton growled and jealousy tightened his chest. "How do you know her?"

The bartender, sensing Braxton's anger, held his hands up and fought a grin. "We went to the same school together. "

Braxton narrowed his eyes. "You two ever date?"

"Nah. Kate was too good for me. Besides, she was always too busy helping her mom out at the bed and breakfast to date anyone."

A tiny pain zinged to his gut. It sounded like Kate didn't have much time for fun growing up. He could understand that. He'd spent most of his youth trying to either avoid his dad's drunken wrath or protect his mom.

"What the hell?" Damon glared at the back of the bar. The rising sound of angry voices had Braxton bristling, ready to fight. The bartender grabbed a baseball bat from under the bar.

"Look, man, I can't help it if the lady can't keep her hands off me." A blonde-haired Were grinned at a bunch of rough-looking locals, while a pretty little brunette clung to his muscled arm.

"What the fuck? Jayden?" Damon yelled across the bar. Jayden looked up from his seat.

The bartender scowled at Braxton. "You two know him?"

"Yeah. " Damon rubbed his hand down his face as Jayden

made his way over with the female hanging off him like a vine, refusing to let go. "What the hell are you doing here?"

Jayden gave the female a panty-dropping grin and unwound himself from her. "Braxton said he needed some intel." Jayden jerked a thumb in Braxton's direction.

Braxton grinned and shook Jayden's hand. "Thanks for coming, man. I have to say you look a lot better than the last time I saw you." The last time he'd seen Jayden, the Were had just been rescued by the unlikely duo of Ava and Granny. A pack of rogue Weres had kidnapped Jayden when he'd gotten too close to discovering the female they'd kidnapped and planned on using as a sex slave. The rogue pack had beaten Jayden with a baseball bat until he looked like hamburger meat.

Jayden shrugged. "Quick healer." He raised his eyebrows at Damon. "Didn't know you were here, brother."

Though not brothers by blood, Jayden and Damon had both been raised by Granny.

"Barrett sent me to get Braxton."

Jayden snorted. "Looks to me that Braxton's too damn big to be fetched up for Barrett."

"I get all the shitty jobs." Damon narrowed his eyes.

Jayden laughed. "Well, you did luck out when you got Ava."

Damon grinned, his white teeth flashing against his five o'clock shadow. "Yeah, I did."

Braxton had learned that Damon had been sent out on a mission to rescue Ava from a pack of rogue wolves. The two had spent a lot of time in close quarters and one thing led to another.

The image of Kate naked and under him flashed through Braxton's mind. It made his chest ache as he wondered what it would be like to be mated to your one and only lover.

Braxton shook his head to clear his thoughts. "Do you have some information for me?"

"Well, after you escaped the cops…"

"Fuck. You didn't tell me the cops arrested you," Damon growled at Braxton.

"I thought you knew. Didn't Barrett tell you?"

"He told me that the Assassins were after you. Nothing about the cops."

Braxton shrugged. "Doesn't matter. Get back to what you were saying, Jayden."

"The cops found the murder weapon." Jayden leaned in closer and lowered his voice. "It was thrown in the culvert outside the driveway."

Braxton couldn't breathe. "What was it? A knife?"

"No. A hammer."

"Damn," Damon breathed out. "Takes a lot of anger to beat someone to death with a hammer."

"That's not all." Jayden leaned closer. "His neck was slit with the claw of the hammer. Apparently they knew he was a Were and wanted to make sure he was dead."

Braxton's stomach lurched. What a fucking way to go.

"Wouldn't one of the neighbors have heard someone being beaten with a hammer?" Damon glared at Braxton.

"They did. The neighbors called me thinking it was my dad beating my mom. Again." Braxton gritted his teeth. "That's why I went over there."

Damon gave him an understanding nod. "And that's how the cops assumed you were guilty."

He swallowed. "It didn't help that my mom accused me of killing him in front of the police."

"Damn," Jayden breathed out. "That's fucked up."

"My whole life has been fucked up." Why would he expect anything else?

"Yeah, but it's the present that counts. You've got to leave all that garbage in the past and start making decisions that will guarantee you a better future," Damon offered.

Braxton and Jayden stared hard at Damon.

"What?" Damon scowled.

Jayden shifted his weight uncomfortably. "Jesus, man. You sound like fucking Dr. Phil."

"You're not going to hug me now, are you?" Braxton arched his brow.

"You both can go fuck yourselves." Damon gritted his teeth.

Jayden sighed and smiled. "Now there's the Damon I know." Jayden slugged him playfully in the shoulder. "Don't go around saying shit like that. It's scary."

Damon returned the slug to the shoulder, knocking Jayden backward on his ass before heading out of the bar.

* * *

KATE JERKED upright in the chair at the ringing of her phone. She'd fallen asleep trying to wait up for Braxton and Damon to get back from town. She'd tried to talk Braxton out of going, but she knew it was fruitless. Braxton was going to do what Braxton wanted to do, and there was no talking him out of anything.

She reached for the phone and rubbed her stiff neck. Next time, she was going to wait up in bed instead of the chair.

"Hello?"

"Kate. Hope I didn't wake you." Oliver Bigsby's voice gave her chills over the phone.

She frowned and glanced at the wall clock. "It's two o'clock in the morning. Why are you calling this late?"

"I was just going to let you know that the police are investigating that murder at my construction site."

"You couldn't wait to tell me in the morning?" What a douche.

"I was just trying to be nice and warn you." The polite tone turned haughty.

"Warn me about what?" She never should have answered the phone.

"I thought I'd warn you that the police are looking into any new people that are in town. Like your guest."

Kate felt her blood go cold.

"Which guest are you referring to?"

"You've got more than one?"

Kate smiled. "Yes, the Bella Luna is full."

Bigsby cleared his throat, apparently not expecting this new turn of events. "Well. I don't know what to say, Kate."

"Congratulations would be nice. If this keeps up, I won't have to worry about foreclosure." Kate smiled, hoping he'd catch the sarcasm in her voice.

He snorted. "It's going to take more than a couple of days of being booked to make up your late payments."

Kate felt the smile slide off her face. "How do you know that?"

He tsked. "Oh, Kate. You're so innocent when it comes to financial matters. You know, I could come over and help you with your books sometime."

"No thanks." Kate gripped the phone. She wanted to pull his condescending face through the phone and punch him in the nose.

"Well, you know my offer stands."

"Good night." Kate slammed the phone down on her nightstand.

"What's wrong?" Braxton's voice filled the doorway.

"You're back."

"Yeah. Tell me what's wrong." Braxton glanced at the phone. "Who were you talking to?"

Kate sat down on the bed and sighed. "Bigsby."

Braxton growled.

She cleared her throat. "He was letting me know that the police were looking into the murder."

"That's newsworthy, why?"

"He also said the cops were looking at anyone new to Eureka Springs."

Braxton narrowed his stormy eyes. "Meaning me."

"I told him I had lots of guests at my place, not just one."

Braxton grinned. "I bet he loved that."

She bit her lip. "Yeah, but he also said it would take a lot of booked weeks in order to catch up on my mortgage payments."

"How the hell does that little prick know how much you owe?"

"That was exactly my thought before I hung up on him."

Braxton reached for her hand and tugged her up. She melted against his strong chiseled chest and closed her eyes, inhaling his warm male scent.

"It's going to be okay. You won't lose the Bella Luna."

Kate's chest ached, a sickness filling her body like a child missing her home. It had nothing to do with the fear of losing the Bella Luna and everything to do with losing Braxton.

Shoving away her sadness, she looked up into his gorgeous face. "What about you? Did you find out anything tonight?"

"Not really. At least not anything about my father's murder." His hands went up and down her back in a slow, comforting caress. "Have you been waiting up this whole time?"

She laid her head on his chest and nodded. "Just wanted to make sure you got home okay."

He stiffened against her. Damn, she probably sounded

like a nagging wife. That was the last thing a man ever wanted to hear.

She took a step back and faked a yawn, holding her hand over her mouth. "I'm going to bed." She slid underneath the covers, making sure her back was to him. She squeezed her eyes shut, waiting to hear the door shut behind Braxton.

The covers flounced as Braxton crawled into bed and settled in behind her. When he wrapped his large hand around her waist and pulled her back against his stomach, Kate's heart lurched.

He hadn't left. Not yet. But she knew he would.

Kate pushed away the painful truth, focused on the warmth of Braxton's body, and snuggled in deeper.

CHAPTER 11

"*Y*ou think he's here?" Brutus turned to Killian, who was leaning up against the Eureka Springs sign.

"I think the fucker is dead." Lorcan shrugged. "I've never seen any Werewolf live after taking a silver bullet. Just doesn't happen."

Brutus scowled at his men. His gut told him different. "If he's dead, then where's the body?"

"Maybe he got eaten by a bear." Lorcan shrugged.

Brutus and Killian eyed Lorcan.

Brutus rubbed his buzz cut and growled. It was obvious Braxton had never made it to Branson. He was here in Eureka Springs. He knew it.

"No one has seen him here. We've asked all the bars."

"You asked in all the Were bars. You need to go ask in the human bars."

Lorcan snarled. "Human?"

"Yeah, you're not afraid of going into the human bars, are you?" Brutus taunted.

"Hell, no. I just don't think they're going to be so open in answering our questions. They may not know we're were-wolves, but they sense we're something dangerous."

"We're out of options. Both of you get to the bars and see what you can find out. I'll make a call to the Louisiana commander and fill him in. I'm sure he's not going to be too damn pleased with any of us right now."

* * *

"KATE, THIS IS A GREAT PLACE." Barbara smiled over her coffee. "I'm shocked you don't stay booked up all the time."

Kate sighed. "I wish I would stay booked. With the economy like it is, people tend to look for the cheapest place to stay."

"I disagree." Danielle cocked her head. "I think people are willing to pay for the ambience plus the extras you have, Kate."

Kate snorted. "Not lately they haven't."

Barbara set her coffee cup on the dining table. "How much advertising do you do?"

Kate sat in a side chair next to Barbara. "Well I'm on the Eureka Springs list of Bed and Breakfasts. We've always just thought word of mouth and referrals were enough to get our name out there. That's what my mom always said."

"It's not enough." Felicity shook her head. "You need a webpage."

"The Eureka Springs Bed and Breakfast list is on a webpage."

"You need your own, something unique and eye-catching, with photos of the Bella Luna inside and out." Felicity's eyes lit up. "I could help you. I'm a website designer by day."

"Really?" Kate felt her hopes rise and then quickly fall. "I'd like that, but I don't have the funds to pay you."

Felicity exchanged a look with Barbara. "What if we bartered?"

Kate shrugged. "I'm afraid I don't have anything to barter with."

"Actually, you do. What if I designed your webpage and set it up for you now in exchange for staying here a couple of days in the fall? No charge."

"I don't know that I'll still be in business in the fall." Kate blew out a breath, feeling more depressed by the second with this conversation. "I'd hate for you to do all that work and then me not be able to hold up my end of the bargain."

Felicity laughed. "I can guarantee you I'll bring you customers by the droves with my webpage. Trust me, Kate, you'll still be in business and doing better than ever."

Kate smiled. For once, that tight feeling in her chest was gone. Besides, she had nothing to lose.

"So, what do you say?" Felicity waited expectantly with her hands clasped under her chin.

"I say, you've got a deal."

* * *

FOR THE NEXT FEW HOURS, Kate waited anxiously to see what Felicity had come up with. She tried to get a peek, but all the writers shooed her away from the upstairs bedroom where they were ensconced. She was surprised to see even Ava and Granny involved in the process. With Granny in the mix, she hoped the old lady wouldn't talk the writers into putting something obscene on the website.

Kate rounded the corner to the kitchen and ran head-first into Jayden. He'd come back to the Bella Luna with Braxton and Damon from their trip into town. With no room, he had to sleep on the couch.

"Whoa." Jayden reached out to steady her.

"Sorry about that." Kate stepped back.

"No problem. I was just about to go find you."

"Me?"

"Yeah. I didn't get to pay you last night for staying."

Kate waved her hands. "Don't worry about it. Sleeping on the couch isn't exactly part of the bed and breakfast amenities." Ava had managed to finagle a room out of Felicity so Ava and Damon could have a bed. Lord knew they needed one. It was either they have a bedroom to themselves or everyone walking in on them having sex in the strangest places.

Kate's cheeks heated with the shock of walking in on the couple getting it on right in the kitchen on the island. And Ava hadn't even been embarrassed. She just smirked and kept riding Damon.

"I'm still going to pay for staying. I already asked Braxton what the rates are." Jayden pulled his leather wallet out of his jeans pocket and plucked out six one hundred dollar bills and handed them to her.

Kate frowned. "But this is too much for one night."

Jayden gave her a sheepish grin. "I have a feeling I might have to stay a few more nights. It just depends how long Braxton needs me."

Kate smiled. "How long have you two been friends?"

"Not that long. He helped me out of a tight spot." He raised his left sleeve of his T-shirt, revealing a long, nasty scar.

Kate covered her mouth with her hand and then met his eyes. "I thought Weres could heal."

Jayden pushed his sleeve down. "We do. Unless someone pours salt in our wounds."

"Oh, God." The pain he must have suffered would have been agonizing.

He shrugged and gave her an easy smile, the kind that

made girls go gooey inside. His eyes lit on the plate of freshly baked cookies she'd prepared for the evening's refreshments.

"Go ahead. Since Damon's been here, I've learned to bake four times as much."

"Cool." Jayden grabbed four oatmeal raisins and headed out the door.

* * *

DESPITE THE LICK of cold wind against her skin, Kate lifted her face toward the sun as she walked down the sidewalk in town with Felicity and Danielle. She had agreed to go with the girls to take some pictures of the town so they could use them for her website.

Kate stopped long enough to pet a black lab being walked down the small sidewalk of Spring Street.

"I think we should have taken the picture of the street from the top of the hill." Danielle examined the picture Felicity had just taken on her digital camera.

"We will. I wanted to get some pictures at the bottom of the street looking up the hill. That way I can capture some of the shop signs in the photo."

Felicity squinted and shaded her eyes with her palm. "Isn't there some kind of religious statue here?"

"You mean the Christ of the Ozarks. It's only a few minutes from here." Kate slipped her sunglasses up on top of her head. "What would really be pretty is Thorn Crown Chapel."

"Isn't that the church made of glass?" Danielle looked at Kate.

"Yes. It's especially gorgeous at night when it's all lit up." Kate waved her hand. "But they only do that during the holidays."

"We can still get a great picture with all the snow on the

ground. Maybe we can come back during the spring and get a picture with all the flowers blooming. That way you could change out your pictures with the seasons."

Kate felt a smile spread across her face. "That's actually a great idea."

She just hoped she was going to be in business in the spring.

* * *

"Come on, Ava."

"I'm not going." Ava crossed her arms and plopped down on the bed. The writers were busy getting all dolled up to go into town to celebrate the launch of Kate's new webpage for her bed and breakfast. Even Granny was going.

"It's going to be a girls' night. Don't you need a girls' night out?" Barbara patted her hair down.

"Nope. I need a night with my guy." Ava fell back on the bed and crossed and uncrossed her legs. It was a nervous habit when she was apart from Damon, whether it be a day or a week. Hell, it hadn't even been a damn hour and her nerves were lighting up like a summer storm.

Felicity snorted. "From the sounds that keep coming out of your room, you should be exhausted."

Ava sat up and narrowed her eyes at the girl. Felicity stiffened and took a step back.

Ava smirked. Smart girl.

When she'd walked in and saw Felicity touching Damon, Ava had wanted to rip the female's throat out, right there. Damon had pulled her away and they'd gotten into an argument in the bedroom, which lasted all of ten minutes. Then came the makeup sex. Oh. My. God. The makeup sex.

Ava went wet just thinking about it. She crossed her legs as her body heated. "Are you sure you're talking about me, or maybe you meant Kate? 'Cause that girl can make some noise."

Kate went wide-eyed and looked around the room.

Ava grimaced a little at her obvious discomfort. Damn, maybe she shouldn't have said anything. Kate did look like the innocent American girl next door.

Kate let out a giggle. "Maybe it was me."

An hour later, after the last eye was lined and every lip was painted, the girls were finally ready to go. Gathering up their purses, the women piled into the van. Ava stood at the window as the van disappeared down the driveway and felt the tiniest twinge of regret at not going.

* * *

"ARE YOU SURE IT'S SAFE?" Myrtis glanced up at the biker bar that was built into the side of the mountain.

"I guess so." Kate bit her lip. "I've only been in here once. But it was during the day. It was rented out for a friend's birthday." It was Beau's twenty-fifth birthday.

Felicity turned in the driver's seat and gave Kate an incredible stare. "You mean to tell me you've lived here all your life and you've never been to this bar at night?"

Kate shrugged, feeling like a dork. "It never really looked like a place to pick up a nice guy."

"Right. Because by looking at Braxton the word *nice* automatically comes to mind." Felicity arched her brow in disbelief.

"Braxton is definitely not nice. Or safe, for that matter," Kate muttered.

Felicity and Danielle gave wide-eyed looks. "Just how dangerous are we talking? Like bang me standing up dangerous? Or go down on me in the laundry room while the spin cycle is on dangerous?"

Kate's mouth dropped open. How the hell did they know about the laundry room?

"Holy shit. I knew it. He did do dirty things to you in the laundry room, didn't he?" Felicity's mouth gaped.

"I don't care how many ways he's banged her. I need to get inside and get me a drink." Myrtis threw open the side door of the van and climbed out. The others followed like ants.

Kate hurried out of the van before any more questions could be directed to her. She was going to have to tell Braxton no more sex until those writers left. She smiled, knowing he wasn't going to stop having his way with her at every chance.

As she stepped through the door of the bar, the scent of cigarettes and beer hit her in a nauseating rush. Now she remembered why she wasn't the bar type.

She waved her hand in front of her nose, trying to dispel the noxious odor as she looked around. It was crowded tonight with lots of large men in leather, jeans, and tattoos. The few women that were there were beautiful with a lethal edge about them. It was that same deadly edge that Ava carried.

Granny walked up to the bar, eyeballed the bartender, and slapped her hand down on the counter like a woman on a mission. "Give me a pomegranate martini."

The hulking bartender lifted an eyebrow before his gaze slid to the rest of them. "We don't serve that here."

"Hmph. Then give me a Sea Breeze."

"Fresh out." The bartender leaned across the bar. "Why don't you ladies head over to the rooftop bar across the street? I'm sure they'd have more of a selection than what we have."

Kate cleared her throat. "Actually, that might be a good idea." The hair on her neck stood on end, and she couldn't fight an involuntary shiver. The idea of visiting a biker bar had suddenly lost all its appeal.

* * *

BRAXTON PULLED up into Kate's driveway and slid out of her SUV. The throaty rumble of twin Harley Breakouts sped up the driveway. His heart squeezed at the sound, knowing his Harley was at the foot of the mountain, forever gone.

Damon and Jayden pulled up and parked their bikes near the side of the house.

"You look like a soccer mom, dude." Jayden grinned, putting his kickstand down.

Braxton held up his middle finger.

Damon snorted. "I'm not sure how you managed to fit your large ass behind the wheel. Looks claustrophobic."

"You have no idea." Braxton bent his head from side to side, stretching out the kinks. Since he'd lost his bike on the highway when he'd been shot, the only transportation he had was Kate's SUV. The only thing he liked about driving it was her scent and how it clung to the inside. It almost made him forget about his Harley. Almost.

"Where have you guys been?" Ava stood at the door, arms crossed. From the look on her face, she wasn't happy with Damon.

"We were checking out the crime scene at the construction site." Braxton offered.

Ava turned her attention back to Braxton and Damon. "How could you guys find any clues at the construction site with all the snow that's still on the ground?"

"That's what I tried to tell him." Damon pulled Ava into his arms for a possessive kiss.

Braxton looked away, jealousy stinging the pit of his gut.

He wanted what Damon and Ava had. He wanted a life with Kate. He wanted the impossible.

"You're grasping for straws, my man." Jayden slapped him on the shoulder as he passed him and entered the house.

What other choice did he have? Sitting around on his ass waiting for the Assassins to show up and put a bullet through his head was not an option. He'd take grasping for straws any day.

Braxton shoved his hand through his hair and looked at Ava. "Where's Kate?" It was too late for her to make another run to the grocery store. He glanced down at his watch. Eleven o'clock. He cut his eyes at her darkened bedroom window. No matter how late he came home, she was usually waiting up and she always had the bedroom lamp on.

Ava snorted. "She went into town with the ladies to celebrate her new website."

Jayden laughed. "Where the hell did they go? We just drove through Spring Street and half the damn town already closed up shop for the night."

"Felicity talked them into going to that bar. She said she needed to go to a biker bar for research on her next novel." Ava shook her head.

Braxton froze.

"What's wrong?" Ava looked between the three of them.

"The only biker bar in town is a werewolf bar." Braxton glared at Ava.

"Shit. I had no idea." Ava's mouth dropped. "I should have gone when they asked me, but I was anxious to see Damon."

Damon caressed her cheek. "You didn't know. It's not your fault."

Jayden frowned. "Where's Granny?"

Ava paled. "She went with them."

Braxton grabbed Jayden's keys and straddled the Harley. He'd make better time on the motorcycle than the SUV.

"They're walking into a lion's den. I've got to go get them out before something bad happens."

"Not without us you're not." Damon hopped on his bike and Ava climbed on behind him.

Jayden scowled. "If you think I'm letting you go without me, you're crazy. My grandmother's in there. Do you know how dangerous that is?"

Braxton nodded. "I'm sure Granny's safe."

Jayden looked pained. "It's not Granny I'm worried about. Do you have any idea how much damage that old lady can do? The last thing I need is to be put on probation by Barrett because my Granny has been up to her antics again." Jayden stood beside his Harley and shook his head. "Dude, it's my bike and I drive. I never ride bitch."

Braxton grinned. "This time you do.

* * *

BRAXTON'S MIND raced with every imaginable thought as he tore down the winding streets of Eureka Springs to reach Kate. He thought about how many werewolves he was going to kill if they laid one finger on her. He thought about how he was going to strangle those crazy writers for putting Kate in danger. And he thought about Jayden, who for the first time in his life, was now sitting behind him hurling a string of profanities at him about riding bitch on his own Harley.

Braxton slid the Harley to a stop and whacked Jayden in the face with his booted foot as he dismounted. Hard rock music bled out into the night from behind the closed doors of the bar.

"Fuck, Braxton." Jayden growled and rubbed his face.

"Sorry, man, but Kate's my priority." Braxton hurried across the parking lot.

Jayden shook his head. "All this trouble for a female. I swear I'm never going to get mated."

Braxton frowned. "We're not mated."

"Yet. You two are not mated yet. But you might as well be." Jayden rubbed the side of his head. "You're just as pussy-whipped as Damon."

"What are you two bitching about now?" Damon asked as he parked his Harley beside them. Ava hopped off.

"I told Braxton I'm never mating."

"That's good. 'Cause no female will ever want you." Damon smirked.

Jayden flipped Damon the bird.

"Cut it out." Ava stepped in between the two males. "Braxton's going to need some backup. So get your heads right."

Braxton didn't have time for their bullshit. He bounded up the steps to the bar, taking them two at a time, with his friends right behind him. He opened the door and stepped in. Music, smoke, and whiskey hit him square in the face.

Through the haze of smoke the bar was full, every table and booth occupied with Weres. He scanned the room until his gaze landed on Kate. And his stomach bottomed out.

* * *

"I THINK we might need to be getting back to the Bella Luna." Kate worried her lips with her teeth as her gaze darted across the crowded room.The longer she was here, the more she became uneasy.

"We've only been here an hour," Felicity whined through her drunken stupor.

It was an hour longer than Kate wanted to stay.

"Granny just ordered another round of shots." Felicity's slurred words made Kate's stomach knot. Felicity was a handful sober. Kate had a feeling that Felicity was a whole lot of trouble once you gave the girl alcohol. All the more reason they needed to leave.

Another round of shots were placed on the bar in front of the women. More alcohol was the last thing these women needed. Since they'd arrived at the bar, they had been throwing back drinks like sailors. Kate couldn't quote the legal limit of intoxication, but she was sure these ladies had exceeded it.

"If you want to drink, I'm sure Braxton will be more than happy to serve you guys at the house." Kate smiled, hoping they'd agree.

"Braxton's eye candy. That's for sure." Felicity slurred her words as she grabbed onto Kate's arm for balance. "But he's yours. And I need to get some inspiration from a single hottie. You know, to get my creative juices flowing." Felicity gave her a wink.

"Hmph. I think the juices you want flowing are your lady juices." Myrtis sneered. "Not your creative juices."

Kate cringed.

"How about that one?" Barbara pointed to the back of the room where a dark-haired male sat at a table, eyeing their group with either curiosity or interest. Kate wasn't sure which it was, but he made her skin crawl.

"He's been sitting there all by himself since we got here. I don't see a ring, so I'm guessing he's single." Felicity narrowed her eyes at the guy.

Kate shook her head. "I don't think that's a good idea."

"Why not?" Felicity set her empty shot glass down on the table. "He looks dark, dangerous, and hot."

"He looks like he just got out of prison." Kate opened her purse and began to search for her cell phone. There was no way she was going to get these women out of here on her own. She needed backup in the form of her werewolf houseguests.

"Prison?" Barbara cocked her head. "Yeah, I could see that. Although, I was going to say he looked like a pirate."

"What is it with you and pirates? You don't even write that kind of book. You write Highlander." Myrtis grinned.

Barbara shrugged. "I might want to branch out. Test the waters. Pirates are very hot right now."

"You mean test your inner erotica." Myrtis laughed.

"I'm going to talk to him." Felicity pushed away from the bar.

Kate grabbed her arm. "No, Felicity, please don't do that."

Felicity twisted out of her grip and smiled. "Don't worry, Kate. I'll be fine." She turned and walked toward the mysterious man.

Damn, this wasn't good. Her gut clenched. She needed help. Throwing up her hands, she hurried after Felicity.

Felicity stopped in front of the biker and rested a slim hip on the table.

"I notice you're not wearing a wedding ring," Felicity purred.

"No, I'm not." The stranger cocked his head as a smirk played on his lips.

Kate looked around nervously. A lot of the men in the bar had turned around in their seats as a hush stole across the noisy bar. The tension in the room seemed to increase tenfold.

"Felicity, we've really got to be going." Kate gritted her teeth and grabbed Felicity's arm, but Felicity shook off her grip.

"I don't want to go. I'm making a new friend." Felicity leaned over and ran her finger down the tight T-shirt-clad chest of the stranger.

A deep growl erupted from behind them. Kate turned.

Standing two feet away, a brunette wearing black leather pants and vest and a scowl so intense it made Kate shiver, eyed them both with contempt. She was one of the women Kate had noticed when they first entered the bar.

The woman grabbed Felicity by her hair and held her off the ground, her feet dangling in the air. "That's my mate. No one touches my mate."

Mate? Kate's stomach turned. Holy shit. Her intuition had been trying to alert her to the danger. They were in the middle of a werewolf bar.

* * *

BRAXTON WATCHED in horror as a female Were lifted Felicity off the ground by her hair. If he made a move to interfere, the entire bar would erupt in a fight, putting all the women in danger. More importantly, it would put Kate in danger.

"I can't fucking believe I'm about to do this." Ava shoved past Braxton and tapped the female Were on the shoulder.

The female turned. Ava reared back and slammed her fist into the female's face. The female let go of Felicity and slid to the floor in a heap.

Ava grabbed Felicity by the throat. "You, little girl, better learn to keep yourself in check. Next time there's not going to be someone around to save your skinny little ass, and you will get more than you bargained for. Do you understand what I'm saying?"

Felicity looked at Ava with wide eyes and nodded fervently. "I understand." She held up her arms in front of her face and grimaced. "Are you going to hit me too, Ava?"

"I ought to. For coming in here and trying to start trouble." Ava released her hold and glanced at Kate. "Kate's too nice to say it, but you are nothing but trouble. If I were her, I'd kick your ass out before you do something that hurts her business."

Felicity swallowed and slowly lowered her arms. "I'm sorry, Kate, I didn't mean to endanger your business."

* * *

KATE WANTED to kiss Ava for saving their ass, but that was going to have to wait. Right now she needed to get everyone out.

She fell into step behind Ava, who was marching Felicity to the front door.

A large hand clamped down on her waist and pulled her down into a hard lap. She blinked, too shocked to speak.

"Hey, sweetheart, you looking for a good time?" A burly biker with eyes so dark they appeared black held her down with his massive arm around her waist. He reeked of body odor, cigarettes, and bad breath. Kate tried to pull away, but his hold was like steel.

"No. But, you need to be looking for a breath mint," Kate said as her anger slowly built up within her. She knew she should be afraid, but for some reason her anger overrode every other emotion at the moment.

A vicious growl shook the room. Braxton filled her line of vision as he yanked her free and crushed her against his chest. The biker's protest muted in her ears as Braxton's murderous growl seemed to vibrate the entire room.

He turned and shoved her at Jayden. "Get her out of here."

Jayden hurried toward the writers with Kate tucked protectively against his side. "Party's over, ladies. It's time to go home." He opened the door and began herding the women out.

Kate turned, frantically trying to find Braxton. She froze.

Braxton had his hand wrapped around the biker's thick neck, holding him off the floor. "Do not touch what belongs to me," Braxton growled.

Kate's heart leaped into her throat. The dynamic of the bar had shifted and all the men were shoving chairs back and circling Braxton, like animals ready to attack.

Kate started forward. She needed to help Braxton.

Damon grabbed her arm. "Don't. Go with the others. We got this." Damon looked past her as Felicity was the last one out the door. Damon grinned, his eyes changing colors to an odd yellow. He dropped to the floor and shifted into a wolf right before her eyes.

Hell erupted.

Braxton punched the biker who'd grabbed her. The biker landed with a thud on the scarred wood floor. The man looked up, growled, and shifted into a large wolf.

Terror paralyzed Kate to where she stood, unable to run from what she was actually witnessing. Braxton howled as his muscled body shifted into the massive grey wolf she'd found on her front steps.

Braxton lunged, his teeth bared, pinning the wolf to the floor.

"Go!" Ava grabbed her by the shoulders and shoved her through the door.

Kate stood on the steps, unable to move as chaos erupted behind the closed door. She knew what Braxton was. But seeing him shift from a man into an animal was something her brain couldn't comprehend. It made what he was, a werewolf, frighteningly real.

"Kate, are you okay? Are you hurt?" Jayden grabbed her by the elbows and studied her face.

She swallowed and nodded slightly. "I'm fine."

"We have to go. If those writers find out what we are, then we will no longer be safe." Jayden narrowed his eyes. "Braxton said you knew what we are, but they don't."

Kate frowned. "You don't think they'd tell, do you?"

Jayden gave her a droll look. "Are you kidding? They're

writers. They put all kinds of shit in those books. I'm sure a book about Werewolves that ride Harleys would hit the New York Times best sellers' list in a heartbeat."

Kate felt the blood drain from her face.

"Come on." Jayden pulled her down the steps and helped her into the van before sliding into the driver's seat. The women were all accounted for. Even Granny was there.

Kate turned around in her seat and met the old woman's gaze. "Granny, where have you been? I haven't seen you for the past thirty minutes."

Granny waved her hand in a dismissive gesture. "I was in the bathroom talking to one of those Wer...ah one of those girls. She was asking me about my sex toys. She said she'd been having some trouble out of her boyfriend who had a wandering eye. I told her she needed my edible panties with matching bra in beef jerky flavor."

"Dammit, Granny. I told you not to talk about your sex stuff in front of me." Jayden grimaced as he started the vehicle.

"Jayden. It's not sex stuff, it's my business." Granny glared.

Kate had a feeling Granny's "business" was a topic of contention between the two.

"Well, don't talk about your little business in front of me. I'm about to lose my dinner over here." He threw the van in reverse, backed out, and sped out of the parking lot.

Granny stuck her chin in the air. "My 'little business' made me over a hundred and fifty thousand last year, just so you know."

"A hundred and fifty thousand?" Myrtis poked her head up. "Damn. Maybe I need to peddle that instead of writing."

"It's a money-maker, that's for sure." Granny looked at the lady. "If you're interested, you could sign up under me, and I could help get you started."

"Enough talking about that kind of stuff." Jayden took a

sharp turn onto a winding street and the ladies slid to one side of the van.

"Yeah, let's talk about how Felicity almost got her ass beat." Myrtis glared at Felicity. "I think you owe Ava a big thank you for helping you out."

Granny perked up. "Wait, what happened? What did I miss?"

Kate shook her head. "Felicity flirted with the wrong guy and the girlfriend walked up. Ava ended up knocking the girl out before she could hit Felicity."

"Hey, how was I supposed to know he had a woman?" Felicity sunk lower into the seat, looking embarrassed.

Granny eyed Felicity. "Was she wearing all leather?"

"How'd you know?"

"Because she was the one I was talking to in the bathroom about her man being a dick."

"Granny, language, please," Jayden called out over his shoulder as he took another intense curve. Tires squealed as the ladies slid to the other side of the van.

"I don't feel so good." Felicity bolted up in her seat and covered her mouth with her hand.

"I think you need to pull over." Kate unsnapped her seat belt and frantically began to search through the armrest for some kind of container.

"I think I need to get out." Felicity reached for the door handle. Kate leaped over the seat and grabbed Felicity around the waist before the girl could tumble out down the side of the mountain. Jayden cursed and slammed on the brakes just as Felicity lost her dinner, wine, and shots.

When Felicity was done, Kate pulled her back in the car and shut the door.

"It stinks in here," Danielle called out from the backseat, waving her hand in front of her nose.

"That's because Felicity hit the side of the door. We'll

wash it off and leave the windows open so it can air out tonight." Kate climbed back in her seat and gave Jayden an eye roll. He grimaced as the scent hit him and he pushed the "down" button for his window. Cold air blew inside the vehicle. Kate snuggled down into her coat.

It was going to be a long drive home.

* * *

DAMON LUNGED at the nearest werewolf. They went skidding across the barroom floor. He jumped to his feet and snapped his teeth at the enemy. The Were whimpered and lowered his head as he backed away. *That's right, fucker. Back the fuck up.*

Damon looked for the next target. Instead of another male wolf, he saw Ava in wolf form being trounced by a female. Damon shifted back to his human form, but before he could reach Ava, she had managed to shift her weight and pin the female underneath her. The female wolf whimpered until Ava released her hold.

Damon grinned and rested his hand on the back of her head. Ava growled and snapped until she realized it was him. She gave him a wolf lick with her tongue. The rest of the bar was empty. Everyone had quickly fled after the fighting had started up.

Ava shifted in to her human form and slowly stood. Damon pulled her close, their naked bodies rubbing together in a slow delicious burn.

She pulled away and grinned. "We're going to need some clothes."

A growl and whimper pulled his attention away from her. Damon froze at what he saw.

* * *

Braxton's mouth clamped down on the Were's throat, every urge and instinct inside him wanting to bite down and feel the crush of bone and ligaments under his teeth. Bloodlust swirled in his head, drowning out any words of common sense or reality of the situation. He wanted vengeance. He wanted blood.

"Stop, Braxton. You got to let him go." Ava touched his back gently.

It registered that Ava was talking to him, but he didn't release the wolf.

"Braxton. Kate's waiting for you back home," Damon growled, urgency in his voice. "Besides, I think some humans heard us from that club next door. They probably called the cops. You don't need to be here."

Braxton slowly released his grip around the Were's throat. He backed away as he panted out each breath, adrenaline flooding his veins. Cops showing up was the last thing he needed.

Braxton closed his eyes, shifting from wolf to human. Standing up, he glared at the Were who was now tucked in the corner with his tail between his legs.

"We've got to go," Damon hissed.

His chest ached with the need to be with Kate.

"Here, put these on. I brought extra clothes in my saddlebags." Damon shoved some clothes at him. "You go into that B&B with your naked ass, there will be no stopping those crazy ladies."

"Thanks." That was the one hazard about shifting into wolf when you least expected it. You tore out of the clothes you had on. Braxton dressed quickly and glanced around. "Where's Ava? She okay?"

Damon grinned. "She's in the bathroom dressing. Can't have you looking at my female, can I?"

"You boys ready?" Ava stepped out of the bathroom in

jeans, black T-shirt, and a snug leather jacket. She bent over to secure the leather boots.

"Where the fuck did you get that?" Damon's voice echoed in the empty room.

Ava lifted her chin in the direction of the female Were. "I got it out of her bag. Thank God she removed the jacket before she shifted or I'd freeze my ass off on the ride back."

Damon pushed her back against the counter of the bar and kissed her.

Braxton averted his eyes. His cock tightened, and the only thought that stuck in his brain was Kate. He needed to find Kate.

CHAPTER 12

"*S*weet Jesus. What's with these women?" Jayden's wide-eyed gaze bore into Kate as he hid in the shelter of the kitchen. "You would think they would have passed out by now with as much alcohol as they've consumed. I mean, even the old ladies are still going. They're like the fucking Energizer bunny."

Someone in the living room turned on the stereo. The sounds of Britney Spears blared through the house, rattling the windows. Kate peeked around the corner just as Lynn stood up on the couch and started singing into a vase. The other writers waved their cell phones in the air with their lighter apps turned on in tune to the music.

"Sing it, girlfriend!" Barbara yelled.

Kate ducked back in the kitchen. She was exhausted and irritated and over the whole damn thing. She glared at Jayden. "At least you didn't have to clean the puke out of the van."

"At least you didn't get molested," he shot back.

Kate snorted. "What are you talking about?"

"I'm talking about how Myrtis grabbed my balls as I was

helping her inside." Jayden shivered, cupped himself, and looked away. "Shit, I'm going to have nightmares about this for years."

"What's that?" Kate stilled.

"What's what?"

"I thought I heard someone knocking." She made her way toward the front door with Jayden behind her. He probably didn't want to be left alone in a room with these women. She didn't blame him.

Kate opened the door. Her heart dropped to the floor.

Standing in front of her was one of the largest men she'd ever seen dressed all in black leather. She glanced over his shoulder and spotted a Harley Davidson parked in the driveway. Her heart turned to ice. This was no man. This was one of the Assassins.

"Where is he?" The Were glared down at her.

"Who?" She swallowed, trying to keep her expression neutral.

"Braxton. I'm here for Braxton."

"Who are you?" Her heart stopped.

"I'm Lorcan." He narrowed his eyes on her." I can smell a male's scent on you. So don't try to tell me he isn't here." He stepped into her space and growled.

Jayden shoved Kate behind him. "I'm the male you smell, you dumbass. There's no one by the name of Braxton here." Jayden lowered his voice. "And if you had any sense you'd get the hell outta here and stop harassing my girl."

Lorcan growled and shoved Jayden back, knocking Kate into the wall. The Assassin stepped past them both. His gaze swept the room.

Kate clenched her fists, her nails biting into her palms. She was tired of people bulldozing over her. First foreclosure, then Oliver Bigsby trying to intimidate her into selling him her home. She was tired of trying to wrangle these crazy-ass writers to keep them from getting hurt, and now a large werewolf was trampling through her house like he owned it. She was so fucking over it.

"Look, asshole." Kate shoved her finger in the Assassin's chest. "I said there's no one here named Braxton. I didn't invite you in, so you need to leave." Each word was punctuated with a jab to his hard chest.

Jayden pulled her away and met the Were face to face. "I don't think the lady invited you in, so you need to leave."

"I'm not leaving until I find Braxton," Lorcan growled.

"Holy shit." All three turned at Myrtis's voice. The writers were craning their necks over her shoulder.

Kate grimaced and held up her hands. He probably looked like a serial killer to them. "It's okay. He's leaving. There's nothing to be worried about."

Barbara stepped around Myrtis, her gaze running up and down Lorcan. "What's your hurry, big boy?"

Big boy? What the hell?

Lorcan growled and eyed the group of women. They jumped.

Jayden got in Lorcan's face and bristled.

Granny came around the corner with a bottle of Grey Goose. She stopped short and looked between the two werewolves. "What's going on?"

"I think that's Jayden's boyfriend." Myrtis sighed.

"Yeah, I think they're getting ready to kiss." Lynn smiled and clapped her hands together.

Lorcan looked confused. Jayden looked horrified and took a quick step back.

"He's not my boyfriend!" Jayden looked around the room with wide eyes. "Why the hell would you think he was my boyfriend?"

"Nothing wrong with being gay. In fact, I've been

thinking about writing a male on male novella myself." Lynn poked her glasses up on her nose.

"I'm not gay." Jayden held his hands up and shook his head. He turned his wide-eyed gaze on Kate. "Do I look gay?"

"How about you, big guy?" Myrtis walked up to the stranger and grabbed his massive bicep. Her eyes widened. "Holy shit, Barbara, get over here. I can't get two hands over his arm."

A very intoxicated Barbara tripped and fell into Lorcan, who automatically caught her. She smiled up at him and latched onto his arm like a leech.

Lorcan tried to pry her off, but Barbara wasn't going anywhere.

Lynn and Myrtis emerged from the living room with their hands behind their backs. Kate frowned. Didn't they have sense enough to know this guy was dangerous?

"So, you're not gay?" Lynn licked her lips.

Kate blinked. Apparently the quiet one in the group was more adventurous once she got some alcohol in her.

"No, I'm not, you crazy bitches," Lorcan thundered. Kate jumped back.

"So, you like women." Barbara smiled up at him.

"I like females," Lorcan thundered, glaring at the women.

"Good. Cause we like you." Lynn pulled something that looked like a riding crop from behind her back and swatted Lorcan across his thigh, dangerously close to his crotch. He let out a growl.

"You like that?" Lynn gave the Were a sultry look. "Want me to hit you higher? I heard guys like a little sting with their sex."

When Lorcan realized the tables were turned and the ladies weren't the least bit intimidated, he took a step back.

"Do I look gay to you?" Jayden murmured near Kate's ear.

Kate shook her head, trying to concentrate on what the Assassin was going to do next.

"Lynn, where the hell did you get that thing?" She needed to get that thing away from the woman before the werewolf ripped them all to shreds.

"From Granny's sex supply box," Lynn purred and kept her eyes on Lorcan.

"Are you crazy? Give me that thing." Kate held out her hand.

"Nope. I got a feeling this one likes it rough." Lynn brought the crop down on his thigh again, this time a little higher.

"Yeah, I bet we could go all BDSM on his fine ass." Granny poured herself a shot of Goose and downed it.

Jayden grimaced. "Jesus, Granny! Stop talking like that!"

"Who are you?" Lorcan took a cautious step back from the group of women. "Have you been sent from the Arkansas Council?" His gaze darted from one woman to the next.

"Arkansas Council? If you mean the Arkansas Sex Council, then hell yeah!" Myrtis gave him a big wink. "When we're done, you won't be able to walk for a week. I'll ride you so hard, you might break a hip."

"Eww." Jayden frowned and looked a bit green.

"I seem to have been mistaken. The one I'm looking for is not here." Lorcan's voice wavered as he took a step toward the door.

"There's no mistake. I got everything you're looking for. Just because I got some mileage on me, don't mean I don't know how to make a man purr." Myrtis ran her hand up Lorcan's chest.

"Just wait till she pops her dentures out." Granny tossed another shot back. "That's when the real fun happens."

"I think I just threw up in my mouth." Jayden made a gagging sound.

Lorcan murmured something that sounded a lot like *Oh God* before throwing open the door and racing out into the yard. Kate slammed the door and locked it. Pushing back the curtain, she peered out the window in time to see the Assassin's motorcycle spin a patch of snow in the air as he tore down the driveway.

* * *

BRAXTON RELAXED AS SOON as the Bella Luna came into view. For the first time in his life, he felt like he was coming home.

He cut the engine and slid off the bike. The front door opened and Kate came running out. He caught her and brought his mouth down on hers. The second his tongue snaked inside her mouth, she moaned.

"Get a room," Damon murmured as he and Ava walked past them.

Braxton pulled his mouth away, keeping his gaze on Kate. "Sounds like a good idea."

"Did you tell him?" Jayden came out of the house and onto the porch.

Braxton frowned. "Tell me what?"

"I was trying to, but he kind of distracted me. With his mouth." Kate blushed.

"What's going on?" Damon and Ava stopped.

"The Assassin, Lorcan, was here." Jayden leaned against the porch railing.

Braxton cupped Kate's face. "Are you okay? Did he hurt you?"

Kate waved him away. "I'm fine. He was here looking for you."

Braxton stiffened, his hands falling to his sides.

"I told him you weren't here." Kate frowned. "Maybe he believed me and won't be sticking around."

Jayden snorted. "He won't be sticking around no matter what. Not after what those crazy-ass women did."

"Please, tell me Felicity didn't flirt with him." Ava propped her hands on her hips. "I swear that girl has a death wish."

"It wasn't Felicity this time."

"Then who?" Braxton glanced up at Jayden.

"Myrtis and Barbara, the old chicks. They were the ones trying to sex him up. I almost felt sorry for the guy when Myrtis brought out the riding crop." Jayden shivered.

"She wasn't stupid enough to hit a fucking werewolf, was she?" Braxton's eyes grew round.

"She smacked him twice, told him she has amazing sex skills, and wanted to pop her dentures out and prove it."

"Jesus. Too much information, man." Damon shook his head as if trying to dislodge the images.

Braxton faced Jayden. "She's lucky he didn't go into a rage and tear them apart."

"I think he was more freaked out by the fact they didn't seem scared of him at all. All they wanted was to tie him up and fuck him."

Ava laughed.

"That's not funny." Jayden whirled around at Ava. "They're like a pack of wild dogs. That's without any alcohol in them. They're even worse when they're drunk. I'm going to need serious therapy after this."

Kate shivered against him. "Where's your coat?" Braxton scowled.

"I forgot to grab it." Kate shrugged.

"Come on." Braxton lifted her up in his arms and carried her into the house. He didn't bother putting her down until he reached her bedroom.

"You didn't have to do that. I could have walked." Kate pulled the quilt off the rocker and wrapped it around her shoulders.

"I like carrying you." Braxton's chest tugged. He knew he couldn't stay here any longer.

She reached up and stroked his cheek with the back of her fingertips. Braxton closed his eyes at her warm touch. He couldn't have Kate. He was the only werewolf fucked up enough to want to mate someone he couldn't have. *Figures.*

He opened his eyes. Her beautiful caramel gaze stared up at him, making his heart warm and tingle. She was the only good thing in his life he'd ever had. She was the only woman who would ever hold his heart. He opened his mouth to tell her, but the words wouldn't come out. So instead, he decided he would show her just how much he loved her.

"Braxton…"

"Shush." He placed his finger against her warm lips. She swallowed.

His fingers fumbled at her buttons on her shirt. Slowly, he managed to free her top. He touched her throat, letting his hand glide down across her soft skin, feeling her heartbeat pulsing against his fingertips.

"I can't stay."

"I know. You should probably wait until dawn to leave, to make sure the Assassins have left town."

"You need to know how much I care for you." Braxton cleared his throat and met her gaze. "You need to know how much I love you."

Her lips parted. "Braxton, I…"

"Wait. I need to tell you this, you need to know." He slid her shirt off her shoulders and let it drift to the floor.

"I have felt more alive these last few days with you than I ever have my entire life." He removed her bra and let it fall to join her shirt.

She blinked and covered her naked breasts with her hands.

He pulled her hands away. "Don't. I love looking at you. I

love looking at every part of you." Braxton let his gaze linger on her breasts before kneeling and freeing her jeans and tugging them down her slender hips. From his kneeling position, he kissed her thigh before lifting one leg and then the other out of her jeans.

He hooked his thumbs on either side of her panties and pulled, ripping them from her body.

He lifted his gaze and grinned.

* * *

KATE THREADED her fingers through Braxton's silky hair, loving the contrast of the sporadic strands of blue. She'd never thought she'd fall in love again. And she certainly never thought she'd fall for someone who was totally not her type. Bad boy, tattooed up with blue streaks through his hair, and riding a Harley. Well, *was* riding a Harley. He was exactly the kind of man her mother always warned her of.

Kate smiled.

"What are you smiling about?" Braxton kissed the outside of her thigh, his eyes never leaving hers as his mouth trailed over her skin.

"I was thinking about how my mom would have liked you." Her words came out between gasps of air. Her thighs tingled against his hot breath.

"I bet she wouldn't like me so much if she knew what I'm about to do to her daughter."

"Oh yeah? What would that be?" Kate murmured, too out of breath and out of her mind with desire to really care about talking.

"This." Braxton licked between her thighs, his tongue sliding along her wet heat.

"Oh, God." Her knees buckled. She grabbed Braxton's shoulders for balance.

He chuckled against her tender flesh, setting her body on fire. He took his time with his tongue as he nibbled and kissed and licked until she was shamelessly arching against his mouth.

He closed his mouth around her and sucked. Kate grabbed his hair, holding him against her, demanding he finish her.

She came against his mouth, crying out and trembling as Braxton continued to assault her with his tongue until she went limp.

* * *

HE STOOD and took her into his arms, kissing her hard until he could barely catch his breath. Picking her up, he laid her gently on the bed and quickly rid himself of his clothes.

"You're so beautiful." Kate eased up on her elbows and ran her hand down his chest.

He wasn't beautiful. He was anything but. But her words touched something inside of him that melted away at the hurt in his heart from years of abuse. She brought out the good in him. She made him hope in a way he'd never dared before. He met her gaze.

The desire in her touch and her eyes had him going out of his mind. He needed her now.

He nudged her thighs apart and cupped her, loving how wet and ready she was for him.

Her breath hitched in her throat.

"I need to be inside you, Kate."

She pulled his head down and kissed him, sucking his tongue into her greedy mouth.

Damn, she tasted like hot sex. The animal inside him growled as lust flowed heavy in his veins.

He grabbed her hips and thrust, driving his cock deep inside her wet heat.

"You feel so fucking good." Braxton buried his face in her neck. He wanted to remember this feeling, this sensation, for as long as he had left on this earth.

He took her mouth with a roughness he hadn't intended. Out of desperation, he wanted to claim her, to make her his, body and soul. For tonight he wouldn't listen to the Law or to reason. For tonight, he was listening to his heart. For tonight, she belonged to him.

"Braxton, please don't stop." Kate clung to him, urging him deeper, faster.

Groaning, he rocked his hips into her, gritting his teeth and holding back his own pleasure.

It wasn't until he heard her moan in ecstasy that he followed her over the edge and into blissful pleasure.

* * *

KATE LAY CURLED against Braxton's side, watching the rhythmic rise and fall of his muscular chest. They'd made love two more times, each time more urgent than the last, as if they were both searing their brains with the memory of being connected before he left.

Kate traced the outline of a colorful tattoo along his arm. She glanced up, making sure he was still asleep. His chest rose in slow deep breaths, still lost in deep slumber.

She sighed. She wished she could find sleep. Despite being exhausted, there was a nervous energy skipping through her veins. Braxton would be leaving in a few hours.

Staying here had become a liability. If he stayed, the Assassins would find him and kill him. She would be devastated if that happened.

Rolling over onto her back, she glanced at the bedside

clock. Four o'clock. It would be dawn in a few hours. She had only a few sacred minutes left with Braxton. Then it would be over. She would go back to her normal life of being a bed and breakfast owner.

She'd calculated her money and gone over the figures. She had enough funds to get her business back on the right track and get the Bella Luna out of foreclosure. With the website and new business plan, she could turn the B&B into a profitable business—even more profitable than when her mother was alive.

Her heart stung at the thought. She loved her home and her business, but she wanted something more. She wanted to share it with someone. She wanted to share it with Braxton.

Tears burned behind her eyes, flowed down her cheek, and sank into her pillow.

Her cell phone buzzed against her nightstand. She picked up the phone and threw on her robe before tiptoeing out of the room.

"Hello," Kate whispered into the phone as she crept toward the kitchen. The only person who would call this late was Beau.

"I know what you are hiding, Kate." Oliver Bigsby's voice sent shivers through her body.

"What are you talking about, Bigsby?" Kate eased onto one of the kitchen stools.

"That tattooed guy you've got at your B&B, Kate. That's what I'm talking about. Just saw his picture on the internet news. He's wanted for murder. Did you know that?"

Kate swallowed as her hand began to tremble. "It's a mistake, please don't call the cops."

"If you want to keep your convict safe, meet me at the Thorncrown Chapel in thirty minutes."

"Why?"

"Because, Kate, you've got something I want."

Kate's stomach churned.

"And, Kate, make sure you come alone. Or I'll be forced to call the cops on your boyfriend. Understood?"

Kate gritted her teeth. "Understood." She disconnected and hurried back to her bedroom to change clothes.

She managed to quietly dress in the dark, her only light coming from the tiny sliver of moon slinking through her window. She glanced over her shoulder. Braxton was still asleep with his arm thrown over his head. She wanted nothing more than to wake him and tell him what Bigsby said. But she knew Braxton would insist on coming with her, and the moment Bigsby saw Braxton, he'd call the cops.

She wouldn't risk Braxton's safety. Not even to save her home.

She closed the bedroom door and snuck down the hall into the kitchen. She pulled open the junk drawer.

"What are you doing?" Felicity stumbled into the kitchen.

"Shit." Kate pressed her hand over her fast beating heart and sucked in a breath. "Felicity, you scared the hell out of me."

"Sorry. I need water. I've got cotton mouth. Plus, I think I'm still a little drunk." Felicity took a long pull on the bottle and then frowned at the keys in Kate's hand. "Where are you going?"

Kate shook her head. "I'm going out." She threw her purse over her shoulder, but Felicity grabbed her arm.

"It's still dark. Where could you be going at this hour?"

Kate's mind raced. "I'm going to Thorncrown Chapel. I thought I'd get some pictures at night."

"Cool. I'll go with you."

"No." Kate shook her head. "I'm not sure if I'll get back in time to make breakfast. So I'll need you to do it."

Felicity gave her an incredulous look. "Do you always ask your paying guests to cook their own breakfast?"

Kate sighed and looked at her watch. She was running out of time. If she was late, Bigsby might think she wasn't going to show and call the cops anyway.

"I've got to go handle some business, okay? You can't go."

Felicity's expression softened and she shrugged. "Fine. Just thought you wanted the company. No biggie."

"I'll be back soon."

* * *

THE SECOND KATE shut the door, Felicity ran into the living room where Jayden was sleeping on the couch. She grabbed his phone and copied his number into her cell phone. She grabbed her purse off the chair and dug out her keys. She waited until Kate started down the driveway before opening the front door and heading out into the yard.

She slid into the driver's seat and started the engine, hoping that Kate hadn't gotten too far ahead of her. When she got to the bottom of the driveway, she saw headlights disappear around a curve.

"Please let that be Kate and not the paper man." Felicity rounded the curve and saw Kate's familiar maroon SUV. She slowed but kept Kate's taillights in view, hoping that Kate wouldn't realize she was being followed.

"What are you up to, Kate?" Felicity bit her lip and fought the urge to speed up when Kate accelerated. She didn't know the roads well enough, but didn't want to lose her.

Felicity relaxed when she caught the illumination of Kate's taillights again. She followed in silence for another few minutes before Kate made a turn. Felicity immediately recognized it as the entrance to the Thorncrown Chapel. They'd been here during the day getting pictures for Kate's website. "Well, looks like she was telling the truth, but something's not right."

Felicity turned in and pulled off the road instead of following Kate farther. She grabbed her cell phone and called Jayden's number. When he didn't answer, Felicity groaned. She should have made sure his phone was not on silent. She pulled up his number again from her contact list and sent him a text. Grabbing her keys, she hurried up the driveway.

* * *

KATE PULLED up to the glass church and cut the engine. The moonlight reflected off the glass church like diamonds. Her hands tightened on the steering wheel as her heart lurched. She frowned at the illuminated church. They didn't keep the lights on in the chapel until after Easter services. It was still the dead of winter in January.

The door swung open. Oliver Bigsby stood in the doorway, sporting an obnoxiously big grin. He probably got the church's pastor to give him a key as well as light the chapel in exchange for a large donation. What a douche.

Bigsby crooked his finger, motioning her inside.

She wanted to give him a finger of her own. Instead, she gritted her teeth and grabbed her purse.

"Kate. Glad you could make it." Bigsby opened the door wider, letting her enter.

She glanced around at the glass structure. It never ceased to amaze her that the entire church was composed of glass with steel beams for support. Tiny tea lights were lit on every surface, from the altar to the small tables in front of every window. Candles were lit on the stairs leading up to the altar, and on the stone wall behind the pulpit, candle sconces flickered. The atmosphere hinted at romance, but with the company in there with her, hatred was the only emotion she was experiencing.

"Glad to see you came alone." Bigsby didn't hide the smirk

on his face, nor the sarcasm in his voice. His façade had cracked, and she knew she'd been right about him all along. He was not a good person.

"I'm here like you asked. What do you want?" Kate pulled her purse in front of her like a shield.

Bigsby chuckled. "Impatient little thing, aren't you." He reached out, taking a strand of her hair between his fingertips.

Kate slapped his hand away and narrowed her gaze. "Touching me is *not* part of this deal."

Bigsby snorted, his face grim. "I can't seem to figure you out. You let that tattooed thug in your bed, but won't give me the time of day," he snarled, his eyes full of bitterness.

"How the hell do you know he's in my bed?" Kate fisted her hands.

"It's obvious. I saw the way he looked at you. Not to mention he was half-dressed. I would have figured you'd have better taste than that loser."

"He's not a loser." Kate narrowed her gaze.

"He's a murderer."

"Actually, he's not. He was wrongfully accused, if you must know." Her heart pounded in her chest, not from fear but from rage. If it were possible to make a human spontaneously combust from a mere look, Bigsby would be a pile of gray ash right now.

"Yeah, right." He gave her a look of sympathy that made her want to punch his face in.

"You'll probably end up like one of those pathetic women on those TV dramas about how they married a jailbird." Bigsby gave her a look of pity. "Don't waste yourself on someone like that. You could do so much better." He gave her a slow smile.

Her mouth dropped open as she stared at the idiot in front of her. He actually thought he had a chance with her.

He actually thought that after all he'd done to destroy her business and take away her home, she'd give herself to him. What floored her the most was he actually thought he was better than Braxton.

Kate closed her mouth and crossed her arms. "If I live a thousand years, I will never find a man as honorable as Braxton."

* * *

BRAXTON BOLTED up right in bed as a sense of foreboding filled his chest. He glanced over, expecting to see Kate still asleep. Instead, the bed was empty.

Uneasiness snaked in his gut as he fisted the sheets in his sweaty palms.

After flinging off the bed covers, he tugged on his jeans and headed for the kitchen. Maybe Kate couldn't sleep and decided to start prepping for breakfast. Turning the corner, he entered the empty room.

"Damn it." Braxton looked at the clock on the microwave. It was a little after four-thirty. Where in the hell would Kate go at four-thirty in the morning?

"Why are you yelling?" Jayden frowned as he stumbled into the kitchen. He scratched his bare chest and then opened the refrigerator.

"Have you seen Kate?" Braxton growled.

"No." Jayden pulled out a water bottle and headed back to the couch. Braxton followed him into the living room. "Why?"

"She's not here." Braxton shoved his hand through his hair. "If she were going to leave she would have told some-one. This isn't right."

Jayden sat up straight. "Are you sure she just didn't have to run into town for something?"

"At four-thirty in the morning?"

Jayden frowned. "Maybe she had to go to a friend's house. You said yourself that vet friend calls at all hours. Maybe he called. Did you hear the phone ring?"

"No." He'd been exhausted after the fight at the bar. "But that doesn't mean I didn't sleep through it. I've got to go find her."

Jayden nodded and reached for his shirt. "I'll go with you." His phone vibrated on the glass coffee table. Jayden reached for it.

Then he looked up. "I know where she is."

"Where?" Braxton's hand stilled on the doorknob.

"Felicity just texted me and said she followed Kate to the Thorncrown Chapel."

"Is Felicity with her?" Braxton spun around.

"No. She said she followed Kate when she left." Jayden met his gaze. "Felicity thinks Kate is in some kind of trouble."

"Fuck." Braxton grabbed Jayden's bike keys. "I need these."

"Of course." Jayden threw his shirt on and headed out with him, but Braxton shook his head.

"Go wake Damon. He knows where the chapel is. Ride with him."

* * *

BRAXTON RACED down the winding roads through Eureka Springs, the cold winter air hitting him in his face, but he felt nothing. His mind was focused solely on Kate and making sure she was okay. If she had put herself in harm's way for him, he would never forgive himself.

The sign for the Thorncrown Chapel up ahead had Braxton breathing out a prayer of thanks that he was almost there. He made the turn and his lights bounced along Felicity's darkened taillights. He parked in front of her car.

Maybe Felicity hadn't felt it was safe to pull in front of the church.

Braxton raced up the driveway, making sure to keep to the shadows and out of the moonlit path. Kate's SUV was parked in front of the illuminated glass church. He crouched behind her SUV and peered into the church. Two figures stood at the front of the church near the altar. One was Kate and the other that dickhead, Bigsby.

Rage poured through Braxton's veins. He was going to handle Bigsby once and for all.

* * *

"What do you want, Bigsby?" Kate ground out the words between her clenched teeth. She was done with any sort of polite conversation with this overgrown jackass.

Bigsby looked a little surprised by her tone. "Well, I see you want to get right down to it." He opened his briefcase on the front pew and pulled out several sheets of paper and a pen.

"I think you know what I want." He shoved the paper toward her.

Kate glanced at the papers and then back at Bigsby. "You expect me to sign over the deed to my home."

"I expect you to save your lover's life." He continued to hold out the papers with a smirk on his cruel lips.

Kate cocked her head. "And if I don't?"

His smirk faltered. "Then I will call the cops and that loser will be spending a life sentence in Louisiana."

Kate's heart lurched. She clung to the purse with both hands. The thought of Braxton being locked up forever chilled her to the marrow. She couldn't imagine Braxton going submissively with the police. He'd fight to the death.

She snatched the papers and pen out of Bigsby's hand.

"That's a good girl. I knew with that soft heart of yours, you'd let a man take away everything you had."

Kate froze. "What do you mean?"

"I'm talking about Tom, your ex-boyfriend. You let him get away with stealing all your savings without even pressing charges." Bigsby snorted. "And now you're giving your home away for a man. You'll never learn."

Kate gripped the pen in her hand and eyed the pulsing vein at the base of Bigsby's neck. All she wanted to do was stab that asshole and watch him bleed to death.

She sucked in a deep breath and focused her gaze on the unsigned papers in her hand. She walked to the altar and set them down, her pen poised.

"Kate, stop!"

CHAPTER 13

*K*ate jerked upright. Standing at the door of the chapel was Braxton, looking very angry and incredibly dangerous.

"Kate, I'm warning you, you'd better sign those papers." Bigsby's eyes bulged as he reached in his pocket and pulled out his cell phone.

"Don't do it, Kate." Braxton stalked down the aisle, his gray eyes glinting lethally.

Bigsby fumbled with his phone as he punched in numbers.

She held up her hands to stop him. "No, Braxton, you don't understand…"

"Back off, freak. One more step and I'll hit dial. The cops will be all over this place in a matter of minutes." Bigsby held his phone in the air.

Kate put her hand on Braxton's massive chest. "Braxton, you need to leave. I can handle this."

Braxton dragged his gaze from Bigsby to Kate. His expression softened. "You think I'd let you sign over your house to this douchebag? Just to keep him from turning me in?"

"Do you know who I am? No one speaks to me like that!" Bigsby pressed his lips into a thin line until they disappeared, his face turning scarlet.

Braxton glared at him. "I know exactly who you are. You are nothing more than a spineless little prick that can't get laid unless you pay for it."

Bigsby sputtered, his face growing redder by the second. Either no one had ever spoken to him that way or Braxton had hit a nerve. Kate bit her cheek. Maybe both.

"What do *you* know? You're a murderer," Bigsby snarled.

Braxton turned to face Bigsby. A slow, lethal grin crossed his lips. "Then one more dead body won't matter."

Bigsby yelped and ran for the door. He only made it two steps before Braxton grabbed his collar and lifted him off his feet by his shirt.

Bigsby screamed and flailed in the air like a fish on a hook. He glanced down, realizing his phone was still in his hand. Before he could dial, Braxton snatched the phone away

"You won't be needing this." Braxton squeezed the phone, crushing it into a million plastic shards.

Bigsby's terrified gaze landed on Kate.

"Braxton, let him go." Kate tugged on his muscled arm.

"But…"

"Now!" Kate crossed her arms and tapped her foot.

"Are you tapping your foot at me?" Braxton's gaze drifted to her tennis shoe.

"Braxton." She glared back at him.

An amused grin crossed his lips and he loosened his grip. Bigsby fell on his ass.

"She's not signing her home over to you." Braxton narrowed his eyes at Bigsby as the man scrambled to his feet and began backing to the door. "She is making enough money to catch up on her mortgage payment. She will survive this. And she'll be safe from you."

Kate nodded at Bigsby as Braxton reached for her hand and squeezed. "He's right. In fact, I'm going to the bank today as soon as it opens."

Bigsby froze, his hand on the doorknob. He turned. A strange look came across his expression. And he laughed.

Kate stepped closer to Braxton.

"You have no idea, do you?" Bigsby grinned maniacally.

"What are you talking about, Bigsby?"

"It doesn't matter if you go to the bank with a million dollars, the house will go into foreclosure anyway. The bank president seems to have a secret addiction. Gambling. And he owes me a great deal of money. I promised him I'd forgive the debt if he'd get me your house. I need that land so I can build my next hotel."

Kate's insides petrified. "But...but, that's not legal."

Bigsby laughed. "You are so naïve. There is no legal or illegal. What matters is who has the control. I'm the one with the money and therefore I have all the control." Bigsby barked out a laugh.

Braxton started down the aisle. Bigsby sobered, realizing he wasn't entirely out of danger, and reached for the door.

The door swung open with enormous force, sending Bigsby flying backward into a pew.

Lorcan walked through the door with two other enormous men all decked out in leather and wearing guns holstered to their chests. She forgot to breathe. It was the Assassins.

She reached for Braxton's arm, digging her fingers into his flesh.

"Braxton." The one with the buzz cut appeared to be the leader since the other two men flanked him. He glanced around the room and then back at Braxton, grinning. "I didn't picture you for the praying type. Guess you picked the perfect time to start."

"What the fuck?" Bigsby scrambled to his feet and stood and stared at the three Weres. "You assholes could have broken my nose, you clumsy elephants."

Braxton didn't let his gaze leave the Weres. He'd never met them, but he'd grown up hearing about the three deadly Assassins and what they looked like. The one with the blond hair and blue eyes who looked like a California surfer was Lorcan. The one who had short spiked black hair with gray eyes and looked like he belonged in a metal band was Killian. Standing between the two was the leader, Brutus. He had sharp green eyes and dark brown, buzzed-cut hair.

They were the self-proclaimed apocalyptic horsemen of the werewolf race, bringing death in the shape of a silver bullet. And they were here for him.

Braxton shoved Kate behind him.

"Hey, I'm talking to you!" Bigsby proceed to poke his perfectly manicured finger in Brutus's chest.

Without his lethal gaze leaving Braxton, Brutus's arm shot out and punched Bigsby in the face, sending him flying through the air and landing on the floor. Bigsby didn't move. The asshole was out cold.

"Your human friend is very annoying." Brutus glared.

"He's not my friend," Braxton growled.

"But I am." Kate stepped in front of him. Braxton pulled her away, but she struggled against him.

With Kate still fighting him, Braxton focused on the Assassins. "Let her leave. Then we can finish this."

"She is free to leave. We have no quarrel with the human." Brutus moved away from the door entrance and motioned her through.

"I'm not going anywhere," Kate yelled.

"Please, Kate." Braxton held her face between his hands,

forcing her to look at him. "I don't want to see you get hurt."

"And I don't want to see you get killed…" she glared at the three Weres "…for a murder you did not commit!"

Braxton's heart convulsed and twisted. God, how he loved this woman, even if she wasn't a werewolf. It didn't matter to him if she were a purple cat, Kate was his perfect match.

"Female, you need to leave," Brutus ordered.

Killian reached inside his jacket and pulled out a .45. "How about this time I put it in your head so you won't feel a thing?"

Kate screamed, struggling to put herself in front of Braxton.

Braxton looked at Brutus and gritted his teeth. "I don't want her to see this."

Brutus narrowed his eyes for a second before nodding Lorcan forward. "Take the woman outside."

"You better fucking make sure you don't hurt her," Braxton growled.

"Fine, rogue. The human won't be harmed." Lorcan smirked and reached her. Kate twisted and bit his hand. Lorcan snarled.

"You sure she's human?" Lorcan growled and assessed the damage.

"Kate, please go with him," Braxton pleaded. He wasn't sure how much more he was going to be able to take before he brought this whole place down around their ears.

Kate glanced at the door and then back at Braxton. She settled down. "Fine. But I'll walk out of here. Without him touching me." She glared at Lorcan, who shot her a glare.

Braxton nodded; he didn't trust his voice at the moment. Instead, he kept his gaze on Kate. He wanted her face to be the last face he saw as the bullet hit his brain.

Kate walked down the aisle with Lorcan behind her. She

was halfway to the door when a woman's scream tore through the church.

Felicity ran through the door carrying a large ceramic flower pot. She hurled it in the air towards Killian. It struck the Assassin on the side of the head with a thunk and then fell to the ground, smashing into a thousand pieces.

"That's from doing crossfit, motherfuckers." Felicity flipped them the bird with both hands.

With blood running down his face in a small river, Killian lowered his pistol and gave Felicity a murderous glare. Felicity froze.

"Why are you not on the ground? That was like a fifty pound flower pot. That shit was heavy." Felicity arched her brow.

"Who are you?" Brutus growled.

"Fuck me." Lorcan's gaze grew wild and he took a step back into a pew. "She's one of those crazy women."

Killian snarled at Lorcan. "Man, why are you being a pussy?"

"She's one of those crazy women, the ones that tried to attack me. She looks all innocent, but wait till she whips out that riding crop." Lorcan eased away from the other two Assassins with a scowl on his face.

Killian took his eyes off Braxton and glared at Felicity.

Braxton saw his chance and lunged at Brutus.

* * *

KATE SCREAMED.

Braxton had Brutus on the ground, one hand around his throat the other delivering a set of hard blows to the face.

Brutus, unfazed, bucked Braxton off. He grabbed Braxton by the back of his shirt and threw him several feet down the aisle, where he crashed on the altar, leveling it to the ground.

Braxton did some kind of martial arts move, flipping from his back and landing on his feet.

The other two Assassins nodded at each other and made a move toward Braxton.

While Brutus and Braxton were equally matched, there was no way it would be a fair fight once the other two were-wolves joined in the action. She wasn't going to let that happen. Kate ran and jumped on Killian's back, wrapping her arms tightly around his neck.

"Really?" Killian sighed impatiently as he shot her a glare over his shoulder. "You are no match for me, you know this, right?"

"Killian, quit flirting and get your ass in the fight." Lorcan shook his head and started to jump into the fight.

"Hey, hottie,where do you think you're going?" Felicity stepped into Lorcan's path.

Kate craned her neck over Killian's shoulder and frowned. Felicity had no idea what she was getting herself into.

"Holy shit." Lorcan paled.

"Hey, you can't say 'shit' in church. It's like a sin or some-thing." Felicity propped her hands on her hips.

"She's just a human, Lorcan. Handle her," Killian snarled and proceeded to unwrap Kate's arms from around his neck.

Felicity's eyebrow shot up. "Handle me. I like the sound of that. And, just for the record, I didn't notice a ring on your hand."

"Ring?" Lorcan frowned.

"Yeah, a wedding ring. So I guess that means you're avail-able for all kinds of debauchery and impure activities." Felicity waggled her eyebrows.

Kate blew her bangs out of her eyes as she struggled to hang on to Killian's neck. "Felicity, they're trying to kill Brax-ton. Stop trying to get laid and help him."

Felicity reached into the back of her jeans and pulled out a Taser.

Lorcan snorted. "What's that supposed to…"

Felicity pressed the Taser to Lorcan's neck and hit the button. Lorcan dropped backward like an oak tree and hit the floor.

"What the hell did you do?" Killian stared down at his friend and frowned.

Kate jumped off Killian's back and headed down the aisle to Braxton. "If he moves, Felicity, taser him, too!"

Kate's heart pounded in her ears as she hurried to Braxton. Brutus now had both hands wrapped around Braxton's throat, while his knee was shoved against his chest to keep him from moving.

Braxton's lips were turning blue as he clawed at Brutus's hands. The Assassin was going to strangle him to death. She grabbed the offering plate off the floor and whacked Brutus on the back of the head.

The Assassin didn't flinch.

Kate brought the offering plate back down on his head again and again. It was like trying to get an alligator off its prey. Brutus wouldn't budge.

Suddenly, a large pair of hands wrapped around her waist and lifted her up in the air. She struggled against the steely grasp. When he released her, she took a step back. It wasn't either of the other Assassins. But judging by his size and strength, he was definitely a werewolf, too.

The stranger's dark blonde hair brushed a little past his shoulders and his angry eyes were a startling shade of deep blue. Dressed in jeans and skin-tight T-shirt, he seemed taller than Braxton.

His angry gaze left hers, and he turned his attention back to the fight. He grabbed Brutus by the neck and lifted the Were over his head and hurled him into the glass wall behind them. The chapel trembled and the sound of glass cracking and splintering had Kate wondering if the whole thing was about to come down around their heads.

"Enough!" The stranger glared at the Assassins and then turned to Braxton and offered his hand.

Braxton stood and rubbed his neck. "Thanks, Barrett."

Kate ran to Braxton's side, burying her face in his chest as he held her close. She didn't know who the Were was, but he'd helped Braxton, so that made him okay by her.

"This is none of your business, werewolf," Brutus growled, stepping into Barrett's space.

Damon and Jayden rushed through the side door and stood on either side of Barrett, effectively creating a wall between the Assassins and Braxton.

"This *is* my business, dickwad. I'm the Pack Master of Arkansas, so you better back the fuck up." Barrett's deep voice shook the cracked glass of the church.

"We were ordered here by the Pack Master of Louisiana," Brutus answered.

"And you are now in my territory!" Barrett stepped forward. "Louisiana commands hold no weight here."

Damon and Jayden smirked and took a step forward.

Lorcan and Killian took a step back.

"I am Law here. And as long as you are in my territory, you are under my authority." Barrett's voice carried through the church, the glass windows trembling under the weight. "So you assholes better kneel before me before I rip out your spleen and eat it."

The muscle in Brutus's jaw twitched, and he fisted his hands. He nodded and he, along with the other two Assassins, knelt before Barrett.

Kate trembled and said a silent prayer that Barrett seemed to be on Braxton's side. Braxton's hand ran up and down her back in a reassuring motion.

Kate leaned closer to Braxton and lowered her voice. "What does this mean?"

Barrett turned his gaze on her. "It means that the fugitive is in my jurisdiction and therefore I will hold a Tribunal to determine his guilt or innocence."

"What about our orders?" Lorcan looked up from his position on the floor.

"When you crossed into Arkansas without letting me know you were here, you forfeited any rights to the fugitive. It seems to be an old law on the books about such an offense." Barrett motioned for the Assassins to stand. "Get up, you're making my neck hurt."

The three Weres stood. Felicity rushed down the aisle toward them.

Kate sucked in a breath. "Damn, I forgot about her."

"Who is she?" Barrett's intense gaze was focused on Felicity.

Kate swallowed, but Braxton answered first. "She's one of Kate's guests at The Bella Luna."

Lorcan stepped behind Killian. "She's crazy. Watch your man parts."

Felicity propped her arms on her hips. "Okay, spill it. Are you guys some kind of vampires or something?"

Everyone grew quiet.

"Vampire?" Barrett set his hardened gaze on her.

Felicity wasn't backing down. "Yeah. I mean how else do you explain how all of you guys are built and ripped? Not to mention how strong you all are." Felicity gave each Were an appreciative look. "So?" She looked back at Barrett.

Barrett arched his brow. "Spartacus."

Felicity frowned. "What?"

"We're so big because we do the Spartacus workout." Barrett's gaze never wavered. Kate felt Braxton chuckling softly, and she bit her lip to keep from laughing.

Felicity narrowed her eyes. Kate held her breath, her mind racing with another plausible explanation because she just knew Felicity wasn't going to buy it.

"Is that right?" Felicity glanced at everyone.

"Yeah." Killian nodded and then flexed his bicep.

Felicity frowned. "Hmph. I'll have to look into that."

Kate released her breath.

"It's not even dawn yet. I think I'll go back to the B&B." Felicity looked at Kate. "Do you want me to wait on you or is everything good?"

"I'm fine, Felicity. You go on back to the house. I'll be there shortly."

"Alright. I'm going to bed." Felicity started down the aisle and turned, a smile playing at the corners of her lips. She looked right at Lorcan. "Wanna come?"

Lorcan swallowed hard and shifted his weight. He looked at his two friends for help, but they kept silent.

"He can't. He's going to have to clean this place up," Barrett stated. Lorcan relaxed.

Felicity shrugged and then closed the door behind her.

"Thanks," Lorcan murmured to Barrett.

"What's with you, man? She's just a human," Killian snarled.

"Actually, she's more than just human. She's a romance writer." Jayden rubbed the back of his neck.

Barrett glanced at his watch. "It's going to be dawn soon. We need to be getting out of here."

The Assassins started for the door. Barrett's hand clamped down on Brutus's shoulder. "Except for you three."

"You three will be sticking around here with me to speak to the pastor of this church about how you'll be paying for the damages."

"What?" Brutus growled.

Barrett's smirk slid off his face. "Do you have a problem

with that? If so, we need to discuss this before the pastor gets here. I'd hate to greet him with three dead bodies in his church."

Brutus gritted his teeth. "There's no problem."

"Good." Barrett turned to Braxton and Kate.

Braxton cocked his head at Barrett. "I guess I'll be heading back with you."

"Yes. There's going to have to be a Tribunal."

"What's a Tribunal?" Kate asked.

Barrett looked at Braxton. "I guess she knows."

Braxton nodded and pulled her close. "She knows what I am. What we are."

Barrett cocked his head, his gaze running down her body as if assessing if he could trust her. "A Tribunal is like a court case where both sides present evidence. Only there is no jury. Only a judge."

"Is it safe to say you would be the judge?"

"Always." Barrett grinned, his bright white teeth gleaming against his five o'clock shadow. He was breathtakingly beautiful, but he did nothing for her. Not like Braxton did.

"I'd like to take Kate home first, before I have to leave."

Barrett stared hard at Braxton. "The Were law states that once in the custody of the Commander of the state, a fugitive has no rights."

Kate swallowed. This would be the last time she'd see Braxton. Probably ever.

"I understand." Braxton nodded, but his body stayed tense.

"But seeing how we have an understanding, I don't suppose it would hurt for you to see the girl home. I'll be by shortly to collect you."

"Thank you." Kate reached out and touched Barrett's arm. He looked a little shocked and then frowned. She snatched her arm away, not wanting to press her luck.

"I appreciate it, Barrett. You've saved my ass tonight." Braxton stuck out his hand. The two shook.

"It's not over yet. You'll still have to prove you're innocent at the Tribunal in Little Rock."

* * *

THEY RODE BACK to Bella Luna in Kate's SUV in heavy silence. Braxton wished for the hundredth time that the stupid truck didn't have bucket seats so he could pull her right up next to him.

He pulled up to the bed and breakfast and cut the engine. The darkness of night was giving way to the purple light of dawn. Only a few more minutes and the sun would be peeking over the mountains.

Kate got out and shut the door. Braxton followed.

His gut clenched as he tried to imagine not being able to see her every day. He hadn't realized just how much he'd miss her. Why had he found his perfect mate, only to lose her? The thought made him feel empty inside.

"Kate."

She stopped, one foot resting on the steps, the other on the ground. The way she held her shoulders, straight and stiff, made Braxton realize she was barely hanging on to her emotions, as well.

He pulled her back against his chest, holding her tight and burying his face in her neck. She melted against him and rubbed her cheek against him.

"I'm not sure how this will all turn out," Braxton murmured against her neck. "If I can't prove my innocence then…"

Kate jerked in his arms and turned to face him. "But you are under Barrett's protection now." She stared at him, wide-eyed.

"I am under Barrett's protection for the Tribunal. Barrett will see that I get a fair trial, but he won't declare my innocence if I can't provide any evidence."

"So there's no hope then." Kate's eyes filled with tears.

He caressed her cheek with the back of his fingers. "There's always hope, Kate. You taught me that."

She reached up on tiptoes and wrapped her arms around his neck, bringing his mouth down to meet hers. This kiss was different, a combination of urgency and longing, and it almost brought Braxton to his knees.

When he finally pulled away, Braxton continued to gaze at her. "I'll come back to you. When this is all over, I'll come back."

Kate nodded slowly. "I'll be here." She turned and hurried up the steps.

Braxton bristled; a strange sense of foreboding crept across his skin.

A metal click echoed in the stillness of the predawn. Braxton sprang toward Kate and shoved her down to the wooden floor of the porch just before a gunshot rang out over their heads.

Braxton stayed still, covering Kate's body, while his eyes searched frantically in the dark. A shadow shifted.

"Don't move," Braxton whispered to Kate.

"Only a coward would shoot in the dark." He called out to the shadow at the end of the porch. His eyes quickly focused and adjusted. The figure was female.

"Braxton." The familiar feminine voice purred as she stepped forward into a puddle of light from the front porch sconce.

"Wendy?" Braxton blinked. "What the hell are you doing shooting at us?" He slowly stood, careful to make sure he kept Kate behind him.

"I'm not shooting at you. I was aiming for her." Wendy glared at Kate.

"Who is she, Braxton?" Kate asked as she peered around his shoulder.

"She's one of the dancers at the club I used to work at." Braxton narrowed his gaze on Wendy. She'd always been slim; as a dancer it was a requirement. But standing in front of him was a ghost of the girl Braxton once knew. Her skinny jeans clung to legs that were nothing but skeletal, and he expected any moment for them to buckle and snap. Her dirty green jacket covered the rest of her, but her hollow cheekbones gave evidence of drug use. Probably meth, if he had to guess.

"Braxton got fired because of me." Wendy's hand trembled under the weight of the gun as her dilated pupils darted between them. "He came to my rescue after one of the customers hit me."

"Why don't you put down the gun and tell me why you're here." Braxton held his palms up, keeping his voice calm and even. The sky lightened slightly, slight streaks of pink and orange coming over the mountains.

"You need me, Braxton." Wendy fixed her dilated gaze on him as she rambled. "I am the one who has set you free."

"Set me free?"

Wendy's eyes darted from him to Kate and then back to him, her chest heaving with emotion, or maybe it was withdrawal.

"Yesss!" Wendy snarled, her lips drawing across her brown-tinged teeth. Were her teeth always this discolored?

"I saw how unhappy you were, having to deal with your abusive father. I understood you, Braxton. I know what it's like wanting to leave, to escape, to run away to something better, something safe." Wendy trembled, the gun wavering dangerously in the cold morning air.

"I know that you stayed in Shreveport for your mom, to try to protect her from that fucking monster." Wendy gritted her teeth. "I did you and society a favor."

Every muscle in his body tensed and his gut clenched tighter. "Wendy, what are you saying?"

Wendy jerked her gaze back to him. "I killed your father."

Kate gasped. He reached back to take her hand, squeezing it.

"I killed him for you, Braxton. I did it so you would be free to leave and we could start a life together." Wendy shot him an impatient glare.

"A life...together?" Braxton had always treated all the strippers with respect and never led any of them on. In fact, he'd made it a rule not to date anyone from work.

Wendy's eyes glazed over. "You were the only man who'd ever protected me. You even got fired for me. And you didn't get mad at me when you lost your job." Wendy frowned, looking lost in her thoughts. "It was then I knew what I should do. It was almost like divine revelation."

Or totally psychotic, Braxton thought to himself.

"I went over to your parents' house. Your father was alone, drinking and watching TV. I went in through the back door, which happened to be unlocked. There was a hammer lying on the kitchen counter, so I grabbed it. He walked in on me in the kitchen and that's when I attacked." She shrugged. "It was easy enough, he'd had a lot of beers and after the second whack to the head, he fell to the ground. Every time I hit him I was thinking of you, Braxton. Only of you."

"And because of you Braxton is accused of murder." Kate poked her head around his chest.

Wendy shook her head. "I wasn't counting on that part. I thought his mother would get blamed since everyone in town knew she was abused. I figured if it went to trial, the jury wouldn't send her to jail. Juries are very sympathetic to battered women."

"How did you find me?"

Wendy shrugged. "I've been following you since you escaped the cops. I lost you after you passed through Eureka Springs. But I went on ahead to Branson to wait for you. I figured we would find each other again."

"Did you have anything to do with that construction worker?" Braxton shifted, easing a few inches closer. He needed to get closer. If he lunged now, she might shoot and hit Kate.

Wendy's gaze hardened. "After a few days of waiting in Missouri, I decided to backtrack, to see if you headed in a different direction. I came back here. I met a guy there who said he knew who you were and offered to take me to you. I didn't realize he was lying until he lured me out to some construction site and tried to force me to give him a blow job. I tried to get away but he hit me. I grabbed the first thing I could grab, which happened to be a nail gun. No man will ever lay a fucking hand on me, ever again."

"So you killed two people." Braxton shifted forward again.

"I killed two worthless shits," Wendy shot back. Her gaze landed on Kate and she leveled the gun. "You would have come to me, Braxton, if she hadn't gotten in the way."

"Put the gun down and I'll go with you now." Braxton's heart was hammering as he took a step toward Wendy. He'd never hurt a woman in his life, but if the drugged-out stripper took a shot at Kate, he was going to rip her to shreds.

Wendy looked from Kate to him and cocked the gun with shaky hands. Trembling, Wendy leveled the gun at him and shook her head. "You're lying. You're just like the rest of them." Her shoulders shook as tears ran down her face. Her outstretched arm shook as she kept it aimed toward them.

It was light now and the ladies in the house would soon be waking up. If he didn't do something quick, there would be more people put in danger.

A limb snapped, breaking the quiet of the morning. Wendy jumped and turned, glancing toward the trees behind her.

Braxton lunged and tackled Wendy to the ground. A gunshot rang out into the morning, sending an ominous chill down his back.

Wendy cried out, struggling under him. Braxton shifted his weight to keep from snapping her fragile bones, but kept a steady grip on her hands. He looked over his shoulder. "Kate, are you okay?"

It seemed like forever until he heard her sweet voice.

"Yeah. But I think my rocker has bitten the dust." She stepped to the side. The bullet had struck her white rocker, shooting off a leg. The chair slumped to one side.

Braxton let out a breath and forced his heart to slow down. For a brief second, he thought the bullet had hit Kate.

"Get off me!" Wendy hissed, her bloodshot eyes shooting daggers at him. "Get your hands off me!"

"You've certainly changed your tune. First you're offering to blow me, now you don't want me to touch you."

Wendy screamed and tried to bite him. Braxton held her down.

"What the hell is going on?" Myrtis stuck her head out the door. "Sounds like the damn O.K. Corral out here. And this is not conducive to a hangover."

"Holy shit. I knew I should have waited and come back with you!" Felicity pushed past Myrtis and stared at the scene on the front porch.

"Then we both would have been shot. Braxton saved my life."

CHAPTER 14

The cops were called and arrived within minutes. Barrett, Jayden, Damon, and Ava pulled in right after. Braxton filled in the cops, as well as his friends, on what happened, including Wendy's confession of killing both men.

After being questioned by the police, Kate walked inside to check on her guests. She glanced at the clock on the microwave. She was an hour late getting breakfast ready.

She pulled out a skillet from a bottom cabinet and put it on the stove. She'd just have to do something easy and quick this morning. Eggs and bacon would have to do.

"What are you doing?" Myrtis stopped in her tracks as she came into the kitchen.

"Breakfast." Kate pulled out a carton of eggs from the refrigerator, but Myrtis snatched it out of her hand. "What?"

"Don't worry about breakfast. We already ate."

Kate frowned.

"Barbara whipped up some pancakes. It's one of her specialties." Myrtis placed the eggs back in the refrigerator.

"Oh, well, I can adjust your bill…"

Myrtis cut her off. "You've got bigger problems to worry about than making a bunch of crazy women breakfast. Don't go adjusting the price. You've had your hands full with us over the past few days. In fact we might owe you money for all the trouble we caused."

Kate chuckled.

"So, is everything going to be okay?" Myrtis nodded out the window at the police car where Wendy sat.

Kate nodded. "Yeah, I think so. Braxton's been cleared of his father's murder. Wendy will have to face murders in both Arkansas and Louisana." Kate shook her head. "My problems of keeping the Bella Luna look very small in comparison."

"I don't think you'll have any problems keeping your home now. After this weekend, all the girls have agreed to come back in the spring and fall for a writing retreat. We know a lot of other writers that would be interested in coming here. You've got everything—beautiful home, charming town, and you're a wonderful and attentive host."

"Thanks, Myrtis."

Myrtis winked and then motioned out the window. "I think your boyfriend is looking for you."

Braxton's gaze searched the yard until he saw her standing at the kitchen window. He smiled and crooked his finger, motioning for her to come to him.

Her stomach dipped deliciously.

"I'll go see what he wants." Kate pushed away from the sink and grabbed her jacket. When she stepped onto the porch, the winter wind took her breath away. She sucked in another breath and searched for Braxton. The lawn was littered with cop cars and Harleys. Since the cops arrived, people from town had shown up to find out what was going on. The cops had since parked a cop car sideways at the end of her driveway to prevent any more nosy neighbors from driving up.

She met Braxton's gaze across the lawn. Pulled by an imaginary gravitation, Kate walked toward him.

She stood a foot away from him and stared, trying to memorize every detail. He would be leaving and she would only have her memories.

"I saw Barrett talking to the cops."

Braxton nodded. "The cops said I need to head back to Shreveport so I can make a statement and be cleared of any charges. Barrett said he would make sure I got there." Braxton laughed. "Apparently Barrett has some kind of *in* with the cops in Arkansas. He knew each one of them by name."

"Are they werewolves?" Kate leaned close and kept her voice down.

"No. Barrett's just very well connected." Braxton grew serious. "Maybe he can help with your home."

"I already have," Barrett said.

They both turned to the Arkansas leader.

"While you were talking to the police, I was talking with Kate." Barrett propped his hands on his hips. "She filled me in on everything. Including how Bigsby tried to blackmail her." Barrett gave Braxton a rare grin. "I told the cops and they are going to be heading over to Bigsby's house and the bank president's house today. They might even have some info on Tom Hudson and that money he stole from you, Kate."

"Thank you." Kate felt the weight of worry lift off her shoulders. But it was bittersweet. She might have her home, but she wouldn't have Braxton.

"That's great. Thank you, Barrett." Braxton reached for her hand and squeezed.

Barrett narrowed his gaze on Braxton. "You still need to come back with me to Little Rock to fill out some paper-work, absolving you from any involvement in the murder.

And, as you were wrongfully accused, you are also free to make a claim against the Commander of Louisiana for sending those assholes after you."

Braxton chuckled. "I'm just glad it's over." He shook his head. "I don't think I'll be filing a claim. Although I would like for them to compensate me for my Harley."

"I've already talked to Louisiana about doing that. It should be here within a week. Hope you like the Harley Breakout." Barrett's smirk slid off his face as he looked at Kate and froze.

"What?" Braxton looked between them.

Barrett leveled his intense blue eyes on her. "Where did you get that?"

Kate gulped and followed his gaze to her pendant. She picked up the gold crescent moon and shrugged.

"My mom gave this to me when I was a little girl."

Barrett narrowed his gaze. "Tell me, do you have a mark like that moon? Something that you didn't have at birth?"

"What's going on, Barrett?" Braxton pulled Kate close.

Kate gasped. Slowly, she nodded. "Yes."

"And, it was after you were bitten." Barrett cocked his head.

"How did you know that? It happened years ago when I was a child."

Barrett rubbed his hand across his mouth and averted his eyes.

Braxton stiffened. "I want to know what's going on."

"Tell me something, Braxton. How do you feel about Kate?"

"I don't think it's any of your business," Braxton snarled.

"As Commander of Arkansas, I think it *is* my business. I make it a point to know what's going on with all my Weres." Barrett arched his brow.

"I'm not part of your Arkansas Weres."

"Ah. So you plan on going back to Louisiana." Barrett nodded. "I see."

Kate's heart ached. She knew this was coming. He didn't have a reason to stay anymore. She was being stupid for even entertaining the thought that maybe he would. Kate pulled away.

"I didn't say that." Braxton reached for her hand.

"It is against the Were law for a werewolf and human to mate," Barrett stated.

"I know that." Braxton glared.

"Good." Barrett nodded cheerfully. "Wouldn't want you to go breaking any laws since you just got off the hook for murder."

Kate started for the house, but Braxton grabbed her arm. "Kate, wait."

Kate froze. She didn't know how much longer she could hold back the tears.

"So, how do you feel about Kate?" Barrett crossed his arms over his massive chest.

"I love her."

Kate couldn't breathe. She had literally forgotten how to breathe.

She turned and faced Braxton. He was declaring his love for her.

Kate sucked in a breath. "But, I guess in your world that's not enough."

"Actually, it just might be," Barrett offered.

They both turned. "What do you mean?"

"Kate, the mark you carry is a result of you being bitten by a wolf."

"I know."

"No, not an ordinary wolf. A werewolf."

"What? I've never heard of a werewolf biting a human." Braxton frowned.

"It's because it is against the law. The werewolf that bit her probably was killed as a result."

Kate stared at Barrett. "So, what does this mean?"

"It means that your mother knew a werewolf had bitten you. The pendant you wear is a sign of the wolf blood that runs through you."

"Are you saying I'm a werewolf?" Kate's eyes grew big.

Barrett laughed. "Not exactly. I doubt you will ever shift into full wolf form. But it does mean you have enough wolf blood in you for it to be legal for a Were to mate with you."

Kate's knees buckled. Braxton grabbed her in time, pulling her into his arms.

"You okay?"

"I think so." A laugh escaped her. "It's just a little shocking is all."

Braxton cupped her cheek. "Kate, do you still want me?"

Kate blinked. "Of course I still want you. I love you."

He brought his mouth down on hers before she could say another word. He kissed her thoroughly before pulling back.

"Will you be my mate? Forever?"

"Absolutely." She frowned. "Does this mean I don't get a wedding?"

"You can have anything you want. A wedding, reception, honeymoon…"

Barrett cleared his throat. They both turned.

"Since I'm in the neighborhood and it is under my authority that Arkansas Weres mate, I could make it legal now."

She looked at Braxton and smiled. "Okay."

* * *

BARRETT LED them through the back of the house and into the forest. Patches of snow still clung to the ground, and from the smell in the air, Braxton knew there was more bad weather to come later that day.

The Arkansas commander stopped at a large oak tree and faced them. Braxton held his breath while Barrett spoke, giving his blessing on their union. He watched Kate's beautiful face. She stared back at him, her eyes full of unshed tears of happiness.

All his life he'd never dared to believe he would be given such a gift as Kate. She was smart, funny, and beautiful as hell. And he silently vowed to do everything in his power to make her happy all the days of his life.

"Since Kate is not full-blood werewolf, blood must be shared to bond you two together." Barrett produced a knife from a holster inside his jacket. Braxton held out his hand and Barrett made a shallow cut. He did the same with Kate's hand.

Barrett then made a cut in his own palm and held it against Braxton's palm and then Kate's. He then pressed Braxton's palm and Kate's palm together.

"You are no longer two bodies. Instead you are one body, one heart, one soul. From this day forth, you will be forever entwined. None should ever come between you."

Barrett nodded once and then walked away, leaving them the privacy of the forest.

"You okay?" Braxton caressed her cheek.

"I'm better than okay. I'm wonderful." Kate kissed his wound. She gave him a worried look. "We haven't even talked about where we would live. I mean your mom is in Louisiana..."

"We will live here. At Bella Luna." Braxton pressed his finger to her lips. "My life is with you. I never thought I'd be so blessed to have someone like you, Kate."

Kate smiled dreamily up at him. "I think I'm the blessed one. So what do we do now?"

Braxton arched his brow. "I've got an idea or two."

"I can't do that now. I've got a houseful of guests…"

"And, we've got Damon, Ava, and Granny to tend to them." Braxton picked her up in his arms. "Which means I'm planning on having my way with you, even if I have to lock the damn bedroom door."

"So, what are you waiting for?" Kate gave him a sassy smile.

Braxton smiled as he carried his mate, the love of his life, back to their home.

EPILOGUE

*B*raxton grabbed his clothes off the limb of the oak and quickly dressed. The last thing he wanted was for the guests at the Bella Luna catching him butt naked after coming back from his midnight run.

Kate said she would wait up for his return with a midnight snack.

He grinned. He was going to eat more than just the meal she prepared for him.

Freshly fallen snow crunched under his feet as he jogged toward the bed and breakfast. His heart warmed in his chest as the soft glow of the home came into view.

The back door opened and Kate stepped into sight.

"I told you that you didn't have to wait up." He crossed the threshold and pulled her into his arms. He kissed her thoroughly.

She broke the kiss and gave him an uncomfortable laugh.

"What?" He frowned.

"Braxton, there is someone here to see you."

"It's kind of late for Barrett to be popping in." He looked around but didn't see anyone.

"It's not Barrett." Kate's eyes grew serious.

"Then who…" The words died on his lips as his mother stepped out from the living room.

"Hello, Braxton." His mother looked different. Thinner. And the circles around her eyes darker,

"Mom." He swallowed the lump in his throat. "What are you doing here?"

He looked down at Kate.

She wrapped her arm around his waist and looked up at him. "Why don't we go into the kitchen and I'll fix some coffee."

He didn't take his eyes off his mother as they headed into the kitchen. Kate reached up on her tiptoes and kissed his cheek before making coffee.

His mother clutched her worn purse in her hands clearly uncomfortable. She looked around the kitchen and then back at Braxton.

"You have a very beautiful home, Braxton." She admitted.

"It's Kate's home. She inherited it from her mother."

"It's our home." Kate corrected. "We are mated so what is mine is yours and vice versa."

He looked at her and smiled. She always made things right in his heart.

"Please sit." He motioned to a barstool at the kitchen island.

"No, I'm not going to be here that long. I don't want to take up too much of your time."

His stomach clenched. He already knew his mother had always took his father side. Now that the bastard was dead, it wouldn't be any different.

"I didn't kill him, you know." He narrowed his eyes on her.

Her eyes widened. "I know. The Pack Master of Arkansas came to see me. He told me he found the killer."

She shook her head. "Who would have thought? A mere human?"

Kate cleared her throat. His mother caught her mistake. "I'm sorry. I didn't mean to offend you."

"It's okay. I didn't think much of wolves until I actually got to know them." She wrapped her arms around his waist and stared up at him.

He smiled.

"You've done well for yourself, Braxton. Nice home, nice…mate." She nodded slowly. "Better than I ever expected."

"Maybe you should have raised your expectations of me."

"Your father always said…"

"Stop. I don't give a shit what my father always said. He was never a father to me. Beating the fuck out of your own is the most despicable thing anyone could ever do. That goes for animal or human."

She blinked. Startled at his answer.

"You didn't know him like I did."

"Thank God for that." Braxton snorted.

She hung her head. "I made a lot of mistakes. I see that now. I'm sorry. I never should have let him lay a finger on you."

He froze. He wasn't expecting those words out of her mouth.

"I should have given you up for adoption. That would have been the safer bet."

"Give me up?" He took a step forward. "You would give up your own child instead of leaving your abusive husband."

"I had nowhere to go. I had no education. I couldn't support myself let alone a child."

"So you stayed. And let him beat me. As well as yourself."

"You don't understand."

"No. I don't. I won't ever understand." He shoved his hand

though his hair. "Look, I don't think we will ever see eye to eye on that." His heart broke for the woman he'd tried to protect who never once tried to return the favor.

"That's why I came by. To say I'm sorry." She glanced down at the floor.

"What are you going to do now? Now that he's gone?"

She took a deep breath. "I got a job. I clean houses for three of the rich ladies in town. They are nice and pay me well."

His heart lurched. He wanted something more for his mother. "Do you need money?"

"No. I'll be fine." He could tell from her eyes she was lying.

He dug his wallet out of his pocket and pulled out all the cash he had and handed it to her. "Here's a thousand dollars. It's all the cash I have on me."

Her eyes widened. "How did you get that much money."

"He's a Guardian now." Kate handed her a cup of coffee.

"A Guardian? In Arkansas?" His mother blinked.

"Yeah. Who knew." He took the coffee Kate handed him. He raised the cup to his lips and let the hot brew slid down his throat.

"Wow. That's great Braxton." She set down her coffee and slowly put the cash in her purse. "I'll pay you back when I can."

"No. Consider it a gift."

She nodded. He knew it was hard for her to say thank you.

Maybe it was the guilt of what he'd been through. Maybe it was the guilt of her thinking she wasn't worth it. Or maybe she'd had such a difficult life that she'd never been grateful of anything in her life.

"I should be going."

"You can spend the night. We have a room available." Kate offered.

"I can't." She shook her head and headed to the door. She gave one last glance at Braxton before shutting it behind her.

"I don't know why she came." He shook his head.

"I think she needed to see if you were okay." Kate wrapped her arms around him.

"I don't think she ever really thought about my welfare before." He snorted.

"Braxton, I think she has been living her whole life in abuse. Now for once in her life she's out of that. Now is the time for her to heal and rethink her life choices. I am willing to bet that one day, she will realize the truth of what her husband was. And she won't defend him anymore."

"Maybe." He tightened his hold on her "But you know what I realized tonight?"

"What?"

"Just how lucky I am to have you in my life. I want a different life than what my mother had."

"You are the one to break the cycle of abuse. Now your mother has to do that as well." She kissed him.

"You're a good man, Braxton. And I'm lucky to call you mine."

He grinned, his heart full of love for the woman in front of him. "I love you. Now let's go to bed so I can show you how much I love you."

ABOUT THE AUTHOR

Jodi Vaughn is a USA Today best-selling author of over twenty novels. When she is not creating worlds of fantasy, she can be found at home in Arkansas with her family, three dogs, and two very fickle swans who travel the neighborhood in search of greener pastures.

Find her on Facebook, Jodi Vaughn, author.

Follow her on Twitter @JodiVaughn1

Sign up for her newsletter and check out her website http://jodivaughn.com

Find her on Instagram at VaughnJodi

ALSO BY JODI VAUGHN

Werewolf Guardian Romance Series
Her Werewolf Bodyguard (book 1)
Her Werewolf Protector (book 2)
Her Werewolf Defender (book 3)

The Vampire Housewife Series
Lipstick and Les and Deadly Goodbyes (book 1)
Merlot and Divorce and Deadly Remorse (book 2)
Bullets and Booze and Dead Suede Shoes (book 3)
Aces and Eights and Dead Werewolf Dates (book 4)

Veiled Series
Veiled Secrets (book 1)
Veiled Enchantment (book 2)

Somewhere Texas Series
Saddle Up (book 1)
Trouble in Texas (book 2)
Bad Medicine (book 3)
Somewhere in Paradise (book 4)

Cloverton Series

Candy Corn Kisses and Candy Canes and Tractor Chains.

Christmas in Cloverton

Lost Without You

Lost All Control